Praise for Cyn … *Upstairs In The Tent:*

Rogerson i… …d
responsibilit… …s in
life, painful a… …fights
desperatel… …the seductions of easy answer…
The Big I…

The structure of *Upstairs in the Tent* is mosaic-like, layered, and its wide-ranging point of view suits Rogerson's ability to inhabit all of her main characters convincingly. She sketches them with just the right amount of detail, chooses just the right aspects to emphasise … an inviting and readable book by a gifted writer.
Scotland on Sunday

Rogerson's narrative brings together family drama, fantasy and off-kilter romance with warmth rather than sentimentality, avoiding easy endings and instead concentrating on the turns of fate that bring people together.
The Scotsman

The central characters brim with believable inner life; their voices ring true.
The Scotsman

About the Author

Cynthia Rogerson is a Californian living in Ross-shire, in Scotland. Her first novel, Upstairs in the Tent, was published in 2001; her short stories and poems have been short-listed for competitions, anthologised, published in literary magazines and broadcast on BBC radio.

She has four children, an ex-husband in her extension, a very tolerant boyfriend, and some hens.

Love Letters from my Death-bed

Cynthia Rogerson

TWO RAVENS PRESS

Published by Two Ravens Press
Green Willow Croft
Rhiroy
Lochbroom
Ullapool
Ross-shire IV23 2SF

www.tworavenspress.com

ISBN: 978-1-906120-00-9

British Library Cataloguing in Publication Data. A CIP record for this book can be obtained from the British Library.

Designed and typeset in Garamond by Two Ravens Press.
Cover design by David Knowles and Sharon Blackie.
Illustrations by Alec Houston.

Printed on Forest Stewardship Council-accredited paper by Biddles Ltd., King's Lynn, Norfolk.

Acknowledgements

Any similarity to certain individuals, alive or dead, is entirely deliberate. You other individuals, it is entirely coincidental, and you are being paranoid. Whereas it is all true, none of it happened.

For editorial help, thanks to: Michel Faber, Angus Dunn, Andrew Greig, Eva Youren, Fee Murray, Janet McInnes, Caroline Bowes.

For help with credibility and history: Florence Nelson, Donald Gunn, Carolyn Jones, Maggie MacDonald, Katy Setz.

For technical help, thank you Alan.

For the signatures, thanks Andrea, Lyndy and Christopher.

For taking a chance on me, thank you Sharon and David.

For the wonderful art, thank you Alec.

For Manuel's face, and for cheering me up in every way, thank you Pete.

For inspiration, thanks to: George Jones, Barbara Jones, Michael Jones, Carolyn Jones.

Apology

I make no apology for the fact this is a story about death. All stories are about death. Oh yes, they are.

Some stories are simple and sparsely peopled; I much prefer these, but this book is not one of them. Instead, despite my best intentions, it is like a chaotic house with too many people living loudly inside it. I do apologize for this. It was unavoidable. The following might help as a reference guide:

Joe Johnson – 60 year-old lecherous owner of Gentle Valleys Hospice.
June Johnson – dreamy wife of Joe.
Georgia May Johnson – sexually-frustrated mother of two babies; daughter of Joe and June.
Consuela Gabriella Garcia – beautiful Portuguese woman who apparently died young.
Ghost of Consuela – appears to various folk as a young girl; apparently unaware she is dead.
Fred Snelling – grandfather of Carson and Robbie; resident of the Hospice; given to farting.
Carson Snelling – granddaughter of Fred; sister of Robbie; neighbour of Joe and June; pot-head.
Robbie Snelling – brother of Carson, etc.
Manuel Mendoza – pretends to be a doctor; infatuated with Morag; fat but handsome.
Morag Angusina McTavish – middle-aged woman from Scotland who thinks she is dying.
Connie – long-time mute resident of Gentle Valleys; looks out of windows a lot.

Eleven whole characters – but really only nine. My advice is to treat this story as a fair ground ride. Hold tight and remember to look at the view when you get to the top.

Death before unconsciousness!

– Doonesbury, Garry Trudeau

Part One

Dead people, for a short while, are all about four years old. You knew that, didn't you? Unless of course they never reached that age in the first place. Babies stay babies, and are not afraid. But everyone else is four years old in the beginning, and they just want their mothers. Even if they didn't have a mother, or they did and she was a lousy mother. Mama! they shout. Or God! if they are that way inclined, but it is still really mama! they are shouting. They ache to show her the hurt place, get her to fix it, cuddle up to her smell. They dwindle back to a little homesick kid with scabby knees. They sit in a puddle of pee.

Why am I here? I could ask you the same thing. Why are you here? What are you doing in my kitchen? Do I know you? Why are you people always asking questions? I'm not afraid, but I'm too busy to talk to you anymore. I have work to do. The bread, the beans, and the fire needs feeding.

Excerpt from *The Consuela Chronicles*, transcribed by Father Pedro of the St. Juarez Order, 1941, Santa Maria, California.
Estimated age of Consuela: eighteen.
Location of apparition: the middle of the kitchen table, in Sycamore House.

Monday Morning

There's a place near the freeway where Hispanic men gather who want a day's work, and the men who want to hire them drive by and ask. It's simple.

'Hey, you! Yeah, you. You looking for work?' asks Joe Johnson from his shiny black Jaguar.

'Maybe,' says Manuel. He already has a job, but he's having one of those days when he feels he should keep his options open. Besides, he knows Joe; he built a garden wall for him, but it is obvious Joe has no recollection of this.

'I need some concrete poured and our septic tank dug up. Whaddya say?'

'I say … that's okay.' He shakes his head.

'Good, hop in.'

'No, I say okay. As in: that's okay, but I really don't want to dig up your septic tank. It's going to be a hot day,' says Manuel. Then, on impulse, and because he is the slightest bit bored this morning, he adds, 'Besides, I am really a doctor. I don't do septic tanks.'

'Oh, right. Right. A doctor, huh?' Joe surveys Manuel, taking in his good-natured slouch, his two-day shadow, his illogical attractiveness. 'So what's your name?'

'My name?' He looks for a minute as if he doesn't know the answer. But naivety is one of Manuel's cunning defences. He scratches his belly, and drawls: 'My name? My name is Manuel Mendoza. What is yours?'

'You know any sick people, Manuel? *Real* sick,' ignoring the name question with ease.

'What?'

'You know. Any oldies, sickies, that kind of thing?'

'Uh …'

'Well, you're a doctor, right? You must meet some, you know, goners. Decrepit types. *Past their sell-by date,*' he whispers. Manuel looks puzzled. Is on the verge of walking away, but his instinct for luck tells him to perk up. Look interested.

'Oh, yeah. *Sí, sí.* Lots of them. Poor souls. They are my speciality. It is your lucky day, Señor … Señor who?' extending his broad brown hand for a handshake through Joe's window.

'Johnson,' says Joe grudgingly, as they shake hands. 'Joe Johnson. I think I may have a job for you, Miguel.'

'Manuel.'

'Whatever. Hop in.'

◆◆◆◆

Joe's problem is basically a lack of dead people. Well, not exactly dead, but dying. People out of gas and freewheeling down the last dusty slope. Which would be okay in anyone else's life, but Joe owns California's first European-style hospice. Dying people are his bread and butter. Where are they all? And why are they avoiding him? Increasingly, he finds this hard not to take personally.

Earlier this morning, he overheard his cleaners whispering in the same soft accent that Manuel has:

'So where are the dead people?' whispered the new one called Maria.

'Oh, for heaven's sake! There's no dead people here, stupid. Only living people are here. Living, but a little bit dying. Get it?' replied Juanita.

'*Sí, sí.*' Pause. 'No. Who is this old lady? Is she dead?'

'She's Connie. She just looks dead. Never moves. Just dust around her.'

'What is she looking at?'

'I don't know. Nothing.'

'Who's that old guy?' (Joe had stood frozen in the far corner, an open catalogue in his hands, eyes glued to the page.)

'Señor Joe Johnson. The boss. Kiss his ass.'

'Can I ask him where the dead – I mean, dying – people are?'

'No, no. Bad idea.'

'Why?'

'We're just a little bit short on those today. Be silent, be part of the carpet, and nothing else matters.'

'*Dios!*' swore Maria under her breath, and Joe moved further away, his humiliation capacity saturated for the moment.

Now he drives the car slowly down Fourth Street and tries to explain things to Manuel, whose face remains inscrutable until Joe mentions dollars.

The Haunted House

There is a dearth of dying people in Joe's hospice because it is well known to be haunted, and the last thing a dying person wants to get a glimpse of is a ghost. Previews are only fun if you have a choice about seeing the real thing. Hence the hundred-to-one ratio of hospice volunteers to patients. Real ghosts intimidate the hell out of auditioning ghosts. This would be obvious to anyone but Joe. He thinks a ghost is an asset. He actually bought Sycamore House because of Consuela.

Re-named Gentle Valleys Hospice, the house is well-maintained and the interior still looks new. But, millimetres underneath, sleep the older layers of paint and paper. And behind these stretch the old wires: like a faulty nervous system, like Parkinson's disease. The old bulbous lead pipes bulge like varicose veins. And above the skirting boards, invisible unless you look hard, is the line where the old floors used to be before the wood worm epidemic of 1932.

The outside skin, likewise, looks new – freshly painted last year, a classy magnolia, soft and elegant. But in places around windows and near roof seams, the sun is already causing the paint to crack and peel, revealing previous lives. The Vietti's house and, in places, the turquoise and purple era – when a bunch of hippies hung American flags out of the windows, and roamed the halls with filthy bare feet and Jefferson Airplane blaring.

This is a house with history.

Long before this area was called Marin County and this particular patch was called Fairfax, there were grassy meadows overlooked by hills. Gold in summer, green in winter. Damp wooded ravines of sequoia, hazelnut and oak with cities of squirrels in their branches. There were buzzards and eagles, racoons and skunks; the occasional deer, thirsty and headed prance-footed for the creek. Indian families camped by hidden waterfalls, cooking acorn mush on oak fires, their dogs asleep in the heat. This lasted for a long time. Centuries and centuries, the same, till the missionaries insisted on having their day, which was bad news for the Indians.

Then, a time of working folk drifting in, Irish and Italian and Portuguese, building rickety wooden houses by the creek. And richer folk from the city drifting in, building slightly less rickety houses by the creek to use for parties and fishing on weekends. And a few shopkeepers opening shops to sell provisions to all these folk. And a lot of bars full of men chewing tobacco and talking about gold and trains and women back east. It was a rough place, but nearly everyone in it was glad to be there. Finally, in 1855, a Virginian called Charles Fairfax, a Scottish Baron, settled with his lovely wife Ada, and decided that giving the area his name was as good a starting point to being a proper town as it was going to get.

Along about then, a San Francisco banker called Algernon Vietti built a house in a meadow by the creek about half a mile from the shops and bars. It suited the meadow, and improved the landscape in that mysterious way that buildings so rarely do. Artists from Carmel and San Francisco painted it. He called it Sycamore House. It looked like this:

There were a lot of Viettis. A lot of baptisms, first communions, confirmations and weddings. They were consistently a rather ugly, but confident family – squat in physique, large-nosed and facially very hairy. Unequivocal ugliness, in their case, seemed to free them up to enjoy life. They had a young Portuguese cook – the proverbial dark-eyed beauty

– who was so loved by these Viettis, men and women alike, that she was not judged and turned away when it was discovered that she was going to have a baby without the benefit of a wedding ring.

No, no, no!

They were a big-hearted family, Catholic to the bone – that is, they were delighted to find someone on whom to practise their big-heartedness, right on their doorstep. In fact, in their kitchen. This cook, this slender Señorita Garcia whose first name is lost to history, was pampered and spoiled – though not let off any cooking duties, for no Vietti woman could cook worth beans. She gave birth prematurely one morning in 1908, in front of the kitchen range. Initially scowling and scrawny, but later gorgeous, the baby was called Consuela Gabriella. By the age of three she bore an uncanny resemblance to Frederick, the young son of their married gardener, Frank Snelling, but this was not remarked on with any intention of retribution. The Viettis liked to forgive everyone – and besides, men were like that. Consuela was considered a great blessing, and allowed to assist her mother with the cooking and firewood when she was old enough.

Unlike her mother, Consuela's name is not forgotten, because she is who she is. Famous, that is. Not for anything special she did, but because she kept doing it long after she was expected to stop. Over and over again, and not in chronological order. She left the house in 1931, aged twenty-three, when she married unwisely, moved to somewhere near Stockton and everyone, even her mother, lost track of her soon after. Consuela simply disappeared, as people do now and then. But somehow, for some reason, Consuela did not leave Sycamore House. Or grow older. Perhaps it was case of homesickness, and she *could not* leave. It was a very nice house, and probably a very nice life.

People love ghosts, really. Once a place is known as haunted, all sorts come to investigate. These kinds of people cannot resist trying to make something of it: usually money. Why should they deprive the public of such an interesting and articulate phenomenon? People, especially twenty-first century atheists, love low-brow comforting philosophy. Think of Kahlil Gibran. Think of *Desiderata.* Think of *The Little Book of Calm, The Alchemist, The Celestine Prophesies.* And so, Consuela Garcia became commercialised and *The Consuela Chronicles* can be bought today for a mere $29.99 (ISBN 4-999164-818905).

The Chronicles begin in 1933. Though no proof was ever found, everyone assumed that Consuela was dead, had died somewhere around Stockton of something or other, and had returned to haunt her childhood home. The sightings increase dramatically during the spiritualist thirties and forties, and again increase during the hippie era of cults (1966 to 1977); after that, they peter out. The truth is, she still haunts the house. But being the kind of place it is now, she is hardly noticed. Except by Connie, of course, but then she would notice.

The first person to record seeing Consuela, though not the first to actually see her, was Lucia, the granddaughter of Algernon Vietti. Lucia, even at fourteen, was an especially vigorous version of the Vietti women, with a black moustache and hairier-than-average armpits. (Vietti women could plait their armpit hair, and sometimes did.) Lucia had loved Consuela, missed her when she married and moved to Stockton, and was consoled by the fact that she at least had her ghost, which had conveniently regressed to her own age of fourteen. Secretly, she suspected that Consuela was a saint. And that, by appearing to herself, she bestowed some silvery saint-dust on her too. What did Lucia and Consuela chat about? What do saints and would-be saints talk about? Mostly boys, of course.

'Kissing boys looks a bit wet and messy-looking, don't you think?'

'Sure, I can't think of a single reason anyone would want to do it on purpose. It'd be like eating something you can't swallow. Like chewing tobacco or gum.'

'Petey McClarty down the town did it with Bella Sugaree. I saw them.'

'This Bella probably got tricked into it. She probably scoured her mouth out later with soap, poor thing.'

Lucia did not tell her father about her visitations; he was entirely as un-superstitious as all bankers must pretend to be. She recorded their conversations in her diary. She was not afraid at all, though the floating thing did bother her. Consuela was always a few inches off the floor – though not when she was outside, which was a puzzle. Then, her bare feet were always planted firmly in the grass.

The Vietti servants lived on the top floor, under the eaves. In the painting you can see what might be a child's face looking out of the top right window. Hard to tell, but it might be. It is always tempting to see what one wants to see, especially with so little tangible evidence. Tragically, there are no photographs of Consuela. It is still hoped by some that her wedding photographs will turn up in a garage sale somewhere near Stockton, though it is equally likely they could turn up in New York. Naturally, witnesses to her appearances have tried cameras; in fact, Consuela herself has prompted them to use them.

'Is that a camera? A real one that works? Take my photograph, please,' she would say. 'Oh, please, please try.'

'We can try, but I don't think it'll work, Consuela.'

'Course it'll work,' she'd say, and fuss with her hair and apply lipstick. Once she even ran to put another dress on.

'Smile, Consuela! Yes, that's right, lift your chin. Turn to me a little. That's good.'

Click click click. But in the end, the photographs never showed anything but empty rooms and gardens. In many ways, Consuela is a naïve ghost who has not read enough ghost stories to understand her limitations, especially regarding cameras. And she is not spooky, either, even if she does appear slightly cranky sometimes. Well, quite a lot of the time.

There are seventy-two 'genuine' recorded instances of Consuela visitations. The only pattern seems to be that she rarely appears to people who wait for her: the Consuela pilgrims who stare into corners and will her to appear. She favours people who are thinking of something else entirely, and quite often people who have no idea that the place is haunted. Her estimated ages during these sightings are mostly between four and ten which, if one subscribes to Consuela philosophy, is accounted for by the intensity of a child's perceptions. Like a magnifying glass when the sun hits it just so, she simply burned her most concentrated childhood moments through to other times. Her older self, witnessed far less frequently, perhaps lived lighter; skimmed the surface.

Increasingly impoverished years of Viettis passed, and in 1966 the house slipped out of family hands and became a commune. Mostly College of Marin students with a penchant for Sufi dancing, draft-dodging, acid and marijuana. Consuela was sighted quite a few times during these years, but half the time was mistaken for a stranger passing through. In her appearances as a young adult she was occasionally propositioned by pony-tailed young men with dilated pupils – she was, after all, lovely with her flowing simple dresses and eyes dark enough to drown in. At least three boys wrote poetry about her, and one named his daughter after her. Another boy, who later became the well-known Berkeley artist John James, drew a picture of Consuela:

As you can see, she had a rather heavy brow, a generous mouth and high wide cheekbones which gave her eyes an almost oriental appearance. But John James insisted that this drawing hardly captured her beauty, which had much more to do with her actual presence. She had a swiftness about her, he claimed, even when she sat still; an intelligence that not only shone from her eyes, but mysteriously from her entire being, as if her skin, her limbs – even her bones – were organs of heightened perception. 'It was as if she radiated an extreme awareness of her surroundings,' said John James. When it was a happy awareness she was very beautiful; but even when it was a cranky awareness she was still beautiful. No observers have reported her as anything less than a startling beauty.

(Note the small scar on her left forehead. It does not exist in descriptions of her earlier manifestations; presumably she acquired it during late adolescence, and it may or may not be related to her bike accident in 1920.)

By the time of the commune, many other houses had been built around the old Sycamore House. The windows no longer looked out onto a meadow, but a street of expensive redwood homes with decks and gleaming BMWs in double driveways – though there was rarely any sign of life. Just the occasional Hispanic gardener humming to himself, or Asian nanny sedately pushing a German stroller containing a sole offspring.

In 1993, Sycamore House was bought by one of these neighbours: Joe Johnson, the man who thinks ghosts should be popular in hospices and hires men off the street to sort out his septic tank and other more interesting problems. A man of retirement age with broken capillaries, naughty blue eyes and an unusually dreamy wife. He, especially at his age, saw no reason to pretend that old age didn't lead to death, and everyone knew that a proper death required the proper accessories. Expensive things that only a dedicated hospice could provide, based on the British model. Not just the care, but an actual place. If it was good enough for the Brits, damn it, it was good enough for Americans. Like the Jaguar, and Fawlty Towers, and the Beatles. Marin citizens, being both liberal and rich, have already promised him endless tax-deductible funds and volunteers, to allow any terminally-ill person a bed for free. Joe was optimistic, hoped for a Consuela revival.

But his timing, as always, was bad. Gentle Valleys Hospice waits, mostly in vain; an unfashionable portal to the unknown. Hub around which things happen. Or cease happening.

Joe's House

You can just see it from the hospice, about half a block away. The front door hides discreetly behind giant ferns and oleander bushes. In fact, the entire house is camouflaged with greenery, which lends a shadowy underwater effect to the interior. Inside, like a fish in a bowl, is Joe's wife June Johnson. Handwriting can be as informative as a photograph, or a descriptive paragraph; here is Junes' signature:

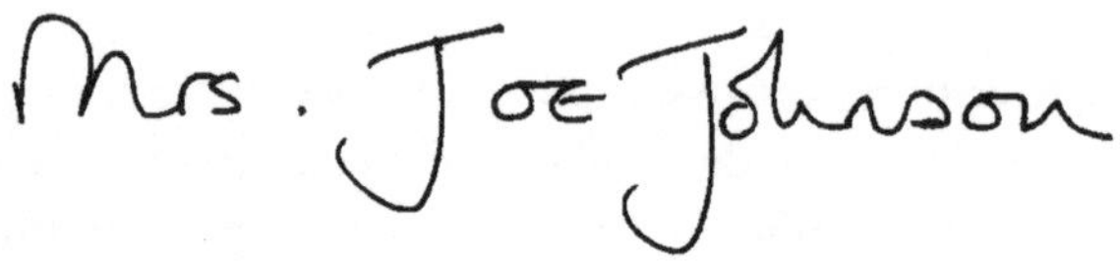

June is in the suspended state that she experiences every time her husband is not near. Vacant-eyed, slow to move. She is wondering whether it is worth vacuuming the bedroom. Would it take too long? Would it even be noticed? She stares and stares at corners softly padded with whorls of golden retriever hair. She decides they look like rodent nests, and yawns. Takes her sixty-six year-old body into the living room to sit down. She picks up the book that she has supposedly read a hundred times. It is June's classy-looking Penguin, and she promptly closes her eyes and goes into her trance state. Not sleep, because she must remain upright, and this means she can't completely let go. But she is not awake either. After a quarter of a century of practise, she can enter the waking dream state more quickly than any Zen Buddhist, and her dreams are a sight more pleasant. They are *spacious*. Sometimes she senses Consuela, or laughter where there should be silence; and aromas of wood smoke where there is only air-conditioning. She does not think this odd; her house, after all, was built in the extensive Sycamore House gardens. On the other hand, if her husband Joe ever saw Consuela, he would immediately stop drinking and be grumpy for days. Luckily June is mistress of Stress-free-ville, and uncritical of most things that come her way. Which is why she has no wrinkles yet, unlike her daughter Georgia-May, who runs around in circles as if her fretting could have the slightest impact on anything. Georgia-May will learn one day that the 'don't worry' gene is planted deep. Or she won't, and she'll end up the most wrinkly lady in town.

Joe is an energetic man and therefore wrinkly. He likes to get things done. It is ten-thirty and already he has closed the deal with Manuel, done his morning hospice round, and is now walking the dog. Moze is the most recent in a very long line of golden retrievers: all called Moze, all stupid, all smelly and all doted on by Joe and June. It is going to be another blistering day, but right now the sun still feels like a blessing. It is a blessed place to be: a leafy Fairfax lane on a summer morning.

Joe stops to listen to Norma, a neighbour, complain about Joe's dog. How Moze poops in Norma's garden and actually comes inside her house to have sex with Toodles, her passive male pedigree poodle. This is fortunate Marin County we're talking about, where people have time to get in a tizz about such things. Unlike June, who conserves her energy, Joe is quick to anger, especially when he suspects that he is clearly in the wrong, and delivers what he thinks is a scathingly original retort.

'Look, my dog can go where it likes. And if you have a problem with that, call the sheriff!'

'But Toodles *hates* sex, Joe. You know that,' says Norma in a mellow tone. 'Simply hates it. Moze practically rapes him.'

'Like Toodles really objects. Get real, Norma. Your dog may be gay, but it is physically impossible for Moze to rape Toodles.'

'I never said Toodles was gay, Joe. You know he's not gay! He's just, well, uninterested,' – in a less mellow tone, colour rising in her cheeks like a spreading stain. 'He's an only dog, and he's not used to company.'

Suddenly, Toodles barks hysterically from inside her house, and Norma gives a little scream as she notices that Moze is no longer next to Joe. She is menopausal, and things like this drive her insane. She races in to haul Moze back out with Toodles in hot pursuit, his neatly-coifed rear end humping away at thin air.

'This is not funny, Joe. If it happens again – well, I'll just have to – well, do that thing. I'll call the sheriff, Joe. I will!'

Norma bristles and returns to her house to slam her redwood door, tinkling her wind chimes angrily. A current of discontent quickly ripples through the air of the magic kingdom. But it is an old running battle and the ripples are gone in seconds.

Joe continues on his walk, re-playing his clever words. Silly old bag; she's just frustrated and lonely, that's what her problem is. He knows what she needs. He has been a very handsome boyish man for most of his life, and though externally he is starting to look his age, his inner self is still this attractive boyish man. He can't break the habit of viewing all women as creatures with hearts that he has the ability to break. He walks with a slight swagger, and is actually more attractive than he deserves to be, given all his wrinkles and bulging middle. Nearly seven decades of sunny weather have not been kind to his Celtic skin.

Moze pauses in front of a house and starts to pee, then decides this would be as good a place any to dump, and squats.

'Shit, Mozey-Wozey,' says Joe softly. With a small smile he heads towards home, while Moze squirts out a considerable mound of steaming diarrhoea on the front step of the house. Joe never carries a poop scoop. On principle.

He enters the house to find his wife nodding over an upside-down copy of *Sons and Lovers*. She has managed to keep her legs crossed very demurely at the ankle but her mouth droops open slightly, and a fly has decided that her nose is a safe enough place to rest for now. Joe gently blows off the fly.

'Asleep, honey?

She opens her eyes, instantly comes to when she sees Joe. Gets the look of love in her eyes, coy, girlish, and says,

'I'm not asleep.'

'I didn't say you were.'

'You said *wake up honey*.'

'No, I didn't. But as a matter of fact, you were asleep. Honey.'

'Joe, you always twist things. I just told you I was resting my eyes. Not asleep.'

'Okay, honey. Where are the car keys?'

'Where are you going?'

'To try and get some patients, of course. We're down to just smelly Fred Snelling and conked-out Connie. It's depressing. We need at least four more. Someone's got to work around here.'

'Oh. I knew that, Joe! Where will you go?'

'Somewhere. I don't know. I hired some Mexican guy this morning to help me. The keys?' Joe starts lifting up newspapers, phone bills, tubes of Moze's eczema cream, discarded socks, half-eaten candy bars.

'What Mexican guy?'

'I don't know, June. Mannola. Minnoola. How should I know? I put the keys here last night. Have you been cleaning?'

'You hired him? And don't you accuse *me* of cleaning!'

'Well, not exactly. I told him I'd hire him if he brought some patients in.' He peers under a table, behind sofa cushions.

June looks puzzled, so Joe elucidates:

'If he brings, like, a dying person to Gentle Valleys.'

'And what job would you give him?'

'He could be the hospice doctor. We could use a resident doctor. Anyway, he wouldn't really cost very much.'

'But he's a doctor, Joe?'

'He's a Mexican, June. Don't you listen?'

'Oh, right. Where did you meet him?'

'The usual place. I asked him if he could do the septic tank for us, and he said no.'

'So you asked him if he could be our doctor instead?'

'Well, kind of. He did offer. And he's dirt cheap, June. Don't look at me like that. Now where are the keys? In the kitchen?' June gets up and follows him to the kitchen.

'Why don't you just leave them in the car like I do? Then you'd never lose them.'

'Because I don't want to lose the car. Did you put them somewhere?'

'Well, obviously, but there's no need to get snappy with me.' The beginnings of a smile on her lips, her cheek muscles tensing.

'You don't know where they are, do you, June?'

'Of course I do.' A giggle in her eyes. She could be thirty.

'Where are they, then?'

She smiles broadly. 'I'm not telling you.'

'June, this is not a game.'

She laughs out loud, giddy, a ten year-old.

'I'll let you know when you're getting warm,' she says.

'Oh, this is stupid.'

'You're cold. Freezing.'

He has his angry face again, slightly flushed. Starts to leave, then yanks out a kitchen drawer. Dried-up felt tips, lead-less pencils and empty spools of thread spill onto the floor, roll under chairs and come to a halt in dog hair and fluffy dust.

'This place is chaos. I'm not doing this with you, June. Did you buy my beer?' Opens fridge.

'Warmer. Hot, scalding!' she says, almost jumping out of her seat.

And there they are. The keys are sitting in the clean butter dish inside the fridge. Of course.

She laughs.

'June. You're sick.'

'Oh, come here and give me a kiss.'

'Why the butter dish? Is that where keys go now?'

Moze returns, walks in the open front door and passes through to the living room, unnoticed by Joe or June.

'That's right.'

'You're so weird. I'm off.'

'Wait, don't forget my shopping list.'

'Where's the list?'

Laughs hysterically, almost crying. 'Right here, where it always is.'

He goes to take it from her, but she isn't letting go.

'A kiss first,' she pants between wheezes of laughter.

'No.'

'One baby kiss. A kiss, or no list, and no dinner.'

'Christ's sake, then.' He kisses her quickly. Then long and deep.

'Joe,' she says, coming up for air. 'Have you been skinny-dipping again? You taste like chlorine.'

'Course. You were there, silly.'

Somewhere on the Golden Gate Bridge a lovely little breeze full of brine and smog blows the shopping list off the dash board, out of the window, to be swept out across the Pacific Ocean. A very grand destiny for a Johnson list containing the words: mayonnaise, wine (white), Saran Wrap, dog food and coffee.

Cynthia Rogerson

Snelling Beings

Keep very busy, mostly sleeping, watching television and eating donuts. In their late twenties, they are just on the verge of not being able to get away with this any more. The creases of grease will settle into permanent lines; their waists will require much elastic. All this soporific activity means that they are fairly oblivious to lots of important things. Like despite the fact that their grandfather Fred Snelling lives in Gentle Valleys Hospice and they have known Joe and June Johnson their entire lives, they haven't noticed the emptiness of the hospice or Joe's desperate search for patients. This is not because Joe is secretive – he tells everyone; he gets quite boring about it – but because the Snellings are exceptionally lazy and self-centred.

They look alike and they have the same birthday, but they are not twins. They are brother and sister, Robbie and Carson, born exactly one year apart. (Carson is the girl.) Over time, many astrology enthusiasts (including their mother when she was not dead) have claimed their kinship came from the stars and planets. But they'll have none of it. They smoke cigarettes; smokers generally don't swallow astrology.

Today, four houses down from Gentle Valleys Hospice and across the road from Joe and June Johnson, these Snellings are in their yellow house listening to *The White Album*. Very loud. Old-fashioned for the turn of the century but then it is Fairfax, some corners of which are renowned for time-eddies; suitable for second-generation hippies and old hippies with grey pony-tails and vintage VW buses that now cost more than they did originally. Basically, it is still the sixties, with better coffee.

Recalling the sixties, their grandfather Fred Snelling once said: 'Oh, it was a wild time, a windy time.' (He'd shivered.) 'And it was like people were spinning away; it was like everyone was blowing away, and some got lost. Oh yes, some did.' That was back when Fred talked some sense, and he relayed the past to them poetically, if not always coherently. And he would know: his daughter, their mother, had been a Class A flower child. Bare feet, patchouli, no bra, Vietnam protests, the lot. She gave birth hippie-style: wedding ring-less, at home on bean bags, with sitar music followed by placenta stew eaten by scented candlelight.

Of course, kids never know their own luck, and Carson and Robbie grew up thinking they'd missed an important era. Though they have the edge time-wise – being further from death – they'll never know the exhilaration of hearing the Dead live in Golden Gate Park and dodging the riot police in Union Square. Everything their parents did to rebel is now politically correct, missing the entire point. These days, the only ways left to rebel are to litter intentionally or to be gay. There're only about twelve people who still find gayness shocking, which just leaves littering. And tossing a Coors bottle in the bay is just not thrilling enough.

Listening to John Lennon hammer out *Revolution* acts as a rejuvenator. (They are unaware that their mother used to nurse them to this music; they are also unaware that their mother nursed them until they were four years old. Fred disapproved; said it looked obscene.) The song stirs them up, causes their hearts to pump more blood, just like songs associated with oral gratification should. They are draped around the kitchen furniture singing along with John and Paul, playing a little air guitar, a little slap-on-the-table drums; letting the music send the old message to their muscles. Maybe providing enough impetus to actually leave the house. Maybe not. The message is: you are free, you can waste time, life is full of unlimited possibilities. You are young, you are young young young: are not yet twenty.

Like when they'd been teenagers in the mid-eighties. Slipped the noose of old Fred; hitched to Baja with a couple of hundred bucks between them to vegetate on beaches. Or, more unusually, rode a freight train to Denver in a brand new Chevy strapped to the top deck. Or rode the midnight express from Watsonville to San Diego, hunkering down on a windy flat-bed freight car loaded up with trucks. Wild times. Especially the freight train adventures, which were Robbie's idea. They never saw anyone else doing that. You would think that this took some courage, but they didn't really value their own lives enough to be afraid. Between trips they took odd jobs – sometimes very odd jobs – and quit the minute they had enough to go on another adventure.

These days they have less energy, probably smoke too much grass, and are too easily satisfied by nostalgia to create anything new to be nostalgic about later. Danger, especially, has lost its appeal. Hitchhiking has become so uncommon that drivers regard hitchers with suspicion. Marin, like themselves, is currently placid.

Carson, in particular, has difficulty with ageing, but then twenty-nine *is* old for a child. Like being too small for your age. She feels older now than she will at fifty-nine. She has recently, secretly, bought a tube of expensive eye cream which promises to reduce wrinkles. Of which she possesses one. Robbie does not feel as old as Carson but then he is one year younger, marginally more handsome, and therefore less vain.

Their house belongs to them outright, given to them by their grandfather Fred. So their need to earn money is not enormous. They work in San Rafael, about eleven miles away, at Café Ole; earn enough to pay for gas, groceries and the occasional ounce. They often watch television all night, old movies and talk shows, smoking joints and eating doughnuts. There's not been a single sensible act in the yellow house for years. Dishes left in sinks till they were beyond washing, beds permanently unmade and dirty socks adorning whatever they landed on when flung. Quite often lampshades. Cigarette butts on the bathroom floor along with a half-dozen empty toilet paper rolls. Sloth for the pure and simple sake of sloth. It's like they are still defying their parents to *make* them do chores.

They were orphaned at twelve and thirteen by a fluke car accident. Their father was smoking a joint, sloppily rolled with too many seeds. As he was passing it to their mother, several seeds crumpled out of the joint, red-hot, and burnt his bare leg. Causing him to swerve into an oak tree. Counsellors, teachers and doctors tried hard to persuade Carson and Robbie that they were deeply scarred and traumatised by their tragedy, but it just wasn't true. They had already entered that selfish era of adolescence and mostly saw their parent's disappearance as an inconvenient defection. As in: *It's not my fault! Look what they did to me!* They will both, at different times in the future, and as they approach the ages that their parents were at the end, feel quite shocked by their youthful callousness. They will weep a little for their flower children Mom and Dad. Well, Carson will weep and Robbie will take up bourbon for a time. But at the time, and even now, they saw their parents as old. Sad, certainly, but not too premature a death.

People say it is such a blessing when siblings are close, and so sad, so very sad, when they are not. But when siblings are very close they can form a kind of mafia and live in an exclusive world with their own rules. A kind of blood clique. Carson and Robbie have not bothered learning to get along with other folk, because they don't need to. They feed each other's cynical regard for every other human being. Basically they are snobs, in the deepest most dangerous sense.

Are Carson and Robbie Snelling universally unpopular, as they deserve to be? Not at all, for two very good reasons. First and foremost, they are stunning to look at – both of them – and have been since birth. In an amoral, careless, androgynous, pale-to-the-point-of-transparency way. The importance of beauty cannot be underestimated; they are exempt from all sorts of things. Like trying. And behaving.

Reason number two, only slightly less important, is the irony that many people love nothing better than people who don't care if they are loved. They want leaders, and leaders must be indifferent to people's opinions. Leaders set trends they are not even aware of setting, because if they cared enough to be aware, they'd not be leaders. The Snellings are even popular, in a mysterious way, despite despising:

People with no vices.
Do-gooders and volunteers of all kinds.
Anyone more popular than them. In fact, every 'in' group that ever was.
People who never run out of milk or bread.
People who cried at 'Titanic' and laughed at 'Bridget Jones.'
People who write not only Christmas cards, but Christmas card lists.
People with neat clear handwriting.
People who always return library books before they are due.
People who invest in burglar alarms.
Young people who buy life insurance and pensions.
Anyone who claims to know the meaning of life.
Happy optimistic types who drive newish economical hatchbacks.
Barry Manilow fans.

And basically all sorts of people for no reason at all, except that it is so liberating to not like them. Especially:

The people who like Snellings, who hang around them, absorbing Snelling insults and put-downs.

They tolerate:

Genuinely hard-up people.
People who pick them up hitch-hiking.
Hispanics, in general. Especially guys like Manuel Mendoza.
The lady with a glass eye who works the midnight shift at the 7/11 near them.
Old people and kids.
People who make no bones about who they are, like ostentatious rich people.
People who know life is short, like dancers; out-going types.
People of all ages who don't wait to warm up to things. Plungers-in.
Father O'Reilly at Our Lady of Happiness, but only because he's an alcoholic with spiritual doubts.
Anyone who makes them laugh, for any reason whatsoever. (This often involves folk from the despise list, so quite a lot of overlapping occurs.)
Policemen, because no-one else likes them.
Musicians, because they are magicians.
People who eat dessert before, or instead of, dinner.
Anyone who happily (the operative term) lives in a very messy house.
Georgia-May Johnson, even though she has a lot of qualities they despise. (In fact, they more than tolerate her. They need her.)
Joe Johnson, who has given them a lot of their values, though he and they will never realise this.
June Johnson, who has mothered them to within an inch of their lives, and still makes a birthday dinner for them.
Fred Snelling, who encouraged their hedonism and made French toast every Sunday, when these things mattered.
Underachievers everywhere. Wasters.
Misfits and losers, anyone shunned, anyone they can patronise. Lonely souls like Morag McTavish at El Sombrero. Late risers.
The ugly guy with no teeth who panhandles at Fourth and D.
The banjo player with the three-legged dog, in front of the San Francisco Macy's.
Anyone who they can't con, who likes them anyway.

They love, no, adore:

Themselves. A lot.

These Snelling lists are appropriate, for one of their strangely endearing (to some) habits is to compulsively make lists. Robbie, marginally more list-oriented than his sister, has even written a list of reasons why he makes lists. This is recorded on the back page of one of the notebooks that he keeps buying, intending to keep a diary:

Reasons to make lists:

> *To prove I am thinking clearly and am not just a neurotic list-maker.*
> *To remember what to do and buy, obviously. To have in front of me my thoughts, which while internal, are too numerous and incoherent to be comprehensible.*
> *To attempt, however futilely, to pin down the over-spilling universe.*
> *To keep track of my favourite albums, ex-lovers, current lovers, concurrent lovers, and future potential lovers.*
> *To record past petty crimes so as to avoid capture.*

Bad, bad, bad! They are so bad, these Snellings! They borrow money and expensive items of clothing from their friends and never return them. They never write 'thank you' notes or remember birthdays. They steal sometimes, even from friends, without shame: little things like tapes and candy bars. Sometimes things they have no need for whatsoever, but just because the impulse takes them. They use other people's toiletries when using their bathrooms, like lipstick, deodorant and toothpaste. They think it's a fun night out to sneak into concerts and movies for free, using back doors and fictitious names on guest lists. They have eaten several times in cafés without paying. They do not return library books ever, and have joined eleven county libraries. They have joined the same book and record clubs many times, under false names. They are impulsive liars. They exaggerate and fabricate for no other reason than the sheer joy of creating a world in which they are the stars.

When they have gas money, they drive an old yellow (to match their house) Volvo sedan which they have never bothered to insure or register. The previous owner, a Penny Smith from Larkspur, keeps getting their parking tickets and occasionally scans the faces on streets and in supermarkets, hoping to spot the Snellings and tell them just what she thinks of them. Not a lot. A lot of people think not a lot of them. (Well, you don't, do you?) This is okay by them. This is funny to them.

If they do have a moral code – and it cannot be emphasised enough that they have never thought seriously about moral codes – it's to be especially nice to people they have been horrible to, after diplomatic intervals. It's not much of a moral code, but they have never once broken this. By their own unconscious standards, they are honourable people. For instance, they always use the cafés they have ripped off. They often recommend these cafés to their friends. They leave generous tips.

Sex is a problem, but each finds that casual affairs (usually with each other's friends) pretty much do the job. Just to reassure themselves that they're not totally dysfunctional sexual beings. But always, they are relieved when the new lover is gone and they can pick their nose and relax again. Once or twice they have had to pick their noses first, in order to encourage the withdrawal. Because who can compete with their shared frame of reference? Who can make them laugh as hard? Their world is inviolate and softly padded with whorls of decadence, like June's dog-haired bedroom floor. Nothing is as easy as being together, and nothing is more fun than being bad together.

The CD ends, and they both move to push the play button again. Then pause simultaneously, like they often do.

'Let's go to San Anselmo and see Georgia-May,' says Carson. Georgia-May is Joe and June's daughter, and their oldest friend. In fact, she has transcended the friend category – she feels like an extension of themselves, and both Carson and Robbie feel mysterious little jolts when they meet people who know Georgia-May well, as if surprised to find she has an existence separate from them. She is *their* Georgia-May.

'Yeah. Call first, see if she's home.'

'Nah, she's got babies, she's always home. Or within ten minutes of home, having a pit stop somewhere. A gutter.'

'True. Poor Georgia-May. All those little hands, grabbing at her,' says Robbie who, thinking of Georgia-May breast-feeding, suddenly realises that she is the only woman friend he hasn't tried to sleep with. Why not? Now that she's so firmly ensconced in domesticity and unavailable, she should be attractive. But whoaa, he tells himself. They watched each other have toddler tantrums, splashed in each other's puddles of pee.

'She loves it. Earth momma, our Georgia-May.'

So the music has worked. They leave their house, the sore thumb on the block. It is the oldest house aside from Gentle Valleys, having been built for their great-grandfather, the faithful life-long gardener of the famous Viettis of Sycamore House. Pristine and picturesque for decades, until Fred was past it. The garden has not been weeded in eleven years. An anonymous slipper has been lying on the parched grass since last winter, as are a few of Moze's dried up faeces. None of this stops the Snellings from loving their house. It reeks of Snelling smugness.

They hop in their car and head to San Anselmo to visit Georgia-May Johnson, one of the few people they visit on purpose and not just because they want to borrow something. They sing snatches of an old song. A road song; takes them back to a desert highway and bottles of *cerveza* and tiny sweet bananas. They have been such great little pseudo-hippies, Robbie and Carson. Damn good times. Isn't it pretty to think so, whispers a cynical voice from their cerebral archives of movies or books or even lovers. Hard to keep it all straight. The past is a blur. If you can remember the sixties, you weren't really there. (But hey – they *weren't* there. Just born in a hippie conservation pocket.)

As they drive away, they nearly hit Joe Johnson's new black Jaguar. This makes Joe's face look funny and they laugh – laughing at people being their main hobby. They laugh, and then they laugh at themselves laughing because they're stoned and they know they're bad to laugh at Joe's fright. Oh, they are so funny! Ha ha ha ha.

It is Joe's daughter they are going to visit, and he doesn't know this but would hate it if he knew. Joe thinks they are a bad influence on Georgia-May, and has done since they were all kiddies walking off to school together. He glares and his face makes them feel corrupt and naughty.

They stop at a red light and a lady in a green car stopped on the other side of the junction starts honking furiously at them and waving her fat fists.

'Jesus Christ, lady. What's your problem?' says Carson, flicking her cigarette ash out the window and casually giving the lady the finger. Robbie is the driver, and is not noticing people in cars.

The lady gets out of her car and starts to hurtle towards the Snellings with a menacing glower.

Is it? Is it? It is!

'Hit it, Robs – it's that lady again. You know, the one we got the car from. Penny Poo Poo Pa Doo. From Larkspur.'

'Shit, the light's still red.'

But the traffic flow has ceased and Robbie eases across. They both hear Penny's fingernails scrape the side as she attempts to stop them.

When they stop laughing they put another tape on, worn out from so much pointless mirth.

◆◆◆◆

Unaware of the impending Snelling invasion, Georgia-May unlatches her most recent baby from her chewed-up breast, and very slowly settles her onto her bed. Then turns to her computer to write. She tries to write something every day, to stop the haemorrhage of brain cells induced by the first pregnancy, but it feels like plugging a bursting dam with an eroded dummy. Nevertheless, she writes. She has honed her imagination with countless witty and comforting put-downs, imagined after the events in which they might have had some use. She also feels she contains enough inherent dishonesty to be a good novelist. Is it a novel? It is starting to unravel into something. She frowns and concentrates, then starts flicking away at the plastic computer keypad.

Her house is not perfectly orderly, but it exudes calm and domestic serenity. This is one reason Robbie and Carson gravitate towards her. She is their mother figure, even though she is the same age. Despite not caring enough to keep the cutlery drawer crumb-free or the toilet bowl scum-free, they find it soothing to be in the presence of someone who does care enough to do these things. You can see by her signature that Georgia-May cleans her cutlery drawer at least twice a year:

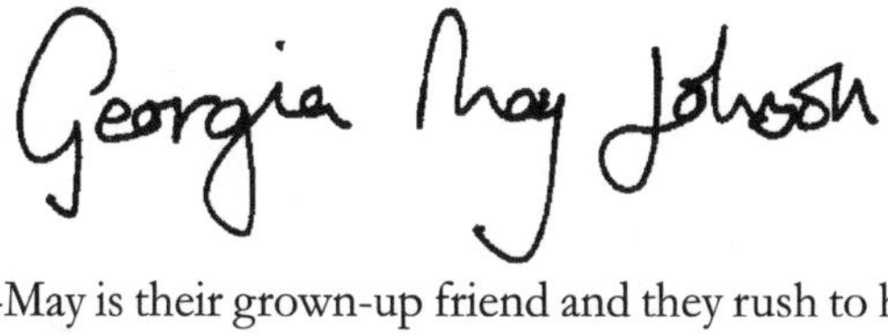

Georgia-May is their grown-up friend and they rush to her whenever they feel insecure, which is a lot recently, for some reason – probably to do with their age. Georgia-May loves baking bread and remembering birthdays and being a mother and keeping to her budget and saving for little outings. She has plunged enthusiastically into the pool of maturity, while they haven't even dabbled their little toes. Georgia-May, in true

Johnson style, owns a golden retriever, but with a slight illicit thrill has purchased a poop-scoop. She has not told her father yet.

On top of this respectable poop-scoop, Georgia-May even has a respectable husband, a shadowy nameless figure that she hasn't become truly acquainted with yet. Her young children are like static and she just can't receive him. He's like an annoying fly on the other side of the screen. Visible, noisy, and irritating some days. Buzzzzz.

She writes and after the first few minutes of hesitancy and stiffness, she disappears into it. It is a wicked story, and it is the easiest story she's ever written. Already written years ago, stored up in some grey-celled closet, waiting for now.

She can see the reviews already: *Despite being yet another autobiographical first novel, this book shows immense originality and humour. A work of art.*

Morag Angusina McTavish

Away across the county, about ten miles from the Snellings and Johnsons in Fairfax, there's a neighbourhood where freeway smog accumulates and sits like puddles of soup in the flat streets and yards. It's called Ben Nevis – Ben being Gaelic for mountain. There is no mountain in sight, nor is there anything else Scottish – except, of course, Morag Angusina McTavish, who has remarked on this irony with boring frequency. Several ironies, in fact, if you count her presence in an American town with a Highland name.

Ben Nevis is a nice place to live, with nice people living there, but it is a far cry from the shady green lanes of Fairfax. It's too new, for one thing. The streets are all in straight rows, and the houses all built by the same contractor. There are no tall trees. The tiny houses look like rows of characterless pastel shoe-boxes, each with tiny strips of yellowing lawn.

They have their own shopping mall – Golden Hills, or just Goldie for short – and they use it. Lately, Fairfax types have begun to encroach on this territory, realising the bargains to be had. Even though they hardly require such cut-rate savings. The parking lot is dotted with the occasional glaring Jeep Cherokee and Audi. Nothing has happened yet, but the real estate agents are sniffing around the area, sensitive to the potential value of the land should the aristocracy of Marin ever decide to slum it. Fashions of the upper classes are so unpredictable – one year they all want to look elite in BMWs and Saabs, and the next it's cooler to be unpretentious, drive old American cars. Marin real estate agents, by their job, are banned from entry into the inner circles. So they've had to develop hyper-sensitive social perceptions. The fully-evolved real estate agent is social litmus paper.

Morag Angusina McTavish, who lives in 37 Ben Nevis Crescent, is a lady from the Highlands of Scotland who has no problem with phenomena like Consuela, but who tends to treat them as she does neighbours that she does not need favours from yet. Distantly. In Inverness, the ancient town where she grew up, the air is thick with echoes; so thick that she had trouble sleeping some nights with the noise they made. Before Marin had even one lonely Indian, Inverness was already a thriving capitol.

Her accent is beginning to resurface; her *r*'s are getting more burred every day as her child-self resurges in her loosening skin. There is a similarity between her *r*'s and the *r*'s of her Mexican neighbours. Marrrin, she says, and her own name in her mouth sounds almost like Morrrdage. Her full name has become a sort of mantra lately; some mornings she finds herself saying it out loud.

'Morag Angusina McTavish, will you not get out of your bed and make yourself a cup of tea?'

Perhaps she is delving into it for clues to her past – Morag, after her deaf granny from Lewis. Angusina, after her dad who had no son. McTavish – the long line of short sturdy men from Ayr who steadily married and begat without thinking, and migrated gradually north to Inverness. When she says her name she recites history, summons ghosts, tells herself about herself. And she seems to need to know, these days.

Morag is a neat, small-boned woman who wears feminine pastel T-shirts and tailored jeans. She signs her name like this:

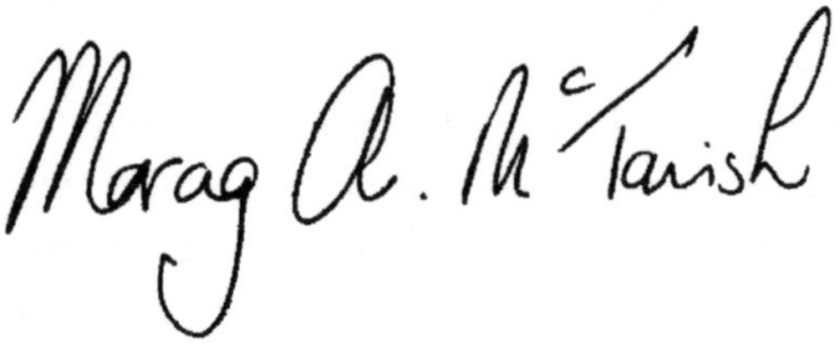

She knows Manuel Mendoza (the man that Joe Johnson has hired as a pretend doctor) because she works with him in the kitchen at El Sombrero in Fairfax; they have a friendship that puzzles her some days. She thinks about him more than she'd admit to anyone; he is one of the reasons she keeps her job there, even though it means four bus rides every day. She doesn't know the Snellings or the Johnsons, though she has seen them many times as they live within a mile of El Sombrero. Joe and June Johnson frequently pass her, waiting at the bus stop. Carson and Robbie Snelling often sit in El Sombrero and eat tacos containing the lettuce that Morag has chopped, despite the unpleasant scene last year about the unpaid bill. Once Georgia-May Johnson's elder daughter threw up in the El Sombrero's bathroom, and it fell to Morag to clean it up.

Morag, at this moment, is surveying her kitchen. (Like women do, like June does, like Georgia-May does, like Carson does not.) She is wondering if the eight years she has spent in it – cooking, eating, washing dishes, mopping, singing, drinking tea, reading – will leave any mark if she leaves, though she has no plans to. She is having one of her transience-of-life moments, brought on by a 1930 penny she found that morning while weeding her garden. It doesn't take much now to send her down this road. The kitchen looks so much hers right now – her pictures on the wall, her bulletin board with photos and dental appointments. She is an extremely tidy and organised woman and her kitchen reflects this. It shouts: Morag! Impossible she could be erased from it – that it will appear bare and neutral to another owner. And yet this is certainly what will happen. Another woman will stand right where she is standing, and have identical thoughts. Perhaps even find this very same penny.

(Other women have already stood on this exact same spot; in fact one of them, Mabel Murray, dropped this penny while fishing the house keys out of her purse in the dark. Mabel also had moments of imagining another woman being mistress of her kitchen, and it made her feel old and sad.)

As Morag contemplates her own mortality she feels a little dizzy, as if she is fading in substance already. She is nothing, she will leave no mark, she does not exist, perhaps she never has. After all, who will miss her, whose life will be altered if she vanished?

Who, exactly, is she, and how has she spent her one and only life? And why is she still, after forty-nine years, asking this question? She sits down at her kitchen table, closes her eyes and is very still for a while. Is she reaching for answers? Reconciling her present to her past?

Who knows what really goes on inside people's minds, what they really do when alone in their houses and rooms, doors shut, especially in the afternoons. Things they never talk about. June reads Penguin Classics to empty her mind. Joe calculates how much profit he is not making. Snellings get stoned, listen to hippie music. Georgia-May eats Twinkies and watches daytime talk shows. Manuel has siestas. Some people masturbate. Perhaps a few of the aforementioned masturbate. Morag has no way of knowing about other people; she only knows what she does. It feels as furtive to her as a private wank, and she certainly indulges with increasing frequency as she gets older.

When Morag is not asleep and not awake – when she is tired or pensive, like now – she often watches a vivid film behind her eyelids.

Oh yes, she just wantonly walks into it without a backward glance. She talks to people, tastes and smells things, feels textures. Sometimes, after hours in this nether land, she opens her eyes and glances at a clock that tells her the astonishing fact that only a minute had passed. She has found a secret door, or window; it can be viewed without entering. Morag is addicted to a hallucinatory time-distorting daydream.

Or it is real?

Morag, in her deepest most superstitious little-girl self, wonders. Maybe it is a timeless place she could inhabit. An answer to entropy. After years of cultivating this habit, certain venues in her dreams have become so familiar that she experiences nostalgia for them. Certain streets and cities are re-visited many times, as are certain houses and flats and people. She often finds new rooms in familiar buildings, and comforting encounters with men she has never met.

Some people masturbate. A lot. Maybe a lot of people masturbate a lot. Morag closes her eyes and stretches time. She finds no answers, but a place where the questions are irrelevant.

Siesta Man

Manuel Mendoza is back home after meeting Joe; in fact, he's gone back to bed, but he is not sleeping. He is luxuriating in the awareness that he does not start washing pots for another hour. It's a kind of cheap thrill that he never gets tired of; the fount of nearly all his happiness: being conscious of the absence of pain or boredom. And when he's washing pots, he says to himself: thank God I am not jobless. He's not a man to let time slip by unappreciated, and he has very low standards too, which helps immensely. Lots of folk would find Manuel's life depressing. He washes pots at El Sombrero for a living, for heaven's sake! He is not in his home country – a foreigner! Unmarried, fat, and forty. And what does he have to show for his life so far? He lives in a part of town that is as ugly as parts of town get in Marin. Much worse than Morag's neighbourhood, which at least has houses. This part of town is comprised entirely of apartment blocks built in the sixties, in a canal area where they are an eyesore to nobody but the inhabitants. Kids who live here tend not to bring their school friends home. Dog-catchers know these streets well, for stray dogs roam night and day, as do skinny cats with missing ears and eyes, rats, mice and for some reason an over-abundance of big black beetles. The garbage here does not tempt the racoons, who tend to favour neighbourhoods like the Johnson's and Snellings'. Even the mosquitoes and ants in Manuel's neighbourhood seem desperate. They suck more blood and seem more resistant to insecticides.

Does any of this bother Manuel Mendoza? Does it look like it does? Look at him.

What Manuel has to show for his life is this: his life. Not such a small thing, after all. And now Manuel's big break has come at last, and all because he started the day thinking that he should keep his options open.

Fred Snelling and Moze Hum

Joe Johnson takes his dog Moze with him to Gentle Valleys Hospice so often that the dog includes the hospice in her home territory. Wandering between them is what she does when she is a little lonely or bored or hungry. Both mean home. Today, while Joe is in San Francisco chasing frail-looking people, Moze scratches at Fred Snelling's door in the hospice.

Come in, old dog, Fred thinks. 'Cococoenenen,' is what he croaks.

Moze walks around in a little circle, then curls up near enough to the bed that Fred can reach over and let his hand be licked. His skin is so dry it is hard to imagine it tasting of anything but paper, but Moze loves to slobber over it and Fred loves the feel of warm slimy wetness.

What a good old dog you are, he thinks, then closes his eyes and hums a tune. It goes on and on, up and down, then up. If Moze could hum, this is what she would hum too: not the accompaniment to a song in her head, but the vibrations of the universe channelling through her throat. Life as sound, pouring into air, drifting. Neither dog nor old man has a thought in their head as they lie, tongue to hand.

Slurp slurp, hum hum. Oh bolomio, hums Fred.

Fred's signature reflects his slipping grasp on the part of life that requires legibility.

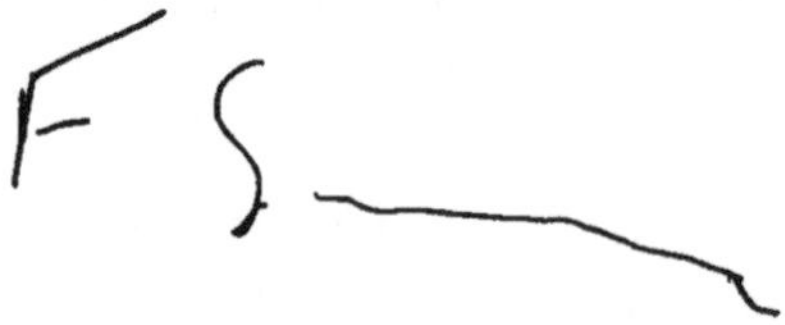

Moze and Fred are old and already they cannot differentiate between floating Consuela and Connie, the old woman who seems to be permanently parked in the window seat upstairs, snoozing with her eyes half-open. Moze side-stepped Consuela today in the garden, a five year-old Consuela who tried to stroke her, but that is the extent of Moze's response. Fred patted Consuela's soft curls after breakfast and remembered who she was, but not her name or her context. Dog and man both conserve their energy to prolong their state. Life is a boat they keep afloat with sleep, humming and licking, not questioning.

Moze's food, meanwhile, sits half a block away, where June has left it in a plastic bowl inside the oven. It is expensive dog-meat and she doesn't want the flies to get it before Moze does. Moze is so slow to eat these days. Another older bowl sits in the refrigerator. On the floor in her tin water bowl another fly drowns, joins the black clump of insect carcasses. The house is quiet, no dust has been disturbed after all, and the rooms breathe slow and calm.

11:52 am, August 14th, 2000, Marin County

Joe Johnson looks for rich death candidates in the Marina District, trawling all the likely places: convalescent homes, park benches, yacht clubs. A good class of patient would be nice. Joe, in a business sense, is hanging on by the skin of his expensively-cleaned teeth. Which he is displaying, to no advantage whatsoever right now, to an eighty-two year-old spinster named Fanny O'Leary.

June Johnson sits in her trance state while ants march calmly over her toes.

Connie sits in her third-floor window seat, and looks at hills. Her eyes light up for no perceptible reason, as if she sees something.

Carson and Robbie Snelling pull up outside their old friend Georgia-May Johnson's house and Georgia-May tsks and sighs. Shuts down her computer and notices guiltily that Chloe has been watching videos for three hours while eating Oreos.

Morag McTavish combs her thin strawberry blond hair, applies apple-red lipstick and walks to the dentist, the old penny in her pocket.

Manuel Mendoza sits next to a middle-aged woman on the bus. This woman moans about her mother-in-law called Edith, who lives with them and is starting to smell really bad. 'Old lady stink, know what I mean? It's like embedded in the walls now.' Manuel smiles in a very doctorly way.

There they all are, in their own important worlds. And around them swish hundreds of other people, also in their own important worlds. It's hard to believe, but they don't really see each other. Some people, like Morag, have to look at old coins to feel transient, but there's stronger evidence in watching people go about their daily lives. Everyone spinning away, oblivious to other orbits. Incapable, even, of imagining other orbits, other suns. It would take up too much space, and they might forget things, like picking up the shirts from the cleaners or defrosting the fridge.

Consuela, of course, thinks she is no different – though she is. This makes her cranky. She's always had an odd nature; you'd think she'd get used it. Consuela has existed on this date and time, and in this county, though not this year.

Sycamore House, Fairfax, August 14th, 1912

There is a four year-old girl upstairs and she is a very good little girl normally: everyone loves her. She may be just four but she understands everything you tell her, and she knows she must stay upstairs until her mama comes to bring her down. This feels right to her, and normally she doesn't mind. She has a doll upstairs, a small rag doll called Lucinda with black boot-button eyes and a little red gingham dress which exactly matches her own red gingham dress. The girl isn't wearing this dress right now; in fact she isn't wearing anything. Although it's morning still, upstairs it's stifling. She began the day with her dress on, as well as her socks and underwear and even a gingham hair-ribbon to match her dress. Her mama gave her a glass of warm milk as usual, and a slice of cornbread thickly smeared with butter and blueberry jam.

'Now, you just wait here, my Consuelita,' said her mama in Portuguese. Then she switched to English – she doesn't want Consuela to have problems in school later. She has big plans for her daughter – Consuela is so bright! 'I'll be back up to get you in a little while, when I finish the baking. You don't want to be in the kitchen this morning – so much flour everywhere! Is like a dust storm down there. Do you know what day today is? It is August 14th – Master Vietti's birthday! So much baking for the party I must do. Those Viettis are such little piglets! Oink, oink, oink,' said her mama, snorting through her nose. Her mama is so funny and so pretty. Consuela never gets tired of looking at her.

But that was hours ago; the milk is gone, as is the corn bread, and Consuela is thirsty again. She cannot remember now if she is supposed to go down and help herself to more milk, or if this is one of those *no no no* days. Days when the downstairs is full of fancy-dressed strangers.

Some days there are fancy-dressed strangers all over the place, even when it is not a *no no no* day. Once she met a man who wore his hair in a pony-tail like her own, and who told her naughty jokes about the Irish men on the railroad. Another time she met a little Chinese girl called Ching, and they played jacks till Ching faded away halfway through eating a peanut butter sandwich. Consuela can never tell that these people are unusual until they leave in their unusual way – by dissolving quite rudely, without preamble. No goodbyes or see-you-laters. Her mama calls these folk Consuela's pretend friends, and doesn't like her to talk to them in front of her. So Consuela tries not to, being a good girl and loving her mama, but it is so hard not to mix them up with ordinary folk. She has entire days when she doesn't speak to anyone for fear of getting it wrong.

She sings a little song, sits in the window seat and sucks her thumb till it wrinkles, then begins to undress. Now she is naked, a brown chubby cherub. The old lady sits in the window seat again, just looks out the window, and Consuela ignores her like she always does. The hubbub downstairs drifts up to her, making her feel lonely – despite the old lady, who is no company at all. (She is one of the dissolving ones. In fact, she is the most frequently dissolving one.) The air is so still that dust motes lazily loiter mid-air; she watches them to see if they move at all. She breathes heavily for a few seconds to make them move, then holds her breath as she worries about breathing the motes in. They look so substantial. She sneezes, which causes an atmospheric change; the motes dance and her particles of moisture glint in the air. It is entrancing.

Consuela is normally a good girl and does what she is told, but her throat is very dry and after so long even the dust motes lose their fascination. She hasn't forgotten that she's naked, but she has forgotten that naked is not the right thing to be, flying down the stairs, out the back door to the ice box in the screened porch.

She is so quick that no-one spots her till after she has had her drink of milk. She gulps her milk, notices how much cooler the air is on her skin and both these things makes her feel good; she smiles by dancing. (She often gets her responses mixed up like this.) Solemn-faced, she lifts her arms, stands on tip-toe, and slowly twirls in the shadowy light. The boy called Freddy comes out to the porch, but she does not stop dancing just because he is watching. He is only seven, he hardly counts. Besides, he is not a Vietti, he is the gardener's son. Finally, when the dance leaves her, she smiles. The sight of her solemnity melting like this, after the beauty of her serious slow dance, makes Freddy unutterably happy. So he pushes her over and makes her cry. What else can a boy do?

Part Two

Mama! Mama! Over here! Here I am, mama, by the lemon tree. Mama! What happened to you! Oh dear, my dear dear mamacita, why is your face all squished and saggy? Why are you making the sign of the cross? Have I done something wrong again? I'm sorry I make you cry. Mama! Come back! Mama!

Excerpt from *The Consuela Chronicles.* Only recorded instance of Consuela appearing to her own mother, Oct. 12, 1951. Señora Garcia had not seen her daughter for twenty years, when Consuela left her house as a young bride. She recalled a time when Consuela, about six years old, came running crying into the kitchen, and said to her: 'Oh, thank goodness, mama. Your face is all right again!' and flung her arms around her. This may or may not be connected to the above transcribed incident.
Estimated age of Consuela: six.
Location of apparition: fruit orchard of Sycamore House.

Life in El Sombrero

Morag is late getting to work, and Manuel gives her his look. His 'typical, of course you're late again' look. A cross between resignation and immense satisfaction that he has been proved correct in predicting her lateness. This is quickly replaced by his simmering dark-eyed look of desire. He fancies her like mad. Morag is not pretty, but there *is* something about the way that her wispy ginger hair, when tied up, falls around her pale face and neck. And, more importantly, something about the way that she doesn't fancy him.

In addition to lust – laced through his lust – is Manuel's perennial homesickness, which Morag should recognise but misinterprets as chronic hay fever.

'What was it this time, Moragita?' shouts Manuel, hands on hips, his voice thick with lust and homesickness.

'I was at the dentist,' she says. 'And my name is Morag. Mor. Ag.'

'Sure thing, Señora Morag.'

'Ah, Manny. Manny Welly-Belly. It's no big deal, is it? I mean, is the lettuce even washed yet?'

'*Sí, sí*, ages ago. And please do not call me that.'

'A wee bittie crabbit today, are we?'

'I hate it when you go all Brit on me. Worse than gringo.'

'Sorry, dear: it's like a rash. It just appears sometimes.'

'Well, get some cream.'

'Or I could just call in sick.'

'You would.'

'I might.'

'Like I would care. Hey, why not just quit? I'm quitting soon too, anyway. I'm getting a better job,' he says in a superior tone which immediately grates on her. As if he is not her equal in the kitchen, not to mention the world – Scotland and Mexico both bordering richer countries. As pot-washer, he might even be below her. She has noticed this; she tunes in to social subtleties.

'Right.'

'You don't believe me? You watch. I won't be here next week. I waltz out of here, say *adios* to Mr. Eric Bo Beric. I will be what I was in Mexico.'

'And what was that? Besides starving.'

'Look at these hands. Guess.' He lifts his graceful long fingers, then wiggles them.

'A masseur?' she asks hopefully.

Why hasn't Morag considered Manuel as a lover? Lots of other women do; he's one of those men who love women, and woman do tend to love being loved. He's not bad at all, once you imagine him out of his pot-washing overalls, which have a constant guacamole stain down the front. Quite a nice chin, always looking like it needs a shave, as if his virility can't be kept at bay by a mere razor. But no, Morag feels nothing, never even has thoughts like this. She thinks – she really believes – that she does not fancy Manuel.

'A doctor!' he says triumphantly. Hey, it worked with the woman on the bus; she's invited him to assess Edith Spagosa, her mother-in-law, for hospice eligibility tomorrow. The ball is rolling.

'Oh, aye, that'll be right, and I'm really a solicitor. Give me just a wee bittie break, Manny.'

'You laugh, but you will see, you will see.'

'I sincerely hope not.'

'Break my heart again with your cynicism! Go on, here is a knife. Stick it in. You never believe me. And why don't you sleep with me any more? Why?' He leans towards her, dripping suds, and whispers, 'When will you come to me again?'

'Ach, away you go with your pathetic fantasies, Manny. You sad boring soul.'

All these words are flung lazily in the heat. They are just a variation on the way Morag and Manuel greet each other five days a week. He flirts, she deflects. Static electricity fills the air, crackles under their shoes, then dissolves unnoticed. If either said anything different, something sweet and soft, or acted differently, then hurt confused feelings would fill the air and sour all the food. Morag puts on her plastic apron, washes her hands, and greets the gigantic colander holding seventy-two heads of Romaine lettuce.

'Aye, you're waiting on me, are you? Well, I'm here now, come to shred you to pieces. Who's first, then?'

She checks her knife for sharpness and begins slicing the lettuce. In the sun from the window, Morag works in a halo of fresh lettuce water. A greenish glow, sweet-smelling and skin-softening. Of course, she never notices, just knows it is her least-hated chore. The tomatoes are far less obliging with their juice, which mainly runs down the counter and drips onto the floor – and occasionally onto her sandal-clad feet. Some nights she has to unpick tomato seeds from between her toes.

'Hey, Moragita – maybe they should buy these new automatic shredders, nice and quick and clean. Then you won't worry about being late. No job, no being late.'

'I don't worry, Manuel. Machines don't have eyes: customers would get bits of slug in their tacos.'

'Taco Bell use shredders. *No problemas* there. You don't hear about Taco Bell getting sued for sluggy tacos. Besides, it's extra protein.'

But Morag doesn't hear, because she has just noticed that Eric is in the kitchen too. He has been in the office, but now he is checking the ovens, sniffing in his authoritative way. Walking (no gliding) down the kitchen aisle towards her on smooth muscular legs clad in khaki shorts. She instantly becomes suffused with lust which, being a woman of her generation, she can only possibly translate as love. She can feel herself swell out – not just her lips, though these are the most noticeable. Every part of her is filling with hot pounding blood. The closer he gets, the more drunk on her own desire she feels. Her pupils dilate. Lettuce slips wetly though her fingers. The knife glints dangerously.

'Hello Eric,' says Manuel.

Eric nods and smiles. Friendly but cool, the face he reserves for all his illegal staff. Ready to disown them at a second's notice, yet happy to pay the lower wage.

Morag breathes shallow little breaths and hates herself for longing for Eric to brush against her.

'Morning, Morag,' says Eric, for Morag is foreign but she is not illegal.

'Hi,' she manages, casually sweeping the hair from her face. Cheek muscles taut, eyelids half-shut. All signals go.

Then she misjudges the knife's edge and cuts her hand – just a slight graze, but the blood is horrifyingly bright against the green.

'Oh shit, Morag,' says Eric. 'Jesus, put your hand over the floor. You're dripping everywhere.'

Morag can't reply because her dream has come true. Eric is touching her. Lifting her hand to see the damage. Holding it like a disgusting specimen. She turns it slightly, so the age spots will not be so blatant against his flawless hand. Most of her skin isn't too bad – still white and creamy after all these years, but her hands are shot.

'Go get a band-aid on it,' says Eric, suddenly losing interest, and Morag's heart plummets and the blood recedes back to where it came from. The fount of all erotic expectations. It's like the sun going in.

So much excitement in one day. First the spell of melancholy after finding that old penny. Then the dentist office, twenty minutes of blissful passivity while the young dentist cradled her head and gently probed her molars. Mortality, then sensuality. Now this. She feels deflated and not far from self-loathing. As she walks to the office for the first aid kit, she has a sudden longing to be married again. That safe, boring state of passionless sex on demand, that Bastille where no other man may humiliate her with her own longing.

Technically, Morag does have a husband. In fact, she has husbands. Her current husband Harry is ensconced in a cheerleader's embrace right now – well, not a cheerleader: more a North Beach stripper. Same thing, anyway, when you were fifty-five. Harry, who always had a knack for good timing, left her two years ago, just as her physical attractions were no longer immediately obvious. Forty-seven is, let's face it, a terrible age. Possibly the worst. It is far more painful than later ages because hope and vanity are still lingering, the last to realise the truth. Hope and vanity cling on to twenty-eight, or thirty-five at the oldest, way past the point of credibility. Forty-seven requires candlelight and certain poses. She is forty-nine now and down to only one good angle – her right side, when her chin is lifted. It takes some manoeuvring to go through life presenting only one angle to men. For herself, she simply avoids mirrors.

Coupled with this injustice is the humiliating and cruel arousal she has begun to experience in drenching waves in supermarket queues, in elevators, on buses. She visits a male hairdresser every three weeks, for the touch of his hands and the un-stated promise that he will make her look younger, more kissable She finds all sorts of excuses to visit the doctor and dentist. The erotic touch of professional impersonal hands on her body while she is prone. She feels forever poised for the big kiss, the big romance, her lips puckered, eyes shut, only to be left on the high tide mark, the sea endlessly receding. When she opens her eyes, she is always alone.

Lately, she's begun to think that this is her fate – to not be kissed by objects of her affection. She continues to oil her skin, do exercises, take vitamins, but more and more suspects that it's all in vain. No man will ever covet her flesh again, and this seems the saddest thing of all – even when she reads about earthquakes and child slavery and epidemics and curses herself for being so shallow. Unanswered lust is a perpetual blade in her abdomen.

She sometimes thinks she would like to give a party (she used to give lots), but is afraid these days that no-one would show up but her weirdest friends like Ethel the Jesus-freak, or Ophelia the vegan healer, or that Dolores from across the road who still wears brown leggings. They'd all sit around being polite and boring and not getting drunk. They would make her suicidal.

Death, plainly, is an option. It has, truth be told, entered her daydreams quite often lately. Clean cheap painless methods; thoughtful wise notes left to clarify things. The tears of joy when the beneficiary (who?) of her life insurance is announced in the sedate grey lawyer's office. Oh, she will be so loved, so missed, *so noticed.* And at the back of the church, Eric will have to jostle with all the other men, grief-stricken and full of regret, for they would only just now be realising the depth of their passion for the lovely and good Morag. Oh, and all the women she's ever fallen out with – the lady at the budget bulk supply store, her big sister Aggie, her old neighbour in Toronto, her pal Fiona McPhee who told her at ten she was a right nosy besom and a thrawn wee bitch – they'll be there too, but closer to the altar. Less ambiguous, but likewise chastened, alongside all her husbands and all the boys she dated just once and in fact every handsome young face she's ever seen from the back of a bus or passing crowd – all these people will be flooding the church with their tears. The minister will have to shout to be heard over their wailing. Ah, the shame of it all, the tragedy, and it'll be too late, too late! Yes, contemplating her death is probably the most reliably satisfying hobby she has these days.

Morag wraps a Mickey Mouse band-aid around her hand in Eric's office and wants to cry for the waste of herself, for the grand romantic gesture she will never enact. She waits till she hears Eric leave the kitchen and go out to the restaurant, then she returns to her mountain of wilting Romaine lettuces. Their juice helps. It is soothing, like a balm. She hums awhile before she notices that the song she is humming is one from her Highland girlhood. A love song. Sad, of course. She sings the words, softly.

'Moragita, sing louder. I can hardly hear you,' shouts Manuel from his steamy deep sink of greasy water.

She tries, but the burst of energy it takes to propel her voice further is too much in this heat, and in her mood. Her throat is filled with the kind of unfocused sorrow that easily comes with habitual funeral fantasies.

'Sorry Manny, you sing for me. Sing for me in Español.'

He obliges with gusto, and even swivels his hips for her benefit. He is a terribly over-the-top flirt, which helps to disguise his genuine flirtatiousness. This way, she rebuffs only the clown Manuel, not the sore-hearted lover. He is not in her realm of possible men who would be heaven to kiss and who would love her true self. Dear sweet Manuel is not even in a three-mile radius of this realm. He is Mexican, he is fat, he is short and, worse of all, he is almost ten years younger. Which makes her feel old.

'Louder, Manny. I can hardly hear you.'

'Never satisfied, woman. I know you.'

Manuel Drinks Wine

The next day, Manuel gets lucky. He gets Edith Spagosa. It is easy: so easy that probably anyone could get Edith Spagosa, but nevertheless he is proud. Edith is delivered and installed, and a dozen volunteers are hovering over her right now.

'This is fantastic, Manuel,' Joe says, remembering the right name for the first time. (This is because he's started on the red wine early today. He doesn't know it's the correct name, but would happily laugh at the coincidence of getting it right without trying.) 'Best news I've had all month. Brilliant!' Joe looks like he might hug Manuel, and Manuel moves backwards a step.

'So, does this mean I will be working for you now, like you said in the car? A job at Gentle Valleys? I am a very good doctor.'

'Sure you are, sure you are. Excellent, you're excellent. Wait till I tell June.'

'About my new job?'

'Got to take the dog for a walk now. Tell you what, come to my office about two on Friday and we'll talk about your job, right? But things being how they are – *certain agencies, being what they are,*' he whispers, 'better to leave it between you and me for a few days. Just till I figure out how to swing it. Understand?'

'A secret job?'

'Just for a few days, my friend. Mum's the word. *Comprende*?'

'*Sí.* I understand.' Manuel's face looks woefully absent of comprehension.

'By the way, where did you find her?'

'On her daughter-in-law's couch, in a nice house over on ...'

'Okay, you don't have to tell me anything else. She's old and she's here. That's what matters.'

'She is sick too, Señor. Some kind of stinky sick.'

'Sick, you say? Even better. You're a genius! And you're a doctor, so you can deal with her stinkiness! I think you people are wonderful.' He has drunk a whole bottle himself, and now he opens another. 'Have a glass of vino, let's celebrate. Look at you! Living the good life here in Marin, and how long have you been here? You people are wonderful.'

Ten years ago, Manuel couldn't speak English. Nor did he know anyone who could, fluently. Hard to believe that someone's life can change that much, but there you go. Manuel lived in another world, and California was as exotic to him as Mexico might be to June, who has never been anywhere. He drove a van on the highway which stretches the length of Baja, delivering soft drinks to cafés, shops, hotels, gas stations. Up and down in his air-conditioned van, playing tapes: it was a fine life. More, it enabled him to rescue people. All his jobs so far have offered him this opportunity, if not overtly. He's been a tow-truck driver, a porter in a hospital, a guide in a tourist museum, a marijuana vendor, a telephone information operator – even a plumber, though his complete lack of plumbing skills proved to outweigh his desire to help.

He was able to give rides to people in his van, to swoop up dusty hot hitchhikers and install them in the cool interior. They talked, gave him lives to imagine. Listening, he sometimes felt a tipping sensation, as if he was pouring into them. He would sit up straighter, keep his eyes on the road, but store bits of those lives for future use. He is a bit of a life kleptomaniac, without ever really thinking about it.

Why does Manuel keep changing jobs? They usually come to an end naturally because he is generally incompetent. Even delivering soft drinks, he leaves too many at some places, not enough at others, and quite a few he just gives away. Or drinks.

Another reason is his short attention span.

There was a period, very early on, when he was married to a girl called Hermandida. He even has three children out there somewhere. He'd been in his late teens, and by his mid-twenties his attention had wandered off again, and he was wanting to try the vagabond hero life of an independent tow truck driver. He had loved his young children in a careless, childlike way, but in later years had trouble remembering their names and ages. After a sordid Tijuana divorce requiring many penance prayers at St. Philomena's, he married again on impulse, one hazy drunk week just before his twenty-eighth birthday. Pretty Rosita from Mexicali. That had lasted almost two years. She moved in with his best *amigo* because Manuel was getting too fat and his *amigo* had a new Corvette. Very reasonable, he thought, and he divorced her without any fuss, using his previous experience to avoid pitfalls.

These wives never became as embedded in his heart as his mother, his dear *mamacita,* though this was no-one's fault, least of all his mother's – who never spoiled him, hardly liked him and shooed him off to his own life as soon as he was sixteen. She is the one who haunts him, the one he sometimes yearns for. Though never enough to write to. The *idea* of his mama is like a muse, she is someone it is pleasant to feel melancholy about, to talk to in his head. To apologise to.

He delivered the cool soft drinks up and down the dusty highway while listening to Tijuana Brass and other terrible music due to the restrictions of owning an eight-track, and one day he crossed over the border quite by accident. Well, not an accident per se, but certainly with no foresight. He'd given a lift to a Californian couple going to Ensenada; had been persuaded by them to come as far as San Diego because the girl was in urgent need of her doctor there, having the most horrendous diarrhoea. Ironically, because nowhere in his heart was the desire to live in California, he had not been questioned by American Immigration. Told them he was only going for the afternoon, and they waved him through. He meant to turn around since he had no legal right to work there, and besides he was late on his delivery rounds, he had no money, he didn't own the van ... and many other very important reasons. He meant to turn around, but one thing led to another – as it can if you really want it to – and then it was too late. He sold the van, sold the remaining cans of Coke, and got a horrendous dose of the runs from the San Diego water supply.

He managed to wangle work here and there, but America was not all it was cracked up to be. Most Mexicans he saw seemed every bit as poor as they had in Mexico, only worse. Because here there was the severe contrast, there was jealousy and discontent. Still, it was a buzz. He felt loose. Fluid. He considered changing his name to Larry or Chuck, but didn't. Being smiling Manuel, the Latino chancer, had a lot more advantages to it than being than a loser who tried to hide his origins. If there was one thing he was excellent at doing, it was being Manuel.

He continued up the coast to the San Francisco Bay Area, despite feeling almost mute with shyness about speaking English. But one day there came that poignant moment that comes to all foreigners if they are lucky: eye contact with a friendly stranger coincided with verbal understanding. A momentous event, no matter how trivial the message.

'Hello, can you tell me where is Highway 101 please?'

'Yes, you go right there, and right again three blocks later.'

'Three blocks.'

'Yes, three blocks.'

And Manuel, like all those other lucky foreigners, laughed out loud, and shook the man's hand, and would have kissed him if the man had not moved quickly away. English had gone from being a flow of nonsense to gradually separating out and finally sifting down into components of sense. It was like looking at an abstract pattern for a lifetime, then one day seeing it for what it obviously was: a face. And never again being able to see the abstract pattern. Magic! First nothing, then face. Eyes. Nose. Mouth. Words with meaning.

He has started to dream in English. But times when he is drunk, or wanting to pretend he cannot understand some unpleasant English words, or wants to say something he hasn't really the courage to say, like *I love you*, he falls back on his Spanish. His words flow then, bypassing his brain, straight from his heart, liquid and warm like warmed-up honey. His personality still lies most truly in the language of his youth. The Manuel that other Latinos know is not quite the same Manuel his new American friends know. The subtle cues of personality can rarely be fully expressed in a second language. For instance, he is considered bright by other Latinos, but simple by Americans.

'I wish I could speak Spanish,' Morag will say to him one day, when she realises she needs more information about him in order to decide.

'I wish you could too. I can teach you,' he will say.

'Oh, is it something I can learn?' For all her innate intelligence, Morag is naïve.

Manuel is continually homesick, but there are not many obvious things to miss about Mexico since all the good stuff seems to be here. And altogether, Marin seems to be a much better version of America than southern California: much prettier, cleaner and richer. (Which makes Manuel wonder if it is heat that causes poverty and filth. It could explain Mexico. And a lot of places near the equator.)

There is one thing, though. He still misses watching dubbed American television programs. His favourite show, *ER*, lost all its appeal once seen on American TV. He hadn't realised just how much a voice defined a person. He'd adored Dr. Green in Mexico; in California, he was disappointed to discover the real Dr. Green was a bit of a drip.

In Marin, it eases his homesickness to find that many town and street names are Spanish. The abundance of Mexican food and music helps too. And the Catholic church full to bursting on Sundays with little girls in fancy dresses, their pretty dark-eyed mothers, savagely handsome young men, and old women very like his mama, dressed in black.

(June Johnson has seen Manuel in the street outside this church and noticed him because she is a kind of periphery person: takes in mostly the things that sidle by in the corner of her vision. She didn't notice him when he worked in her garden.)

Manuel is quick, and it took him about three seconds to realise he was not the only new kid on the block. He was part of a tidal wave of Hispanics. Features are written about them in Sunday papers, special teachers are recruited to teach their children English, popular food chains have added Mexican food to their menu, extra priests were drafted in from predominantly white areas where they were no longer required. As foreigners tend to do, festivals like *Cinco de Mayo* were expanded beyond belief. Replicate and exaggerate home: it is the newcomer way.

One Saturday afternoon while hanging out on Fourth Street, listening to a street salsa band and smelling tacos from a nearby stand – all against the backdrop of affluent modern buildings and tall pale quite lovely people – Manuel suddenly realised that there were three distinct worlds. There was Mexico. There was California. And there was Mexican California, or Californian Mexico – a thriving new hybrid nation of which he was a typical citizen.

Manuel doesn't know it, but his great-great-great-grandparents had lived in California – in fact, not far from where he is now in San Rafael. He has walked almost daily through the ghost of one of their houses. Mexicans pre-dated all the Irish and Italian immigrant waves; the Anglos and Aryans too. And so in a way, although he does not feel it, Manuel has come home to roost. California has finally grown into, or returned to own, its Hispanic name.

Manuel has come to believe, but is unable to explain in English, that everyone is where they belong simply by virtue of being there. When he met Morag last year in the El Sombrero kitchen, he had to alter his theory: If you don't feel like you belong where you are, the chances are you don't belong anywhere, but to a tribe of nomads whose DNA has for some random reason risen in your blood, and so you belong nowhere and everywhere. But everyone else, including himself, is where they belong because they are there. Hence there are no displaced people, only recent arrivals and nomads, wilfully and perennially out of context. A kind of sentimental homesickness runs deep through Manuel, but he feels part of his new world and makes apologies to no-one.

He has continued to find ways to be useful to people. Church usher, taxi driver, waiter, bartender, helper of lost children in parks, guardian of old ladies on dark streets. He loves California, and especially he loves Marin County with its opulent redwood houses, lush valleys and fragrant hills. The bay and Mount Tamalpais and the view of San Francisco. The fog and the foghorn and the sea birds. He likes the way that extreme wealth and extreme poverty share a kind of aimless timelessness – the days drift by painlessly enough, and the streets are busy with people who have a lot of time on their hands because they are either very rich or very poor. He feels a lucky man to be here.

And he is.

Manuel is Mañana Man. Hence his wild fatalism and the chance he has taken with his future. What, after all, does he have to lose? A pot-washer can be bold, and an overweight middle-aged illegal pot-washer can really go to town. He can even go to Doctor town. Do you wonder what his face looks like?

Not much, right? That's because you can't hear him sing or laugh, or smell his masculinity or touch his warm skin. He tastes and smells like the sun; his skin has the solid smoothness of unripe melons, and his voice is soft. Soft like dandelions. Manuel is full of Mexican *mojo*. He knows a lot of women, countless Marias and Juanitas, and he has flings with them all. Fantastically fun flings, that improve marriages (theirs) and break hearts only as much as they want to be broken. He keeps half a dozen women on the back-burners, flirting just enough to keep them simmering but not enough to burn. Morag puzzles him. So self-sufficient, so tidy and composed, and yet she seems to scream *help me* with every speech, every gesture, every breath. How can he resist? He is Help-Man. Señor To-the-Rescue. And so he is her friend, even though he thinks that platonic relationships are nonsense.

◆◆◆◆

'So, how long did you say you've been here?' asks Joe again, pouring more wine for Manuel. It is a bottle of juicy aromatic Rioja from an especially fine little winery near Thinwater, Napa. Joe bought it there not long ago, on a hedonistic wine-tasting expedition with June. Or rather, wine-tasting in half a dozen cool cellars, while June drove. Drinking good wine in the valley twilight beats just about every other pleasure Joe knows. It *always* makes him feel young, and the taste of the wine now is bringing it all back. Some days he can hardly believe it's legal.

'Oh, a few years. A few years, now,' replies Manuel hazily. He has trouble with numbers, especially when drinking.

Manuel, still slightly drunk from Joe's Rioja, spots Morag entering the drugstore and doubles back, even though he has already bought his toothpaste.

'So, *qué pasa*, Moragita? You look for drugs. *Sí?*'

'What are you doing here?'

'I follow you, of course, Señora Paranoia Neurotica.'

'You are so sad, Manny. I'm needing some aspirin for my headaches.'

She turns away and sighs. Manuel looks deflated, but brightens considerably when she turns back.

She notices this effect she has on him, but hesitates to interpret it. She has gone through life misinterpreting people. Is she liked? Envied? Pitied? She doesn't know, and it is so humiliating to make assumptions and get it wrong.

'Why are you looking at me that way?'

He doesn't answer, but smiles slyly and takes a small white card out of his shirt pocket and gives it to her. It says:

Hi. Smile if want to sleep with me.
If not, please return this card, as it is very expensive.

'Jesus, Manuel. Another sad gimmick. Does this actually work with women? '

'You smile? I see a smile.'

'It's a sneer, moron. You're the one who's smiling. Jesus, you look like you just won the lottery,' she says accusingly.

'Oooh, jealous? Look, Moragita, if I win, I share it all with you.'

'Why do you persist in calling me Moragita? Manny Welly-Belly.'

They both have to flatten themselves against the shelves as a half-dozen thirteen year-old girls totter by on heels, clutching cans of hair mousse.

'Because it has more prettiness than Morag. Morag is too short. Too *aggie*. It sound too … too hard and chopped-off.' He demonstrates chopping with his hands.

'Well, I like chopped-off. Chopped-off is how I feel.' She reaches for one bottle, puts it back, then reaches for another. Something that says it will soothe her stomach as well as her entire spiritual and physical being. She needs balm for her being. Being Balm.

'Besides, I never mind that stupid name: Manny Welly-Belly.'

'Yes you do, you hate it. Will you move, please? Mr. Manuel pain-in-the-ass.'

'I do not hate it, Moragita. I think it is sweet you care enough to think of a … a … a mike-name.'

'*Nick*name. Do you? Ah dear, Manny. My head is killing me. Can we not have this conversation some other time?'

'Okay, sure. *Sí, sí*, Moragita.' He moves. 'How about trying this one: *Porposate*. Says "food for the soul."'

'Does not. Can you not read? It says good for the bowel. Jesus.'

'It is same thing. You forget, I am a doctor. You should listen to me, Morag.'

'See, you can do it. My name. Thanks. Now move, you're in my way again. Aren't you here for some reason? Why don't you go do your own shopping?'

'I've got it. See? Toothpaste. I think we finish that game of monopoly tonight, si?'

'I put the board away.'

'You what? *Porqué?* You are a bad loser, Moragita. I win last night, and you are a bad sport.'

'You were not winning. I had all the utilities and railroads.'

'*Sí,* what are those? Nada. Peanuts.I had Park Avenue, with a hotel. I am disappointed in you, Moragita. Deeply disappointed.'

'Oh aye?'

'You are a chicken, and I not think that of you.'

'No?' Morag sighs. None of her husbands has been a Manuel type; she doesn't know quite how to convey her irritation with him in a way he'll understand. The man has no pride, she decides. They've only known each other a year, and she hasn't told him much about herself. For instance, he doesn't know about any of her husbands. Marital status is one of those subjects that she tends to veer from, and that he has no real curiosity about. Yet they seem to be on intimate terms, as if they have always known each other. They take liberties with each other. They are frequently rude. And lately, Manuel is too constantly there for her to evaluate him. She is always herself with Manuel; has no sense of vanity with him and knows this is a rare thing. But can one person be both irritating and a relief? And a man?

Another customer, a fat woman with a basket full of powdered diet milkshakes, flows past them. Morag and Manuel are forced to squeeze up, nearly touching. The fluorescent strip-light above them starts to pulsate.

'No.' He pouts. 'I never think you are a chicken before, but now it is all over. My respect for you is . . .' He indicates flicking dust away with his fingers. 'Vamoose.'

'Well. I guess you'd better come back and start a new game, then.'

'No, too late. I can't trust you.'

'I could open that bottle of wine.'

'Not in a million years will I come again. You cannot bribe me, I am a proud man.'

'Oh aye. Fine. Goodnight.' She shrugs and heads off to the cash registers, telling herself she won't feel sorry for him. But she does. Fools always have this effect on her.

Besides, she can hear his footsteps following her.

Part Three

Some days – in fact, today – I live my life for everyone who's not alive. When I hear the roses, touch chocolate, taste the breeze in the Sycamore trees, I whisper to myself: I am not dead. I can do these things; they're not wasted on me. They're real. Listen up, world, I say. I see you on behalf of everyone who no longer can. You are hereby witnessed. This is how I live. Not every minute of every day, of course, but often enough.

Are you dead? I don't mean to be personal, but I just wondered.

Excerpt from *The Consuela Chronicles*, transcribed by Lola Swarts, San Anselmo, 1937.
Estimated age of Consuela: eleven, though some experts have claimed this is probably an underestimate, based on the fact that she was short for her age and that the sentiment is too mature for an eleven year-old. She was probably closer to fifteen.
Location of apparition: the Sycamore House kitchen. Lola had come to work as a cook when Consuela got married and left, four years previously. She didn't at first attribute this child-ghost to Consuela, as she had never seen her as a child; but she did remember being asked by the twenty-three year-old Consuela if they had met before.

June Gives Bus Money to Carson and Robbie.

She finds them hitch hiking on Miracle Mile. She stops her car, rolls down the window and says, like she always says:

'I am not picking you two up. You know I don't approve of hitchhiking. It's so dangerous! No-one hitchhikes anymore. Why are you doing it?'

'The car's out of gas and we're late for work.'

'Oh! You ran out of gas? How could you do that? Stupid!'

'Yeah, well, you know.' The Snellings look down and scuff their shoes, look chastened.

Cars beep from behind while June rummages in her bag and thrusts two ten-dollar bills at them. 'Here, take the bus! Look, there's one stopping now. Run and catch it!'

(Manuel and Morag are on this bus, on their way back to her house after bumping into each other at the drugstore. Manuel recognises the Johnson black Jaguar and feels quite excited all over again about his new job. Shifts in his seat and makes a little noise he is unaware of making – a kind of satisfied grunt. Morag doesn't notice June or the Snellings, but does notice Manuel's private little grunt and moves marginally further away from him. Difficult on the narrow seat.)

'Oh, too late,' says June as the bus pulls away. 'But there'll be another one soon. Just don't hitch. And don't forget to come for your birthday dinner tomorrow night; I bought you a special cake!'

'Wow, thanks, June,' says Robbie.

'Just go to the bus-stop! Go!' she says dramatically. They begin to walk towards the bus-stop, so that she'll leave. They watch June's car disappear in the direction of their jobs at Café Ole. When it's gone, they stop.

'Well, that was good of her. Though I wish she'd just give us a lift. Let's go,' says Robbie.

'Where?'

'To catch a bus, of course. There's time, come on.'

He begins to walk. It is early evening, and the fog is rolling in about five miles away. Where they are standing, the fog is still just a damp taste.

'Hey, I don't want to take a bus. Let's just keep the money. She won't know.'

Robbie pauses, then shakes his head. 'Nah. Too much hassle. I want to take the bus.'

'Suit yourself. Give me my ten bucks. I'll meet you there.'

'But sis …'

'What?'

'It's not that safe, you on your own.'

'I'll be fine.' She feels strong. Amazon woman; intrepid explorer.

'It's getting late. You'd better not, Carson.'

'Just come with me, then.'

'Nah.'

'Well, see you later then.' She sticks her thumb out.

'Ah, come on, Carson. Come on.'

'Beat you there.'

'Ah, hell, Carson.'

A car pulls up and Carson runs up to it. Gets the needed information from the driver, assesses him briefly (mid-thirties, clean-cut, baby seat in back. Safe-ish) and gets in. Doesn't look back to see Robbie frown and walk off to the bus stop.

A Johnson Dinner for the Snelling Birthdays

June Johnson in her kitchen again, watching food cook, daydreaming. Her pupils dilate, her face slackens, she floats away. She hears nothing but a car toot pleasantly and drive by her window, then nothing but all the early evening household sounds. The birds, the humming of appliances, the click-clickety of Moze's toe nails on the linoleum; a toilet flushing and a door opening as Joe heads back to the garage. And it seems to her that her life is now like this sedate neighbourhood and empty road; just as it was in the beginning, too. Just a few cars passing; usually the same ones. Quiet enough to hear occasional birdsong, to notice the state of the pavement under her tyres. Childhood was good. Now is good. But she looks back to middle age as if it was a congested town. A small but exceedingly irritating traffic jam. A time when she was surrounded by Georgia-May and her little friends: by their needs and wants, by insufficiencies of the emotional kind. Then whoomph! Here she is on the other side of the town, bewildered but relieved, looking back to the hustle and bustle and even further back, to when she'd been young. Before she'd known about the bulge of life awaiting her, though she'd strode towards it every day. As the pot finally boils, June thinks to herself: Life is short. And *so what* if that's a cliché.

The front door slams open.

'Georgia-May! You're early, honey. Where're the kids and their daddy?'

'They'll be here in a while, Mom. They had to do something. I forget what.'

She tries to disguise how happy their absence makes her feel. Reflects, not for the first time, on how much harder it is to be a married mother than not. Today this has been brought on by two things: 1. her husband whimpering in bed all day with a minor cold and 2. all the militant single mothers she mingles with at Chloe's playgroup. Whiny women who preface and end all their statements with the defensive: I can't buy that/ do this/ go there/ be understood by anyone because I am a single parent. As if they didn't mostly choose single parenthood, and have weekends off from their kids. As if it's easier coping with another adult in the house – and a male one at that. As if they weren't almost in the damn majority. Georgia-May visualises a time when badly-behaved children in school will be excused on the grounds that they come from a double-parent family. Married women will be the recipients of welfare cheques rewarding them for all their sacrifices. Support groups for married mothers will abound. *Well, what do you expect*, catty women will whisper to each other in supermarket aisles: *she's married. To a man.* Or: *She's nice, I like her. Even if she is, you know … married.*

Georgia-May feels good and a little guilty that she feels good, but it's only for a while. Not long enough for real guilt. Life in toddler-land is too damn long, especially in the afternoons between one and four. Life is long. And *so what* if it's not a cliché.

'Can I help, Mom?'

'Oh, no, honey. Everything's just fine.'

June is poised over four pots, each steaming or sizzling, and looks – for a moment – in control. Georgia-May goes to the living room and spills her wine, the clumsiness of exhaustion. Before she can get a paper towel to wipe it, Moze has lumbered over and slathered it up. She displays this puppy-like behaviour whenever anyone spills anything. She's not fussy; it can be anything. Dragging melon rinds and chicken carcasses out of the garbage and over the carpet is one of the high points of her day: especially days when she's been left alone for more than five minutes. But most of the time Moze is invisible, a smelly golden shedding old rug in the corner. June occasionally checks her for breathing, hoping that if she's dead, she hasn't been dead too long.

Georgia-May, it has to be said, is not as enamoured of Moze as her parents are. And the feeling is probably mutual. Without fail, every time she comes home, in true jealous-brat mode Moze eats a prized possession of hers or her children's. Within minutes. In the past, Moze has dragged her bloody sanitary towels out of the bathroom, dragged them around the house (usually during dinner time) while Georgia-May got yelled at for leaving the bathroom door open. She hopes that the wine Moze has drunk sends her off for a nice long (possibly permanent) nap. Her own golden retriever is much better behaved, if you don't count the diaper fetish. Georgia-May returns to the kitchen to re-fill her wine glass.

'Are you sure you don't want any help, Mom? And what's that smell?'

'What smell? Oh, my goodness! Out of the way, out of the WAY!' shouts June as she carries a smoking frying pan over to the sink to sizzle down into soapy water.

'Stupid recipe. I hate stupid recipes! Your dad and his stupid cook-books.'

'What was it, Mom?'

'What was what?'

'Never mind. Who's coming tonight, anyway?'

'Just Robbie and Carson. We always invite them for their birthday. You know that, Georgia-May.'

'Oh yeah.'

'Did you forget their birthday?'

'Of course not, Mom. But it's not their real birthday yet, is it? I saw them last week; they came over.' She sighs, remembering the wasted afternoon while they watched old Jerry Springer re-runs, ate the pizzas she'd meant for dinner and finally left, trailing a mess of crumbs behind them. 'I'll give them their gifts on their real birthday. Next Saturday, isn't it? I've never once forgotten their birthdays. Not once.' She sighs again. They haven't ever remembered hers. Not once.

'Wait till I show you the cake I bought for them. I drove all the way to that French Bakery in Sausalito.'

Georgia-May sighs yet *again.* Her mother usually buys her own birthday cake from the local supermarket. On special offer, frequently featuring blue icing that no-one else eats. She is not really a doted-upon only child, but one of three. She is the good boring one who offers to help; who is grateful for inedible blue cakes. Sometimes, for quite ignoble reasons, Georgia-May wishes that the Snelling parents hadn't driven into an oak tree. Only children aren't supposed to have to share their parents with other children. That was the whole point of being an only child. Wasn't it?

'So there's nothing I can do to help?'

'Are you tired, dear? That's a lot of yawning you're doing. No, no. You just go talk to your father.'

'Where is he?'

'Oh, silly me. I think he's still out looking for … you know. People. That Edith Spagosa woman arrived. You know, the one that really nice man from Mexico found for us. But three really isn't enough, so your dad had to go out looking again.'

'Christ, who would have thought a hospice would need to solicit business? It's humiliating. Poor Dad.'

'Oh! Oh, no. I just remembered. He's back. He's in the house somewhere.'

'Did he find any?'

'Now there's a good question. I didn't think to ask. You always hit the nail right on the head.'

'Which means he didn't.'

'Well, you never know. Go talk to him. But maybe don't ask him. You know.'

'I know.'

Georgia-May is not in the mood for talking about morbid things, so she switches on the television instead of looking for her dad. An old British show called *Are You Being Served?* which hasn't been shown in Britain since the early seventies, but which somehow has caught on here. It is bizarrely camp. She's fascinated, as if its popularity might explain something about America to her. Joe comes in from the garage, where he spends most of the time that he's not walking Moze or searching for pre-deadies.

'Want any help, honey?' he asks June.

'Where have you been? Of course I need help; look at this mess. No-one ever offers to help me in this house. How could you just disappear like that?'

Georgia-May hears this; feels irritated and then comforted by its familiarity.

'I was in the garage, honey. All you had to do was call me.' He's using his fourth-glass-of-wine-nothing-is-going-to-faze-me-now voice.

'What do you do out there all the time, Joe?'

'You know, honey. Garage things.'

'Oh, that's nice,' June says – sweetly, now. 'Good for you.'

Georgia-May is further comforted. Home means contradiction and irrational conversations. It means never having conversations. Her mother is a man-lover and her father is an egomaniac. The perfect combination. They see-saw between temper and tenderness every thirty seconds. She considers the great favour that her parents have done her by lowering her expectations of sanity. Closes her eyes and considers the kind of relationship that her lowered expectations have led her into. Remembers with a jolt Adam-from-the-playground. Adam! The handsome dad pushing his toddler on the swing next to Chloe's. They'd pushed their offspring in tandem for a full ten minutes before getting up the courage for offhand remarks. About toilet training and Ritalin side effects. And, eventually, eyes bashfully meeting over their sea-sick offspring, they'd exchanged names. The air had been charged. In fact, Georgia-May blushes right now, remembering. Her left side, from her scalp to her toes, remembers the scalding sensation merely from Adam's proximity. But what does this Adam have that her own husband lacks? What is going on? Has she reached her sexual peak, but is too exhausted to realise? Have her hormones grown so haywire that they prefer a stranger to the father of her children?

Her parents are ignoring each other noisily in the kitchen. The television is blaring; dusty laughter canned in the seventies, sounding stale now. Like ancient French fries forgotten in the freezer, heated and eaten despite the dated taste. Moze farts loudly. Georgia-May smiles for no reason. Interesting how the exact same set of circumstances could sometimes make her feel terrible, and other times fill her with contentment.

An hour passes, in which Carson and Robbie appear. For some forgotten reason, probably stemming from their orphan-hood, they have always just come into the house as if they live there. They come in, make themselves at home, frequently don't bring a bottle of wine, use ashtrays, or bother with polite small-talk. Carson is restless tonight; blames this on Robbie's infantile jokes and the whole ritual birthday dinner. She will take a trip somewhere, she decides. Alone, for once. She just doesn't know *where* yet. Canada? France? Columbia? She sits on the arm of June's armchair, and fidgets and frets while Robbie opens Joe's most expensive wine and pours himself a beer-glass of it. A university application sits in his desk drawer in the yellow house, and a piece of paper sits in his back pocket with *Elizabeth* written on it, and a phone number. Robbie has no need to fret. He will never know *fret*.

Then Georgia-May's husband (a very un-Snelling-like being) arrives with their two children, flowers and a bottle of Chablis. He has even remembered to bring the right diaper bag. Georgia-May experiences her usual mix of pride and irritation. Why can't he be so considerate at home? Meanwhile, Moze comes alive for the toddler; knows Chloe will feed her Fritos all evening. Georgia-May takes her children and Moze off, leaving her husband and father to talk about football. But their heart isn't in it. They don't really get along – for no particular reason – and are always very polite. June is quiet, but busy thinking. Or not thinking; her eyes give no clue. Then suddenly the table is set, candles lit, and the doorbell rings.

'Who's that, honey?

'The pizza boy, of course.'

Of course, thinks Georgia-May and everyone else. It was never going to be a home-cooked meal. Everyone finds a chair. A moment of silence while Joe mumbles grace. Johnsons are very Catholic, in a never-go-to-mass kind of way.

Blesssalor forthesethygifts boutareceive fromthiebounty namof thefathersonholgo.

Everyone joins in on the *amen* and tucks in; strings of mozzarella drape across the table. The only person not sitting is June, who hovers in the kitchen nibbling something black off a frying pan and peering approvingly at the candlelit scene. All her beloved extended family, at her beloved table. A genuine English antique farmhouse table with an ancient triangular burn mark in the middle, produced by Mary Smythe in 1834 while she kissed her illicit true love and forgot about ironing the pinnies. This mark is never concealed by a cloth, but proudly polished and displayed as proof of antiquity and Johnson class.

'What's that noise, grandma?' asks Chloe.

'What? Have you finished all your pizza? Would you like some more?'

'That noise. Listen.'

A sound is coming from another part of the house, below all the table talk and silverware clatter. There is a rocking noise, and a low voice singing.

Carson and Robbie exchange a look. Delighted.

'Isn't that our granddad? Has Fred wandered over from the hospice again? We found him in our backyard one night last week; thought he was a racoon,' says Robbie. 'Is there any more wine?'

'It can't be your grandfather. He's over at Gentle Valleys, sound asleep by now, I should think,' says June, as if nothing could be more ridiculous. 'Joe, isn't that right? They wouldn't let an old man wander out at night, would they? Joe? Joe!'

Joe looks happy. He puts down his glass of wine, turns his mellowed eyes over to his wife and purrs, 'Fred Snelling is just fine, June. Calm down. You know he likes to wander. You know he's not a normal patient. He grew up in the goddamn place, didn't he? He's like Moze.

The boundaries are blurred. The whole block is home.'

'Then where is he? Ssshhh, everyone. Listen.'

Everyone quietens for a moment, and the old man's voice comes through the hall.

'Oh, bololomio; oh, bololololomio.'

'Oh, Christ. He must've come through the back door. He might've fallen in the pool. Did you lock the back gate, June? That's the only way to discourage him. Or racoons. He can't open the gate himself.'

June gets her all-right-I've-been-caught look. Silly smile and defiant eyes.

'Well, so what? I forgot to lock the gate. So be it. With all the commotion, I just forgot. Now go and get him. No, wait. There's no more pizza left. Can we give him this?' scraping the rest of the black shiny objects from the frying pan.

'Mom, what kind of mom are you?' whines Georgia-May.

'Yeah, June. What kind of mom are you?' mimics Robbie in a girly voice.

Chloe spills her juice and starts to cry; the dog gags up something slimy, and Joe opens another bottle of wine, riding on a smooth wave of patriarchal pride. Let anarchy reign, he almost says. Georgia-May's husband is looking at his watch, impatient to get home. He doesn't know why he is here, but this is a familiar feeling, hardly worth recording.

Meanwhile Carson sighs; tells herself this sanctioned craziness is another reason to find a new life somewhere, and goes to find her grandfather. He'd raised them in an increasingly eccentric manner till they were old enough to realise that the only way to have a decent conversation with him was to smoke a joint or two beforehand. Or even during. He never seemed to notice. They could even blow smoke in his face. The higher they got, the more sense Fred made. When they reached their late teens and his job was more or less done, Fred gave them the yellow house and quickly tumbled down the hill of coherency. At first they put him in a nursing home in Greenbrae, but he was kicked out after repeatedly fondling the nurses' breasts. The final straw came when he refused to wear pyjamas, and one old dear named Becky Binlotta died of a heart attack one night upon confronting his dangly bits one inch from her face. It was an accident, Fred claimed; he'd thought her room was the bathroom and hadn't turned on the light because the sight of his own face in the mirror had begun to scare him too much. He didn't want to die of fright. If Becky hadn't woken up and died when she did he might have peed on her face, which might or might not have been worse.

Finally, because he needed patients (and also because of the fling he'd had with Fred's daughter in the sixties) Joe Johnson had invited Fred to live at Gentle Valleys. It seemed only right. He'd grown up in the place. Fred's father, Frank Snelling, had been the gardener for the Viettis. When Frank had retired after fifty-five years service, the Viettis had given him the little yellow house at the end of their long drive. Where Carson and Robbie still live, apathy preventing further change.

The Snellings think, wrongly, that they have lived in the neighbourhood longer than anyone else; are secretly proud of this fact. Think it bestows a kind of superiority on them, as all true locals do. Which is why, unlike Morag McTavish, the Snellings do not feel intimidated by wealth – though they themselves live haphazardly.

Carson finds Fred in the hall, contentedly sucking Chloe's bottle. He makes a rhythmic wet sound and rocks gently back and forth on his feet.

'Come on, Gramps; come have something to eat.' She leads him back out to the dining room, all the while thinking that his arm, which she is holding, has become incredibly thin. It feels as light and as brittle as a chicken bone. She sits him down in front of the bowl of Cheerios that June has provided. Begins to feed him, but too late; he is using his hands and shoving the Cheerios willy-nilly into his mouth where, because he has left his teeth at home, they slosh around and fall back onto the table.

'Give him a bib,' demands sensible serious Chloe. Joe observes this and sighs: she'll be just like her mother, he thinks. Where has he gone wrong? He feels a wetness on his ankle, and looks down to see Moze sucking on his sweaty sock. Good girl, he says, then remembers something.

'Listen up, you guys. I need a favour. I need someone to take Moze to the vets on the twenty-sixth to get her anti-scabies treatment. The Jaguar has a car spa appointment that day, and I can't cancel on Luigi.'

'Ah, Dad. Do I have to?' Georgia-May sighs.

'Of course. I am the King and you will obey. Or one of you will.'

'But that's a Saturday,' whines Robbie. To be funny, not because he cares. All days are equal to him.

Georgia-May's husband's face is full of woe, for he knows who will be left with the children if Georgia-May goes.

'Now, Joe. If the children don't want to ...'

'Oh, it's fine, Joe. I'll do it. Or one of us will. *No problema*,' says Robbie, all manly now. 'No sweat.'

'Oh, you are wonderful. I just love you all.' June has entered the gushy phase of her evening.

'But you love me best, don't you, June?' says Robbie. Who, like Joe, is on his second bottle of wine. His flirtatious, teasing self.

'No, I love you all the same,' says June. Who always takes things literally, and has forgotten for a minute that she is supposed to pretend to love her own daughter most. She too has had some wine. Not much, but enough to be honest. And enough to remember the fling she'd had with Robbie's father. Oh yes, they'd been *those* kind of friends, despite the ten-year age difference and the incurable but sweet respectability of Joe and June Johnson. But not openly: these affairs had been secret and sexy sixties kinds of things. If asked, June and Joe would never admit to these dalliances. In fact, they could probably pass a lie-detector test, so convinced they are of their own innocence. The questions would have to carefully worded to not include sleep or love.

Robbie leans over the table, lips puckered, to June.

'Tell me the truth. I'm the one, right?' He tries to kiss her.

'Stop that! Stop it right now!'

'Look at you, Mom. You're blushing. He's always been your favourite,' sulks Georgia-May who, it has to be said, lacks a sense of humour sometimes.

'Well, you're your dad's favourite,' comforts Carson with an artificial lightness of tone, because she can't help but be jealous sometimes. A dad would be a fine thing to have hanging around in your life. Georgia-May looks both pleased and embarrassed.

'Will someone please feed that old man properly? He's getting on my nerves,' says Joe with the faintest of edge, the wine wearing off. Inches from his brain are embarrassing episodes from earlier today: fleeing old ladies, himself in hot pursuit. Manuel is his big hope now; he is obviously a natural, though Joe can't tell him this: always a mistake to let your illegal employees think you respect them. Joe stands up, feeling the need to apply some brandy.

The evening ends. Five adults and two children dribble through the doorway for what seems like hours, with plenty of reversals and searches for teddies and last uses of the toilet and goodnight kisses. Fred hums, Chloe yawns, the infant cries, and they all leave. Swing music is now audible, though it's been playing all the time, submerged in the human noise. Glen Miller. *Pardon me boys; is this the Chattanooga choochoo?* Joe pours another. Slips back into his early stud-hood. A vague sense of pity for everyone who was not young in the forties.

Georgia-May is outside, waving off her old friends who are supporting Fred between them as they wind over the road to the hospice. Her husband has already taken the girls in his car. She stands for a moment alone, letting the evening sink in. First she is numb, exhausted; then there's a swift pain in her diaphragm that she interprets as the involuntary spasm of love. Georgia-May gets attacks of love like Morag gets attacks of lust. She is love-inclined, but only sporadically and with no warning. *Oh yeah*, she thinks. That's what this family and old friends stuff is. And I keep thinking that I hate them. She sneaks back and watches her parents through the kitchen window. This is what she sees:

They look like one person, don't they? Georgia-May envies them. Not their marriage, but their capacity to love each other. Surely that's the trick: not to choose the right person, but to love the person you choose. Joe and June bend over the sink doing things with pots and pans, ignoring each other, each in their own world. They are limp-featured, exhausted, old-looking. Another quiver of love attacks poor sleep-deprived Georgia-May. Love squeezes her, like contractions. This time with the added flavour of protection, because maybe this is how they always look now when no-one is looking. Do not die, she wills them. *Do not die.* Then, before she begins to cry, she gets in her car and drives off to her own house and her own edible babies and her own sweet husband who suddenly, in their absence, have become the best things since mocha fudge.

Meanwhile, inside June's refrigerator – next to the can of dog food and dead flies covered in plastic wrap – is the chocolate birthday cake, for the moment forgotten. The evening has been too full of distractions and Robbie and Carson themselves have forgotten the purpose of the dinner, since their real birthday is not till next week. June will discover her oversight at about two in the morning, when she is up checking things in the house as she has begun to do over the last few years. Doors and windows, thermostats and dog. She will find the cake and eat half from the plate with her fingers, while standing in front of the open refrigerator. She is always so hungry after having company for dinner. One day she will learn to eat when other people do. About the same time she starts believing she is not twenty-eight. A sad, but nourishing day.

Part Four

Hi. Want to play? I've got a rope. Do you skip? Do you know 'someone's in the kitchen doing a little stitchin, in comes me and out goes you?'

What's your name? Edie? That's a nice name. What's your mom writing? What? Oh, listen. If you don't want to play, that's okay. I've got to go out in a minute anyway. By the way, what happened to your feet? Where are they? Don't be scared; I'm sure your feet are somewhere. Ask your mom. She looks like she knows a thing or two.

Excerpt from *The Consuela Chronicles*, transcribed by Mrs. Olivia Thomson of Terra Linda, 1994, in the presence of her seven year-old daughter Edie. This is the only recorded time in which a small child has been used as Consuela-bait, so to speak. It follows a long period – four years – of no Consuela sightings at all, and possibly reflects the current desperation to revive the ghost.
Estimated age of Consuela: seven.
Location of apparition: the utility room of Gentle Valleys Hospice, which used to be part of the formal living room of Sycamore House.

Manny is Having Another Good Day

A very good day. His steps, as he comes away from Gentle Valleys Hospice, are bouncing, springing, nearly launching him into the hard blue sky. Boing, boing, boing. He carries on until he reaches El Sombrero and stops. Sighs, smiles, and opens the back door into the kitchen.

He pauses to come back down to earth. To let the bounce leak out his rubber-soled sandals. Sssssssssss. It is midmorning, he is late, and he looks at the place where he is supposed to be: the pot-cleaning station with its aluminium sinks and counters, already piled up with refried bean-encrusted pots. He so much does not feel like himself right now that he is almost surprised to not see himself standing there with his stained apron, scrubbing in the steam.

Hey, Manuel. Looking good, he would say to himself, and nonchalantly back out of the door again.

Hey, see you around, man, he'd say back to himself, and admire his own shining eyes.

'Hey, Manny: you're for it,' hisses Morag from the salad station by the window, in her halo of lettuce juice. Right now, in his hyped-up state, he can see each individual water droplet clinging to her feathery carroty hair. Swept up today to reveal a pale thin neck with two mosquito bites. Some of her hairs are colourless, translucent.

'Ah, Moragita.' He moves towards her (the sparks sparkle under his shoes again, the radio loses its reception momentarily) and is about to sweep her northern loveliness into his arms, where she must belong now. She is his angel in fresh green juice, his cohort in foreignness, his dear sweet Moragita.

'Hey, watch it, you. Just because you lost at Monopoly again,' she says in a bored tone, and fends him off with her elbows. Her hands are in yellow rubber gloves since the accident with the knife.

'*Pero mi amor, tengo muy buenas noticias*. Moragita.'

'*Sí, sí,* aye, aye, but first you're in deep dog-house, Manny.'

'*Qué?* Deep shit, you mean?'

'Whatever. Eric is on the warpath, and you're almost two hours late.'

'But I have good – no, excellent reason. You will definitely want to sleep with me now.'

'Shht! Here he comes. Get your apron on.'

'*Buenas dias*, Eric,' says Manny, smiling.

'*Buenas noches* nearly. Where the hell have you been?'

'I have been talking to very important person. I have …'

'I don't give a shit who you've been talking to. You're fired.'

'No, no Señor. I do …'

'*Sí, sí, stupido*. You are so out of here.'

'But you *no comprende*: I come to say I quit. I have a new job. Better job. Real job.'

'Really? Wow, Manny – that's great. What job is it?' asks Morag, letting some lettuce leaves float to the floor.

'This isn't your business, Morag,' says Eric. 'And I would appreciate it if you could finish those without wasting too much.'

'Thank you, Moragita. I have the job I told you I'd get.'

'Where?'

'You know.'

'Do I?'

'*Sí, sí*. I tell you *muchos tiempos*,' excitement causing him to lapse back to Spanish. 'So many times I tell you. Think.'

'Out,' says Eric. 'Now.'

'Phone me,' says Morag.

Manuel leaves El Sombrero, his step only marginally de-bounced, and only for a few minutes. There he is springing again: ah, life is good. Very good indeed.

But life for Morag is not very good. What is wrong with her? She used to be so easy-going, so invulnerable. Her last husband, Harry, has ruined everything. Everything! Deserted, she has shrunk, and diminished people never have the energy necessary to spring. She has shrunk from herself too. An unwanted item, tawdry. Harry embarked her on the worst era of her life because she can't feel good about being alone. She has not chosen it. She is lonely. Without doubt, yes, Morag is lonely. Physically, spiritually, mentally, emotionally, absolutely out-and-out dirt lonely. She aches. And now this! Manuel's departure!

Morag whimpers and softly moans, automatically slicing Romaine lettuces.

These days it is mostly her lower gut that aches, as if her heart, broken and deflated, has sunk along with the rest of her. Like her breasts, her upper arms, her chin, her ear lobes. She aches thinking about her aches. She's glad she has another doctor appointment tomorrow. After all, it's been three weeks since the last appointment, where she'd lain quietly while the doctor took blood for tests and probed her abdomen, pressing softly and asking, *Any pain? Any pain?* with each thrust.

'Yes, it hurts,' she'd said.

'A lot?'

'No. Not a lot.'

'And there?'

'No.'

Damn, she thinks, why did all the pain vanish when she was there? Well, tomorrow the results would be back and she'd get the news. Waiting to learn what her body is up to feels a little like waiting for a letter from some distant foreign country. She has no idea what to expect. She doesn't speak the language, but will rely utterly on the doctor to interpret for her. Going to the doctor is as close to going to church as Morag comes these days.

Gentle Valley's Little Ways

'What do you mean, dead?' asks Joe Johnson, who is very annoyed. 'The nurse just told me she was in bed, sleeping. What do you mean, dead?'

'*Muerta.* Edith Spagosa is dead, as in not very alive any more,' says Manuel, in slow measured tones. It's his first week on the job and he hasn't quite got a handle on his boss's IQ. After all, Joe seems to have no recollection of hiring Manuel to rebuild his garden wall last year.

'No. Impossible. It can't be.'

'*Sí, sí,* this can be,' he says gently. 'Life, it can end. Poof, just like that. First the heart is going boom boom boom, then nothing. *Finito.*'

'*Finito* is Italian. Can't you even use the right slang? You're a wetback, for Christ's sake.' Joe sighs impatiently and paces.

'I am citizen of the world, *gringo.*'

'Don't call me that.'

'Don't call me wetback. I am citizen of …'

'Yes, yes, all right. Enough with the dignity thing. Damn it! And she just got here! When did she die?'

'Well, presumably this afternoon sometime, after the nurse saw her.'

'Damn. Goddamnit!'

'I know.'

'And I got my hopes up again.'

'*Sí, sí,* Well, that's life. Or … not.'

'Manuel …'

'Dr. Mendoza.'

'Okay. Dr. Manuel-who-owes-me-a-helluva-lot.'

'There's still Fred Snelling and Connie. What is Connie's last name, anyway? I can't find her records and she doesn't seem to talk at all.'

'She's just Connie.'

'*Just* Connie? Where did you get her, a park bench? The Sally Army? Did you steal her?'

'Jesus, Manuel, you're a suspicious bastard. If you have to know, she was dumped on our doorstep about five years ago, with her name safety-pinned to her dress and fuck-all else. *My name is Connie, I like cinnamon toast*, it said. Now, if we can move on. We need more patients. Damn it Manuel, doesn't anyone ever get old in this county?'

'There may be some by-laws concerning that, Señor Joey.'

'Mr. Johnson.'

'Either you call me Doctor Mendoza, or I call you Señor Joey.'

'Shut up, you idiot. This is serious. Hospices work in Europe; why don't they work here? I am doomed. Why doesn't anyone want to die here? Do they want me to go bankrupt? Does anyone care? What about all those bleeding heart rich liberals – where the fuck are they when you need them? Huh?'

'Hmm,' says Manuel. 'Probably by their swimming pools, where they have nice tidy heart attacks after a round of tennis and aromatherapy-aided sex with their personal trainer. Thereby bypassing the need for a hospice altogether. Señor.'

'Stop joking. This is dire, Manuel. This place has everything! It even has a goddamn famous ghost. What more could anybody want? We have a dozen volunteers raising thousands every year – all those righteous matrons! We provide emotional fulfilment for them! Plus, we have two full-time nurses to pay, as well as a cook to feed us all, a gardener, a cleaner for the patients and three more cleaners to clean up after the staff, half of which don't seem to speak English *or* Spanish – and you, the wetback illegal doc who is only working because of my compassion, because I am willing to take a risk and give you a chance the American way. Me! With all my wife's credit card bills and not enough fucking patients.'

'Or many patients of any kind.' Pause. 'Does this mean you will be paying me, then?'

'This is an emergency, Manuel. Stop thinking of yourself. It's not just your job and mine at stake, there's this whole fucking infrastructure.'

Joe Johnson looks out the window, his face hard to decipher. Manuel stands up and leans over the desk towards Joe, who turns suddenly with a desperate expression.

'We need more sick people, Manuel. This is serious. Someone has to be dying out there.' Joe lowers his voice to a growl. 'Find someone, Manuel.'

'Yes sir. *Sí, sí,* señor.' Manuel salutes and clicks his heels together, but Joe is too preoccupied to notice. Or notices, and takes it as his due. June has, after all, primed him for dictatorship all his married life. He storms out of his office, down the stairs and out to the garden, where he nearly steps on a little girl in a gingham dress who is making a daisy chain.

'Out of my way!' he shouts to Consuela, who instantly fades. The strangeness of her comes to him, and he freezes and slowly turns around. Nothing to see, just a faint whiff of something he doesn't recognise. Home-made soap?

Morag Goes to the Doctor

Manuel dons his doctor suit and heads for the nearest health centre. His shoulders squared with resolve, the boss's ridiculous words ringing in his ears. As if the terminally sick can just be plucked off trees. Edith was easy, but then Edith was a fluke, albeit a short-lived fluke. He has taken the same bus a dozen times since, but no other middle-aged people have complained about unwanted old relatives. No, there will be no more Edith Spagosas dropped in his lap. To find a patient quickly will mean a tiny act of deception. Tiny acts of deception are Manuel's speciality. His vocation, in a way. Like Morag's weddings. To be honest, he is looking forward to the challenge. He feels just scared enough to feel totally awake, which adds a certain intelligence that his face otherwise lacks.

As he walks, he does what he always does when about to be a doctor. He mentally flicks through all the *ER* shows that he's taped and watched over and over again. Way back, since before that pretty woman doctor left. He rehearses every eventuality – how he'd act, what he'd say, what sharp utensil he'd ask for in crisp confident tones. *Triactiole scalpel, nurse. Yes doctor!* It always sends a little thrill through him, and he shivers slightly, even though it is another hot day. The soles of his shoes make a sticky sound on the sidewalk.

As he approaches the building, he checks his suit over – yes, remarkably still presentable, considering it had belonged to a man much skinnier and taller than himself. Sometimes he catches a whiff of something from the jacket or trousers, and thinks – whoops, there's old Fernando. But mostly he considers it entirely his own possession now. It is light-coloured; slightly past its prime but good linen. It suits Marin very well. Quality but not show-offy. Old money, it says.

At the entrance, he lets his eyes flicker over the reception and strides past the desk with a quick nod and assertive but inaudible mumble that sounds like:

'Dr. Rochel, to see Dr. Waddy-Doody.'

The receptionist takes in his suit and confidence, and responds with an artificial baring of her teeth. He finds himself in a corridor with a dozen doors leading off both sides. Now for the tricky part, the part he must use his instinct to guide him. He is from Cabo San Lucas – his heart is a warm dark place swimming with intuition and music, and it is into this pool that he dips right now. Which way, which way? Guide me, he asks his heart. *Adonde voy, mi corazon*? Then he says a second's prayer to Mary, his favourite blue-robed, blue-eyed Madonna, just to hedge his bets. Also to his *mamacita.* And finds his hand on the third door handle on the right.

'Jesus Christ, Manny. What are you doing here?'

Manuel gives a girlish little yelp. The intercom on the desk lets out an electrical buzz like a startled bee; the lights tremble.

'*Dios,* Morag!' Then, in a whisper, 'What are you doing here?'

'What d'you mean? I have an appointment. This is a doctor's office.' Then she makes a gesture with her tongue, pushing out the space below her lower lip, and makes a *nnnnnn* noise that means that he is beyond stupid: he is an imbecile. It's one of the affectations that she's picked up from the teen waitresses she works with in El Sombrero.

'What are you, the orderly here? Is this your new job? We miss you already, by the way. Pedro can't wash pots for love or money. You should ask Eric for your old job back.'

Manuel shakes himself slightly, straightens up taller, seems to grab hold of the situation at last. It is going to be both easier and harder with Morag. Good luck or bad luck, hard to decide. Maybe he can come clean with her, pay her to play along. Maybe not.

'Morag. Shh, Morag. I always told you I was a doctor at home, in Baja, remember?'

'Yeah, like right. As if a real doctor would ever need to wash pots. If you're a doctor, I'm the queen of ...'

'No, I was not joking. I am a proper doctor, Morag, and my papers have finally come through. I am Dr. Mendoza.'

'Cut it out, Mannie. A joke's a joke. Jesus, who'd you get that suit from? Nice.'

'Thanks, you really like it? It's not too long in the sleeves? Too tight around the waist?'

'It is a bittie long in the sleeves. Who does it belong to, anyway?'

'This suit is my own. And now, if you don't mind, we'll get down to business.'

Someone tries to come into the room just then, and Manuel calls:

'We'll be finished in a few minutes, thank you,' in just the professional voice Morag needs to hear to half-believe it. She studies him. Manuel, a doctor. Well, that will take some re-thinking. He grows taller in her mind; in fact, enters a completely different category. The serious adult category.

'Let's see now,' he is saying, moving papers on the desk. 'Your notes seem to be missing. I wonder if you could just give me your details first. We must be quick today.'

'Got a golf match?' she smirks.

'No, I don't smoke, Señora Moragita.'

'Ha ha.' Morag takes him in a bit more closely now. Observes the fine frayed edges of his trouser cuffs and his worn-down shoes.

'Are you really a doctor, Manny? All along you weren't lying? I'm in awe.'

'If you just fill in your name and address and birth date, we can begin.'

'You can do that. You've been round my place enough times.'

'Well, your age then. If you don't mind.'

She tsks, then writes quickly – a number within a decade of the truth.

He watches in mounting panic, as she pales. He cannot do this.

'There you go, Doctor Manny Welly-Belly. Did my blood test results come back?'

'Test results. Ah.' His luck! He can do this! 'Yes, they did. I've got them here.' He watches in horror as she begins undressing.

'This feels so weird, Manny.'

'Don't feel embarrassed, Morag. I am a doctor,' he chokes.

He feigns nonchalance, as if he has not spent a lifetime persuading women to remove just the outer layers of their clothes. He blinks rapidly and looks out the window till she is standing in front of him with just her jeans on, and her sweet softly sagging breasts eye him defencelessly. She lies down on the bed and he fumbles for his stethoscope. He listens to her chest. Inside his ears, the muted beat of her heart, her blood pulsing.

'It sounds very … um, busy in there,' he mumbles.

He closes his eyes and for a second Morag wonders if he has just given himself a minimal sign of the cross. She observes his dark hand hovering near her white breast, stares at the contrast which is so eye-catching. Pleasing, and somehow soothing to look at, in the same way that watching a waterfall is; motion against stillness, dark against white. Notices with some dismay that although the room is warm, her nipples are standing erect. (They know lots of things that she does not.) He seems to notice this too, and hesitates another second before placing his hand on her breast-bone and listening again to her heart.

He moves his hands down to her abdomen. Prods gently. He is thinking of Cabo San Lucas again. The scene that often comes to him when he wishes he were elsewhere. It is his displacement vision, especially when feeling aroused in inappropriate places. As vivid as a hallucination, as reproachful as guilt solidified. Now his children all stand in a row in front of his mother's house, with the blue door. Bright, bright, almost blinding, so that, at first, when the door opens, he doesn't see his dear *madre*. She is so small.

We are waiting, Manuel, she says. She spreads her hands to include the barefooted children, all suddenly crying and hungry-looking. *Donde esta mi hijo? Ayudarme, por favor.*

'Manny?'

'Yes, sorry. I was …' (*Madre, lo siento mucho*, he weeps in his heart.)

'No, I didn't mean to interrupt, but is everything all right? Only I've had this little ache in my chest as well as my stomach. A long time now, but Dr. Gonigal just says it's wind. Do you hear anything abnormal?'

His face brightens as if he has been given a gift. Then clouds, when he realises what he is about to do. Then brightens again, as he thinks that it is meant to be. Morag will save his ass, and everything will be all right. And no way is she going to drop dead like Edith Spagosa.

'Are you all right, Manny? Your face went all funny just then. All twitchy.'

'I'm afraid, Morag, that there is something. Something quite serious, I'm afraid. Put your clothes back on now, please. The test results are clear. I just needed to confirm.' He fumbles with some papers, drops them, picks them up and pretends to read them.

Her large blue eyes fill and his heart fails yet again. To give such a woman – a friend! – news like this. What kind of sin is this? But then the vision – this time himself in the doorway with the children, no shoes on his feet, the old gnawing in his belly, the television grinding on in the background with Spanish voice-overs. The smell of rancid beef fat and corn flour.

'I have some bad news.'

'How bad, Manny?'

'*Muy malo*. Very, very bad, Morag.'

'I knew it. I just knew it. I've known all along.'

'It's cancer. A very bad kind of cancer that has no cure.'

'Stomach cancer?'

'Actually, well, three cancers, none of them common.'

Silence. A roaring silence.

'Tell me anyway,' in a faint voice. 'What they're called.'

'Of course.' Manuel looks down at the sheet of paper and rearranges letters and words. This is easy because his fear has done something strange to his vision. Reading clearly is not an option.

'Cancer of the tusglapi, thorto cancer and cancer of the gudley gland. None of them curable, I'm afraid. So you will be spared chemo and losing all your hair and vomiting all the time. We can give you pills for pain.' Then, remembering another *ER* episode: 'Near the end we'll give you massive shots of morphine and you can be peaceful and feel nothing.'

'I'm going to die,' she whispers.

'Well, yes. You are. Most definitely.' Happy to be on honest ground again.

'Oh, God. Are you sure, Manny?'

'*Sí,* there is no mistake, Morag. I am so sorry.'

Morag straightens up. 'No, this isn't your fault. This has been coming for a long time. Ever since … Haven't felt right, and it's got a lot worse. I knew it. Funny, though …'

'What is funny, Morag?'

'I feel fine now. Absolutely fine. In fact I feel perfect. This always happens. Isn't that ironic? Oh, Manny – isn't that a killer?' And she laughs, then cries. Just like some alcoholic heroine; like Lady Brett Ashley or Holly Golightly.

'Well, I guess that's that, then,' she says, blowing her nose. 'I'd better hurry: I'm late for work. I only took an hour off to come here.' Blows her nose again and has a thought. Manuel can actually see the thought enter her mind, so closely is he watching her. 'Wait till I tell Eric you're a real doctor – he isn't going to believe it! Oops, three o'clock, got to go.' She stands up to leave.

'Well, but Morag. My Moragita.' He puts his hands on her shoulders and looks into her eyes. 'You're going to die very soon, and you must enter a hospice.'

'Why?'

'Because. You will be happy there. They know how to take care of people like you. How to give you the right drugs. And … things.'

'Really? But I can't afford it.'

'Money *no está importante*. The hospice is a charity. Free. Hundreds of fundraisers, all for you. You must go.'

'When?'

'Oh, any *minuto* now. It is essential that we remove you straight to Gentle Valley Hospice.'

She sighs; sits down, deflated.

'Guess I won't bother getting my veins stripped again, then. Will you cancel that for me?'

'*Sí, sí*. I will take care of everything for you. I will look after your cat. I will water your geraniums.'

'You are a good friend, Manny. But I don't have a cat. Or geraniums. But thanks anyway.' She sighs again; feels, rather than hears, the sound of a myriad doors softy and irrevocably shutting. Life life life, nae more of that stuff, ken. Hen. This, finally, is it. Her plight is so justifiably sad, for a change, that she can almost enjoy the tears.

'I am very sorry, Morag. You will need some counselling and I will arrange that with the hospice. They will take very good care of you there. Lot of rooms, all with TV and room service. Good food, happy place. Honestly, you'll like it.'

Morag squints at him with puffy red eyes.

'How long do I have?'

He just shakes his head very slowly, mournfully, tries not to cry himself. Fails. His tears begin, oh! He could never control them once someone else started.

'A week? A day? Tell me, Manny. I need to know.'

'*Vaya con Dios*,' he mumbles. 'Can I use your handkerchief?'

'All right, don't tell me. Better I don't know. Let the end catch me by surprise,' she wails on the last word.

'You are very brave, Morag.'

'If you say so, Manny.' But then the sense of unreality really descends. She hears a queer buzzing in her ears. Wonders, detached, if this is another symptom.

'A hospice ambulance will fetch you tomorrow. You must prepare all your things, in bags. Tell your relatives.'

'Manny, I have no family here. You know that.'

'True, I am being stupid. I am upset, forgive me.' He too is hearing this queer buzzing, and his voice seems to come from a long way off. Shock is contagious; they are in mutual shock.

'That's okay. I can't believe it. Even though it's what I felt, deep down. I wonder what Dr. Gonigal's going to say for himself now. Wind, indeed!' (Looking cheered, buzzing decreasing.) 'I've half a mind to sue him.'

'See, always a silver lining.'

'What?'

'Nothing. You have stopped crying now, that is good. You'd better go pack.'

'For this hospice place? We'll see.'

'No, not we'll see. You will enter the hospice. Please, Moragita.'

'Oh, all right. Just for you, then. But not today. I have to think. I have a whole house to take care of. In a few weeks.'

'No, tomorrow. Honestly. You'll be needing the drugs they have.'

'Saturday. Three days. I need at least that. I feel sure I won't keel over before then. Unless this is going to be one of those out-of-the-blue things. Is it? Will it come like a heart attack, while I'm laughing, or sleeping or eating a hamburger? Will I have to make sure I'm wearing clean knickers every single second from now on?'

'What are knickers? No, no, don't tell me. Morag, don't worry. You will have some warning. Three days will be fine. Saturday, then. I will see you there.'

'You will? That's awfully nice of you.'

'Oh, I forgot to tell you. That is where I work now.'

'What are you doing here?'

'Oh … also working. They needed me just today, an emergency. Dr. Gonigal was called away to an emergency, so they ask me to come quick. I run.'

'Manny, you surprise me.'

'I thought I irritated you.'

'Well, that too. Intensely. But look at you: a doctor. You do surprise me.'

She sighs yet again, drenched with the most intense emotions life offers: fear and desire, though her desire has not been given admittance to her consciousness yet. It hovers, quivering and pulsating, waiting for a day that may never come.

Manuel smiles for the first time: a tearful, wet smile, his dark pools of eyes shining.

'You will be very happy in the hospice, Morag. Everything will be all right now.'

'And you'll explain to me more carefully exactly what is wrong with me? I can't take anything else in just now, but I'll want to know more about all this, Manny. You know me, I'll want to know everything.'

'I will tell you everything, Morag.'

He holds her hands in both of his and has to fight the most powerful urge to crush her to him, Hollywood style. Lift her up, swing her around, cradle her. Like he does with women. They love it; shriek with laughter. His favourite kind of scene. Then the prospect of death rushes in like a teenage mugger, and grabs it all away. Her eyes have emptied.

Morag Grapples with Mortality

'Eric, I'm not coming back in today. I have to quit.'

'Oh, okay.'

'I'm afraid I'm dying.'

'Well, if you want any references, just let me know.'

'So, I won't be able to work any more.'

'That's fine, Morag. Have a nice day.'

She will not remember this day. It is a bad dream, a time of living in the air, floating, unreal. Of tiptoeing around inside her skin. Of taking the tiniest of peeks through the door of sad possibilities (which she has opened before on low days), and opening it just wide enough to find the even darker door of sad certainties. Dire calamities that happen to other people. But she does not open this door yet. It's enough to notice that it is definitely there.

Her adrenaline is jammed full on. If she smoked, this would be a four-pack day. She flits around the house, mentally organising, as if for an emergency short trip. Must pare down, use her wits, prioritise. She makes a list of who to phone, then phones no-one after Eric's response. Who, after all, are her friends? She realises that she doesn't actually like many people, and time is way too short now to waste on good manners. Ruthlessly throws out all the limp vegetables in the fridge, thinks about funeral songs (*The Lord is my Shepherd*? Followed by Louis Armstrong's *What a Wonderful World*?), tosses away old letters and new tights for work that she will never need now. She moves so fast that she is breathless. Then she pauses to gaze out of a window or at a wall or in the mirror. Finds herself still frozen in that position ten minutes later – no thought, no panic, nothing. Just her mind fainting from all the unaccustomed exertion. An extremely in-and-out day, the most tense, frightened day of her life so far, which manages both to stretch into years and to be gone in a few seconds. Her rapidly diminishing time. It finishes with a dream of someone like Manuel (but not, of course, Manuel; she doesn't fancy him) kneading her breasts and waking from that dream only to wish she could wake up yet again to find that the cancer too is a dream, albeit not as nice as the breast dream. All together, two hours and thirty-two minutes' sleep.

The second day, the sky falls in, and she'll remember this day very well indeed for the copious amount of tears that she produces. She is a novice at crying, and so she makes lots of strange sounds – quite frightening, ugly, ragged noises. (She'll get better and better at this, and within days will master feminine and romantically-distressed sounds.) She weeps and weeps; soaks towels, pillows, carpets. She watches herself cry in the mirror and cries harder for the sheer drama of it. And in between, catches herself having thoughts like: Will the catharsis of crying make her more or less beautiful? More or less ugly? Will the tears wash wrinkles away, or increase them? Should she be drinking gallons of water to counteract the dehydrating effects? She does no packing or cleaning, nothing practical at all. Phones her sister in Scotland, who is out shopping; speaks to one of her nieces, which is easier than speaking to her sister, as she has not spoken to her sister in six years.

'How are you, Auntie?'

Morag gets a sudden attack of shyness.

'Fine, I'm just fine. Just wondering how you are. And everybody.'

'We're fine. Are you coming for a visit this year? It's been ages.'

'Aye, I might. I'll see,' Morag says. Then hangs up, fright-paralysed.

Finally, she sleeps marginally longer than the previous night, by twenty-two minutes.

Day three, dry-eyed for longer periods, with deep depression hovering just, but just on the edge of her periphery like a dark-winged insect. Though it is a distinctly new kind of depression – she hasn't the slightest desire to be dead. Can't derive even an ounce of pleasure, suddenly, from imagining her own funeral. Where did that elaborate satisfying fantasy go?

She begins to pack. One suitcase for the hospice, black plastic bags for the garbage men and green plastic bags for the Salvation Army. It is slightly reminiscent of packing for long trips where she needed only the essentials. Like the three occasions when she left husbands to move to a new life; but this time it feels like moving from her house to thin air.

The exertion helps; she works steadily and even forgets for whole minutes why she is working. She feels less and less attached to anything. Wool coats and prints of Chinatown, *Joy of Cooking* cookbooks and food-processors, cheery floral curtains and comfy sweaters – what do any of them matter? Superfluous rubbish. And only very slightly more superfluous than the things she has chosen to save: a scrapbook, passport, photographs, two small ceramic elephants she has had since childhood, her favourite jeans and matching powder-blue shirt. She can imagine someone (Harry? A stranger? Manuel?) in the near future, looking at the only things she thought worth saving, and wondering why.

All proofs of her existence will take less than a day to dispose of. In a way, dying is like outgrowing every single thing you own. The world will absorb her useful leftovers, like her kitchen table and the hall carpet, and she will disappear without a trace. Like every other human that ever lived, she will cease to live; exit and be forgotten. It is soothing, in a masochistic way, to imagine the huge throng she will soon be joining – far larger, after all, than the group of the living. At last, she will be doing something she is supposed to do. A popular group activity.

She phones Harry.

'Harry, I'm moving out, so you can stop paying the rent now.'

'Ah, Morag. That's great news, honey. I didn't want to say, but money is getting pretty scarce, what with Tilly stopping work to have the baby and all.'

'I'm also getting rid of quite a few things, and some of them are yours. Furniture and what not, if you want to come and have a look.'

'Sure thing, when I get some free time.'

'You'd better come soon, they have to go this week.'

'You're putting pressure on me. I hate it when you do that, Morag. Look, I just can't do it this week. What's the hurry anyway?'

'I'm going into a, uh, a hospice tomorrow and I want the house cleared.'

'You do? Why?'

'Well, I'll not be needing it, will I? Shall I will stuff to you? Shall I do that, Harry?' She makes a mental note to find out about wills. And insurance policies. And funeral homes. This is starting to be a very complicated business. Where did people find the time to die properly?

'Hold on, Morag: the other phone is ringing. Can I call you back in ten minutes?'

Which would have been fine, but he doesn't call back and she calls the Salvation Army to come for the green bags and the furniture. After all, she tells herself, Harry does live quite a distance – two hours away, and he does have ever such a successful business. He will try to get in touch at some point to ask why she is going into a hospice, she has no doubt about that. Probably the prospect of birth cancels anything remotely resembling death. Baby as shield against mortality.

Which reminds her – death as shield against mortality. The way she'd felt when her own father had died. Returning for the funeral to Inverness, soon after she'd left Ian. The way her mother seemed to feel, it was only a matter of minutes before she'd be joining her husband. She'd said:

'I've lived an incredibly long time, it just seems to go on and on, Morag. I wish it would stop, but you know what? I bet it won't stop just now. No, no: it'll wait till I'm back in the middle of things again; it'll wait till I'm looking elsewhere and time is slipping by too fast and I'm fretting about being late somewhere, death the last thing on my mind. But these long, long days are torture. I'm telling you it feels years already since he died, and I'm not sleeping right either. What a contrary thing death is, is it not? But you're too young to know what I'm saying, lassie. Too young at all, and you're doing some queer enough things of your own. I haven't a clue, honestly. Leaving a good hard-working man like your Ian. Like your dad, bless his heart. I wish I could die right now, there's nae point in going on at all, at all.'

Knowing she'd never see her father again was bad enough, but worse to hear her own mother *coax* death. It felt obscene, and she'd left a day early and stayed in a B&B near the airport just to get away. A year later, her mother died instantly after slipping on some black ice and cracking her head. She might have been rushing off to some bargains, mortality nowhere in her thoughts, and been ambushed by death, just as she'd foretold. Or she might have been running from deep despair and aiming her dainty feet at the black ice. Recalling her mother's words, Morag hoped she'd been caught when she wanted to be caught. Not snapped out of a glad-to-be-alive-and-going-shopping day. She couldn't wait to leave Scotland after her mother's funeral; it made her feel so uncomfortable, so exposed somehow, and she has not been back since.

Morag thinks now, on the third day of knowing that she is dying, of that house, her childhood home. Damp grey stone, with the smell of coal fires perpetually a catch in her throat every time she opened the door to come in. Something about a draughty chimney. Highland air – sharp, clear, bloody cold; she hasn't forgotten that, but now, for the first time, she misses it. It may have been bloody weather, but it was her bloody weather. This heat is too drying. She aches to walk without sweating, to breathe without effort. To shiver in July suddenly seems a delicious thing to do. To hurry inside and light a fire. To bundle up in woolly jumpers and vests – not these stupid unflattering cotton sweatshirts that she wears here, but real Marks and Spencer jumpers. Clothes that kindly conceal sags.

She sits on her front step in the glaring midday heat and summons the past. A dreich day, with the rain in the wind, and her dad flinging her some Black Jacks from the pocket of his old tweed jacket, then rolling himself a cigarette with Samson tobacco and green Rizla papers. The way the bits always stuck in his beard. Californian men were so smooth and tidy and healthy. Californian men had no smell. Except Manuel, but then he wasn't really a fully qualified Californian, no matter how many green cards he pretended to accumulate.

(Manuel. His dark brown, almost black, eyes: surely she has noticed them. How could she not? They were eyes to sink into, to drown in, to let oneself be saved in. If saving was a possibility. But she hasn't noticed them yet, in this way. She may never.)

Morag shudders herself back into the present. Stands up and looks beyond Ben Nevis Crescent to the distant Marin hills. Golden dry grass on rounded hillocks, like the blond crew-cut heads on the skateboarding youths on her street. Two neon joggers swish by, both with headphones. The air thrums with insects and the freeway. She closes her eyes. It is happening already. They say that when you die you regress to infancy, and here she is, practically greiting for her mum already. Dying! Her!

Life is bloody short, and no joke. Like coming to a dead end, no room to turn the car around, and realising she knew it was a dead end all along. It feels inevitable, but she can't help gunning the engine anyway. It is such an unending dead end.

Her chest begins to ache again and she dissolves into a puddle, picturing herself as she sits now, forlorn, on the precipice, alone and unloved. A puddle of tears that quickly swells to a loch. With wild swans and salmon. And gentle rain, almost silently joining sky to earth, as rain should and frequently does in the Highlands.

She suddenly knows what she must do. Go back. Return to her

own country, where she belongs. Let her bones rest in the soil that had formed them. Inverness will be her final cradle. She'll write her sister. And her old school-friend Fiona McPhee. (Yes, the very same one who called her a thrawn wee bitch. And yes, she'll tell her, I am *still* a thrawn wee bitch.)

But first this hospice thing, which is beginning to feel a bit like a social obligation. She must, for some reason, not let Manuel down. He is counting on her. She said she would, and so she will. Unable, even at this crisis point, to forget her manners. She can make her escape plans once there, and God knows, escape plans are her speciality. But what is she escaping this time? Not a husband. If she moves fast enough, and often enough, can she elude death? Like the way aeroplane pilots who follow the sun gain minutes, hours, days? Is there a trick to it, after all?

She stretches, notes again the absence of all her physical symptoms – the sore stomach, the headaches. She makes a mental list of more things to get rid of and things to save (but for whom?). The mailman walks up and gives her a small pile of letters.

One postcard of Palm Springs from Dolores of the brown leggings, who is back already, and who always sends cards even though Morag has never sent her a card.

A reminder from the dental hygienist.

A flyer advertising the opening of a new MacDonalds two miles from her and offering her a free chilli flavour fries with her Big Mac.

A letter from American Express, with a gold credit card attached, instant access to a one hundred thousand-dollar debit account, and all that's required is one phone call. One signature. One hundred thousand dollars.

She begins to crush it up, but stops.

Cynthia Rogerson

Good Manners

In a house three houses from Morag's, five women sit at a kitchen table and consider Morag's condition. She has told them, of course, because one of them, bumping into Morag in the store, asked how she was and Morag was honest and said she was not at all well. She had cancer – in fact she had three kinds, each incurable.

These women are old friends and neighbours, which is to say they frequently stop speaking to each other over trifles, like whose turn it is to do school runs, and whose dog has been pooping on whose lawn, and whose kid has been speeding late at night with music blaring, and whose husband has been flirting with whose wife. (Not very different, in friction terms, from Joe and June's neighbourhood, though more densely-layered, since there are simply more people per inch here.) The arguments are part of the friendships, but there is no tension this sunny morning; the women are all bonding nicely, leaning over steaming cups of sweet coffee and home-made coffee cake. What has brought this truce, this intimacy, this almost moist warmth into the kitchen?

Morag's cancers, of course. Morag is suddenly their dear, dear friend, though they have had hardly any arguments with her at all – after all, she has no kids, no dog, and lately no husband either, though she does seem overly familiar with that Mexican man. Morag is friendly but they had long ago labelled her a snob because she has a British accent and because she does not come to their Neighbourhood Watch meetings. A few of them have not, in fact, even liked her very much, but this doesn't stop them from loving her now. In fact, the cancers have given Morag the single most essential ingredient for popularity. The chance for others to feel superior. They haven't felt so good about each other, and themselves, in ages. They swell with altruism and sympathy and importance and gratitude. Huddle and plot ways to alleviate Morag's misfortune.

'I'll make a pot of soup, that's what she's gonna want. Something warm and comforting.'

'Good idea, Maria. I'll make a nice chilli meat loaf.'

'I can bake my lemon cake. I remember she said she liked it once.' (A lie, but then who's noticing? They're all high as kites on sympathy.)

'Oh, the poor dear. I don't know. Weird how it just comes out of the blue like that. I saw her yesterday and she looked normal, but I didn't like to ask her about it. I mean, you can't, can you? But aren't you supposed to go bald or something?'

'She's not getting the chemo. Too far gone.'

'Wow. Scary. When you think.'

'Yeah,' says Dolores, who will later become a death groupie and loiter in Morag's hospice room, fussing over her. She is a good and generous woman, never better than at times like this. She crosses herself and says, 'I think maybe we need a special treat today. Whisky in your coffee, girls?'

A chorus of yes pleases, and they settle down to the next stage. Two non-smokers accept cigarettes and suck on them dramatically, to show the depth of their despondency and empathy.

'I want to do something more. There must be something else, besides just food.'

'Yes, I know. I feel so helpless.'

'We could maybe hold a garage sale. For the hospice.'

'Is she going there soon?'

'Oh, yes. Tomorrow, I think. She's going downhill quite fast now. I saw her this morning, just sitting on her door-step, and she looked shattered.'

'Oh, wow. Any more of that coffee, dear?'

'No. Have some more whisky.'

'I think a garage sale is an excellent idea. We can use my house. But when?'

'Yes, when? The timing is crucial, isn't it? Before or after?'

'Oh, after, I think. Then we can put some of her stuff in. She said she has tons, and has to get rid of it. She said the Salvation Army's coming for it, but we could offer to store it for her.'

'That's a bit tactless, isn't it, Marge?'

'Well,' says Marge huffily, and also drunkenly. 'Waste not, want not. Anyway, there's not enough time before. Isn't she supposed to pop off real soon?'

'I think so. She inferred it was only a matter of days,' says one woman in a sombre tone. 'But who knows.'

They pause in their swigging and each looks into space for a minute, reflecting on the possible repercussions of a remission. Their social responsibility towards someone who does not leave when they say they are leaving, but rudely hangs out on the doorstep. How long, exactly, can they be expected to sustain this sympathy?

Manuel is Fraught

But has so little experience of fraught-ness that he doesn't even recognise it. No, Manuel is not a man accustomed to complex emotions like regret or guilt. So he takes to his bed and phones Joe.

'Joe, I can't come in. I am very, very sick.'

'Yeah, right. Whatever.'

'It is true: I am a very sick man. I cannot move. My head, my stomach. I must have the Asian flu.'

'Uh huh.'

'Or maybe the Bulgarian variety. I have never felt like this.'

'Okay, Manuel. That's good. Fine.'

'You do not believe me.'

Silence.

'And after I give you Morag.'

'Who?'

'Morag McTavish.' Audibly sighs. 'A patient-to-be.'

'Yeah, yeah. Look, Manuel, you've got twenty-four hours to get better, or get another job, right?'

'*Sí, sí.* I knew you would worry about me. That's why I called. Hello? Hello?'

The Day of Departure

Morag greets the two ambulance men with a toast of her tequila sunrise.

'Good morning. You must have come for me. I'm delighted to see you and I am completely ready. Can I offer you a quick drink before we go? Made with fresh-squeezed, a real breakfast drink. My very good *amigo* Manuel taught me how to make this.'

The two young men look at each other and smile. This is a great job some days.

'Sure. We have time for a quick one, don't we José?'

'Why not.'

'That's the attitude. Here you go,' she says, pouring from a big pitcher. She sits on her porch surrounded by boxes and bags. 'Can you fit all these in the ambulance? I need them all. Every single wee itty bitty thing.'

The boxes are brand new and have pictures of things like CD players and gin bottles on them. Some of the bags say *Laura Ashley*, some say *Neiman Marcus*, some say *Banana Republic*, stores which do not have branches at Golden Hills Mall. Many still have the credit card slip attached. Around her neck is a rope of turquoise and silver, and Chanel No. 5 floats above her head.

'Had a shopping spree, did you?' asks one of the men.

'Oh aye. Well, why not?' She hiccups. 'Doc says my number's up, so to hell with budgeting. Let someone else deal with the bills. What do you think of my rings, dear?' She flashes up her fingers sparkling like small explosions in the morning sun. 'Anyway, I got rid of everything else, and you can't imagine how empty a house feels with nothing in it. I felt I deserved a few treats. Not had that many, you understand.'

'Sure. *Muy bonitas,*' he says of the rings. He gives her a smile. Offers her his arm.

'You know what I like about you people? You're so bloody sweet to me. I think I love you, and you know what? More than anything I wished I'd married a man with eyes as dark as both of yours. I just realised. Isn't it incredible? I've only ever had blue-eyed men. No wonder they never lasted!'

'Are you a leetle bit drunk, Señora?'

'Oh no! I'm very drunk! I've been drinking all night, haven't slept a

Jimmy Choo
CHANEL
5
Jimmy Choos?

wink. No more time to waste,' she says, with a finger on each of their chests. 'This is my last morning here. In this kitchen, in this house, on this street, in this town. But it's okay. Funny, I never really liked this house. Not really, really, really, *really*. Not compared to the place where I grew up. Now that was a house. Walls three foot thick. Stone slates on the roof.'

'What about all these dishes and tubs? You don't want to take these, do you?'

'Oh, I'd forgotten,' she laughs. 'That's food, my handsome men. Soup, casseroles, pies and cakes, and I don't want any of it! Take them all if you want, or bin them.'

'But Señora, they look fresh.'

'Aye, fresh they are, but I'm not wanting them just the same.'

'Why did you cook them all?'

'Me! I never. It was the posse of neighbour women.'

'Your friends?'

'Well, I don't know about that. I hardly saw them before. But word got round about me dying, and bingo! The number of hugs I've gotten! But all from middle-aged women . . .' She looks wistfully at the men's shoulders.

'Is that so? They smell delicious.'

'Have them, do. I've gone off food for the moment, and hey, would you like another top-up, I've made a whole pitcher. Special going-away treat.'

'I think we've had enough, thanks. Come along now, you'd better let us carry you.'

'Oh my,' she giggles. 'This is more fun than ever.'

Several hours later, Morag lies in a new bed. She barely makes a mound under the stiff cotton sheets and quilt. On the bedside table is a huge bunch of pink roses in a white vase, with a card propped up, saying – *Hope you feel better, love Dolores*. They have no smell. Morag lies very still, and thinks she can hear someone near, maybe a person, maybe an animal. She holds very still, straining to listen, and the noise stops. It is her own breathing that she hears; her own heart which quickens when she realises this. She looks like a very ill person in a hospice bed, and though none of her symptoms have returned she feels the role already. Passive, weak, faint, on the verge of expiration and in need of ministering hands. It has taken six days to fully possess her, the part Manuel assigned her. It reminds her, again, of her travelling days – time accordions out or collapses inwards, according to events. The imminence of death has stretched out time, so the six days have been equivalent to six years. She lived her entire forties more quickly than the last six days.

Her room is simple, with a colourful Mexican tapestry on the wall, and her own white-tiled bathroom. Extremely comfortable. Somewhere in the depths of the building a vacuum thrums and a radio plays an opera. Outside, two blue jays begin to make a racket in the tree nearest her window. Her bed is angled so that she can look out the window, and she is grateful for their noise, for the drowning of her own self-consciousness.

Then she tries to call someone.

'Excuse me. Is anyone out there?'

No answer.

'I am a little thirsty,' in a husky voice. 'All that tequila, now I'm dry as a … a … isn't anybody there?'

She has been settled into her room by a small squadron of women in white dresses and other women in floral house-dresses and still other younger women with dark skin and voices like Manuel's. She'd imagined, with so many, that at least a few would remain within earshot.

'Just have to find the kitchen myself, I guess.'

Heaves herself out of bed, gets dressed and wanders the corridors, adorned with all her jangling jewellery. Peeks in a room.

'Where is everybody? Dead quiet, so it is.'

She is lost.

'Now where has my room gone?'

Approaches a room where two volunteers are arranging flowers. Hovers, and listens. Feels light-headed, invisible, post-tequila sunrise.

'Too bad about Edith; she was a nice lady. So sad,' one of them is saying, while thrusting pink carnations into a green acne-pitted oasis.

'Yeah. But I don't mind the sad bit, you know? My real nightmare is when they all go home and no-one takes their place.'

'Like now? It's pretty quiet just now. Is that what you mean?'

'Yeah, I guess you're right. With all of us, I hadn't noticed, but yes. It's definitely a lull period. Imagine if everyone just popped off in car accidents or heart attacks.'

'Or got bumped off by pimply adolescents looking for drugs money.'

'No lingering on.'

'No needing constant surveillance, stimulation, flowers. Imagine!'

'No relatives to comfort. No playing with their poor grand-children.'

'Oh! Stop! I can't bear it when the children come,' she says, as if too much pleasure is pain.

'No making lovely glasses of iced tea! No more baking oatmeal cookies!'

'No taking them to bereavement counselling sessions.'

'And getting visits from that hunky minister.'

'And that even hunkier family support worker.'

'Oh you don't really think he's cute, do you? Are you blushing?'

'Not me, of course. I don't think he's cute. But you know *they* could. The sick ones.'

'I suppose. After all, beggars can't be choosers,' she giggles and whispers. This feels like a very naughty thing to say.

Morag listens, puzzled; then smiles, shakes her head. Wanders off and studies a floor plan of the hospice, conveniently on the wall. A nurse rushes past her.

'Excuse me, nurse. I'm thirsty, and I …'

'Off duty, sorry. Ring for a care assistant please!'

◆◆◆◆

'Oh, it's you!'

'Si, Señora Moragita. I work here. Remember?'

She twitches as a jolt jolts her.

'Are you chilly?'

'No. Well, a little.'

'Let me adjust the air-conditioning.'

'I've turned it off.'

'No, you must not do that, Señora Moragita.'

'I love it when you call me that.'

'Moragita? You used to hate it. That's why I do it.'

'No. Señora. So soft. Say it again, Doctor Manny Welly-Belly.'

'Is it the drugs, Señora? You are feeling maybe a little dizzy? A little relaxed? You will sleep with me now?'

'You sad man. No, it's the booze. I stopped taking the pills.'

'But why? They will make you feel better.'

(They were his very best prized painkillers, a little like ecstasy and THC, and if she does not want them, he'll know someone who does.)

'But they made me feel so far away, Manuel, and I'd rather not rush things. You know. Time enough to be distant.' She leans forward, to continue confidentially: 'Yesterday when I went to sign a credit card slip, I couldn't remember how my signature went – if I used my middle initial or not, and how the big letters looked. I've done it automatically for so long, I really hadn't a clue. Has that ever happened to you?' But before he can answer, she giggles and says, 'Anyway, all my pains have gone away. All gone! And look what I bought you – a present!'

She hands him a small box, which contains a gold cross embedded with twenty-carat diamonds, hanging on a simple gold link necklace. It is solid enough to look manly, yet so exquisite that his hands tremble holding it.

'Wow, I guessed right. Thought you'd be into the religious stuff. You former Catholics always are.'

'But Moragita, this is a very expensive present. I mean, how did you, where did you . . .?'

Morag just smiles serenely.

'Now, Manny. It's good manners to just say thank you, you know.'

'Thank you. Moragita.' He puts it on; keeps fingering it.

She sits by the window, more ethereal than ever, and calm.

'Ah.' He frowns. A fact is trying to wing its way to him. Feels like, sounds like, tastes like . . . hmm . . . what?

'What is it? Not more bad news. Is worse news possible?'

'No, it is only that . . .'

Only that you look so extraordinary right now, he might say. There is something so painfully poignant about Morag diagnosed-with-cancer. So poised on the edge; so frightened and yet still talking and walking and making jokes, even. Especially the making jokes. It's only that dying becomes you, *mi bonita Moragita,* he might say. Ravished by death, you are ravishing. Manuel can feel his heart trying to leave his chest. It's a little disturbing. New.

She looks down at what she's wearing: her new white silk dress from

Banana Republic.

'You think I should get out of my clothes and back into bed, Manny? Sip broth and doze away my time?'

'No, no, Señora.' He begins to take her pulse then seems to forget why he is holding her hand. Just holds it. Her skin is so soft, and so white. And her hand is still, not fluttering like his heart.

'You do not ever tan, Morag?'

'Not a bit, I'm afraid. But then where I come from it wouldn't matter.'

She thinks about pulling her hand away, then stares at it lying in his hand. Again, the two skin tones, so contrasting. Funny how her age didn't seem to be in her hands today. The age spots could almost be freckles. And then, the memory of the traitor nipple arises unbidden – that too had been almost virginal. Bodies are such funny things – ageing at different rates in different places. Her face was easily fifteen years older than her breasts. Yet even in her face, it is only the skin that has aged – her eyes, wide and a little lost, look young.

'Are you all right, Manny? Do you have an eye infection? Maybe it's the pollen, but the windows won't open, so maybe not. Here, have a hankie.'

'You are the only person I know who always has a clean cotton hankie.'

'Ach, well. It's an old habit.'

He blows his nose; sits on her bed.

She flutters about with a glass of water and when her hand brushes his, he knows heart pain so exquisite that it nearly makes him cry out, and the light bulb in the ceiling makes a quiet popping noise to signal its imminent death.

Part Five

Being alive is pure luck. Better than finding out one day that the country you were born in just happens to be a rich place, not a poor place. Better than waking up to find it's not a work day or a school day: it's a Saturday in summer. And your skin's the easiest colour to be. And your nightmare's just a nightmare. And the person you married without really knowing has turned out to be normal. Being alive is the only proven miracle. It's wearing clothes that feel wonderful against your skin, and skin that feels wonderful against your clothes, so you're exactly — but **exactly** *— the right temperature, and need to touch someone, you feel so good. I can tell you know what I mean. It's discovering that the shoes you bought on sale, untried, really do fit well, and spring your feet forward. Effortlessly, on good days; and even on stumbling days, they stay on your feet. Until, of course, they do not.*

Excerpt from *The Consuela Chronicles*, transcribed by Xavier Juarez of Oakland, California, 1962. Xavier is credited with solving the missing feet/floating Consuela mystery. While researching the house documents, he came across a bill to Algernon Vietti II, which requested the sum of $612.89 to be paid to a building firm for the extermination of woodworm, and the subsequent replacement of the floors most damaged. The plans show these new floors to be approximately three inches below the original floors, presumably to increase the rather shallow height of the rooms.
Estimated age of Consuela: twenty-one.
Location of apparition: the linen cupboard in Sycamore House, which is now the Gentle Valleys Hospice volunteers' lounge.

Dog Bubbles

Georgia-May arrives at her parents' house to take Moze to the vet. Heads first for the kitchen, as is her habit from the old days. June follows her, as is her habit.

'I'll get you something to eat, honey. What do you want?'

'That's okay, Mom. I'll just make myself a cup of coffee, and maybe some toast. I haven't had any breakfast yet.'

'You sure?'

'Sure. Where's the bread?'

'In the freezer, of course. Georgia-May, you are silly.'

'Silly me. Must be asleep still. So where's the butter?'

'Georgia-May! Stop teasing me!'

'What?'

'Oh, you are just like your father, always teasing me. The butter,' she says in a giggle, 'is in the freezer too.'

And there it is, a cube of frozen yellow by the ice-cream.

'What's it doing there? Oh, never mind,' as she remembers. Everything lives in the freezer in her mother's kitchen. Safe from heat, from ants. Georgia-May fills the old enamel kettle. Puts the burner on high and goes to find a newspaper to read. If she can read and eat and not talk for a few more minutes, she'll be fine. It's been a bad night, both girls up hourly, husband feigning sleep to punish her for escaping this morning. It's all a power struggle, and neither can admit to having a good time without conceding defeat. Each racing to win the suffered-the-most prize. Plus, she has just realised that the novel she is writing is self-indulgent crap. She has to close her eyes for a second when she sits at the table. Her eyelids re-glue themselves. She can hear the kettle begin to boil, then suddenly it is boiling but before she can get up, June screams:

'Georgia-May! Never, *never* put the burner on high. That is so stupid.'

Georgia-May begins to object, to reason, but like the butter-in-the-freezer, gives up before she begins. Reaches for and fails to find her habitual anger. Better to comply. Ants and fire are June's big fears. Also there's Georgia-May's low energy problem.

'Okay Mom. Sorry.'

But June is still bristling. 'Just don't *do* it. If you put the kettle on, you have to stand right by and watch it. Don't put it on high, then go walking away. That is just so stupid.'

Georgia-May sighs. Cannot credit her recent emotional surge of parental love. Surely not. Not this woman, not this kitchen.

'I was just sitting here. I could hear it boiling,' she whines, because she has remembered her function is not to comply – not to say okay, sorry. She must provide the obstinate voice for her mother to rail against. But hasn't it been going on for too many years? Were other families so arrested?

She wonders if Adam has this regression problem at home with his parents. She'll ask him tomorrow. Adam of the playground has progressed to Adam of the cappuccino café while the toddlers are at nursery school. Yesterday they'd stood outside the café, prolonging their parting with an inane and catty conversation about other parents. She'd leaned against him for a moment while laughing at something he'd said which was not, in itself, funny at all, but a sufficient excuse to vocalise her ridiculous bliss. Leaned her full length, chest-to-chest, thigh-to-thigh, helpless with mirth, then drew back, horrified. He, too, stiffened, in the asexual sense.

'Oops, I touched you,' she whispered. 'Is that all right? I don't usually touch people. Except my kids, of course,' she gushed, wondering at her omission of the word husband. Gush, blush, mush. Oh dear.

It is too confusing. It is murky. It is adolescent mud. Georgia-May drinks her coffee in her childhood kitchen, but the coffee doesn't work, the Adam thing is still mud and she yawns repeatedly. It must be the heat. The room is stuffy, feels subterranean. And the window, even with the curtain pulled, is blinding. Outside a bird riot is going on at the bird table. Then suddenly, a cat fight — fearsome growls and feline screams, as the cats who line up to kill the birds get tired of waiting their turn. Georgia-May gets up to see, and finds her father on the deck sitting quietly in the shadows and watching the carnage with a smile. Yes, chaos! he seems to be saying again. As though he hasn't spent his entire life imposing rigid order on his immediate universe.

'Hey Dad. How's it going?'

'Shhh.' He cackles. 'Watch this.' He points to a ginger tom about to eat sparrow.

'You're sick.'

Joe has a thought, something he meant to ask Georgia-May – a nagging thought. A thought that came about when he was contemplating how somehow satisfying it was that Georgia-May has kept her maiden name. She is still his Georgia-May, his Georgia-May Johnson. Joe and Georgia-May. He hasn't dwelt on the irony that it would not be satisfying if June had kept *her* maiden name.

'Hey, Georgia-May.'

'Yeah?'

Listen, he wants to say. Are you all right in your life? You could always move back here. This is your home. I still miss having you around all the time. Not a huge amount, but your absence annoys me sometimes. You've got no right to deprive me of you, when I want to see you, damn it. Especially if your marriage is not one hundred percent. Of course, the girls would want to stay with their daddy, but you could see them on weekends. June is good for wife things, but I like talking to you.

'What is it?' asks Georgia-May again, sitting down. The cat pounces, and Georgia-May braces herself for the sound of small bones being crunched.

'Georgia-May, are you happy?'

'Happy? What's happy? Sure, I'm happy.'

Crunch, crunch.

'Good. That's good.'

'Yeah.'

'Good.'

'Yeah. Happy — good.'

'That's great. Just great.'

She gives her father a worried frown. 'Well, think I'd better find Moze and take her to the vets now.'

'Yup. Think she's in the garage.'

'Dad?'

'What?'

'Do you like that bone-crunching noise?'

Georgia-May needs the bathroom first, but finds her mother scrubbing Moze in the bath.

'Oh, don't mind me, honey. Just go ahead. I won't look.' (Georgia-May does.) 'Just giving the dog her bubble-bath. I always shampoo her before she goes to the vets. It's her psoriasis; I feel guilty we don't do it as often as the vet says.'

'Does she like it?'

'Loves it, don't you, Moze?'

Moze has the vacant bemused look on her face that all retrievers have, no matter what they're doing, and shampoo all around her mouth so that when she opens her mouth and inhales as a prelude to a low doggie chuckle, quite a few bubbles go inside. She exhales and the gust of air blows them out as bubbles.

'Will you look at that! Aren't you smart? You are so smart! I just adore you, Moze,' she says, frothing up her tufts.

'Why is she called Moze, Mom?'

'Oh, you know why, Georgia-May. Our dogs have always been Moze. Heavens, you know why. Silly.'

Georgia-May has a quick wash at the sink and leaves. Maybe she does know. Maybe it is an old family story and she's lost it. She's having one of those days. She doesn't know what she knows right now, and would believe anything. Even her own name sounds slightly too ludicrous to be real, like the name Moze. She wouldn't be surprised to find she was actually Linda or Susan, and that Georgia-May was a delusion that she'd need to forget now.

Home is not always good for Georgia-May. She makes another cup of coffee, the right way – eyeballs glued to the kettle the whole time. Home seems to disconnect her from her adult self, as if the house can only reclaim her child self. No, not even her child self, which was full of seriousness and wonder, and was possibly loveable. No: what this house has preserved, and demands every time she enters it, is her adolescent self, the one she'd like to disinherit forever. Insecure, stubborn, defensive, moody. Her teenage hormonally-haywire self waits to prove that she hasn't changed after all, no matter how many children she has, no matter how many birthdays she remembers or dental appointments she keeps or bills she pays on time. The house knows the truth, and will never forget. Georgia-May, as an adult, is a fraud.

But who cares. This is not a crisis or a revelation, it is the usual stuff. It is so hot; caring takes too much energy. She watches the mailman on his rounds and a jogger who is walking. Marinites in the summer move slow, as if they are dreaming.

June guides Moze back down the hall to the deck to dry her in the sun.

'When are you off, Georgia-May?'

For a second Georgia-May thinks she's referring to her own smelly state of rottenness.

'What?'

'Off to the vets.'

'Oh. Now, I suppose.'

'You're a good daughter.'

'I had a real good mom.'

Both women smile, not looking at each other.

◆◆◆◆

'Hold the dog, please', says the vet.

Georgia-May hates touching Moze. Old dogs have such loose skin. She can feel the muscles and bones slide underneath.

'Feel this?' The vet guides her hand to a hard crusty lump on Moze's belly, where the hair is even thinner. 'I'd operate, but she's too old.'

'What is it?'

'A tumour, almost certainly cancerous, given the other tumours I've found on her back.'

'I thought she just had a doggie version of scabies. My dad, that's what he thinks too.'

'I'm afraid it's much worse.'

'How long has she got?'

'Hard to say, but not long. She could go at any time.'

'I see. Poor Dad.' She forces her hand to stroke Moze.

'She seems all right now, but bring her back in if she seems to be in any discomfort and I'll give her an injection. No need for her to suffer.'

'That kind of injection?'

'It would be the kindest thing.'

'Oh, I agree. Well, she's an old dog.'

'How old is she?'

'Oh, old.'

Georgia-May and Moze get back in the car. Moze slobbers; Georgia-May sighs. How old *is* that dog? Moze had been the puppy bought by Georgia-May to help Joe get over Georgia-May going off to college.

Moze has been the Georgia-May replacement, and served her purpose well. What can replace a replacement? A grandchild? Should she offer her firstborn? After another broken night like last night, she will be tempted to consider this.

Part Six

I am not crying. Go away!

Why are you still here? Are you a dead person? My mama says dead people are completely dead, souls go to heaven and there are no ghosts. And I believe her: she is smart, my mama. But then who are you? What? I can't hear you. It's not a good day for hearing. Where are you going? Good, I'm glad you're going. I want to be alone. It's not a good day for anything. Why do some days hurt so much? Breathing, eating, swallowing, walking. I am not crying. Go away! Hey, where are you going? Come back!

Excerpt from *The Consuela Chronicles*, transcribed by Murdo Bruce, January 17, 1972. It is thought that Consuela was crying from some drama related to World War I, as three Vietti sons were killed in it.
Estimated age of Consuela: ten.
Location of apparition: the middle of Addison Avenue, which used to be the fruit orchard of Sycamore House.

Morag's Messages

'Miss McTavish, can I come in? You've had several phone calls.' A volunteer enters with a piece of paper in one hand, and a bunch of carnations in the other.

'Yes, yes, come in. How lovely. Who called?'

'A woman called Dolores.'

'Oh. Who else?'

'And ... oh! It looks like it's the Dolores woman again. And again.'

'Oh.'

'And she sent these flowers. What a generous friend! Aren't they splendid! Do you want them in a vase?'

'No, that's all right.' Morag takes the flowers and dumps them on a chair.

'Oh, well. I guess they look nice there too. Just two more things, Miss McTavish: I'll go get them.' She returns in a minute, out of breath, partially concealed by the two enormous boxes that she carries. One says *Gumps*, the other says *Treasures for the Treasured*, in gold lettering.

'UPS delivered these,' she says, dumping them on the bed.

'Oh!' says Morag, backing onto the flower-covered chair and not noticing. Crushed pink carnations give out a perfumed gasp. The crazy thing about ordering by phone with a gold credit card was that it was so easy that you tended to forget what you'd bought. Once, Morag received the same item twice, having forgotten she had already ordered it. And these boxes today – she has simply no idea at all what is in them; the whim which inspired their purchase has evaporated. In fact, the purchase act itself might be the bigger thrill. The looking through catalogues and newspaper ads, the phone conversations with chatty people who don't know that Morag has cancer, the quoting of all those little credit card numbers. It is private and it is satisfying. It is a little dismaying to have the solid evidence of her greed plopped onto her bed by a stranger.

'Enjoy!' says the volunteer, retreating quickly with a puzzled smile. She dashes upstairs, two steps at a time, late for her afternoon break in the volunteers' lounge.

Gentle Valley's Volunteers' Lounge

Five well-groomed women in their late fifties/ early sixties sip decaffeinated sugar-free iced tea. Their clothes are muted earth-tones – beige and cream, mostly. They have what used to be called class, before it became a no-class thing to mention class because it infers that only one class is worthy of the name. Good breeding that shows in their healthy vigour, their expensive shoes, their subdued demeanour, and their enormous pure-bred dogs at home. These are all good women, good and honest well-meaning women. They are still performing the roles they were born to, and this is no mean feat considering the decades they have traversed. They resisted the 'flower power' era, but carry minimal grudges for missed sexual opportunities. They meet at Gentle Valleys most weekday afternoons; it is part of their routine. Mornings are devoted to pelvic floor exercise, the mall, hair and doctor appointments. Lunch is spent catering to the overweight retired husbands that they never divorced because divorced women have no class. And afternoons are for girl time, right here in the volunteers' lounge.

Sometimes there are real dying people, like Morag McTavish (unlike Fred and Connie, dithering dyers) who interrupt their sessions of camaraderie somewhat, but these dying people are forgiven because they cannot help dying. And also because they provide a lot of intense emotional conversation. After all, what could be a better topic than a tragedy that isn't happening to themselves, but is near enough to witness safely? In a way, for these genteel good women, the hospice is the respectable version of stopping at a freeway accident to gawk.

But there is no shame in this; it's just what ever single human being wants to do. Gawking at death is as natural as breathing; it's just considered to be bad manners. It's why we turn up the radio when there is horrible news; it's why we buy more newspapers during disasters; it's why we go to the funerals of mere acquaintances; it's why some of us become undertakers, others become friends of undertakers, and the rest are just glad that someone wants to do the job. It's why we love war movies; it might be why we have wars.

But these women are no ordinary gawkers. They are not shallow or lazy or passive. They gawk with infinite kindness and respect. They escort the dying right to the very last terrifying portal, like perfect, calm hostesses. Tactful. Tender. Privileged to be so close to that dangerous place: a life's end. Trusted to accompany a human involved in the ultimate private act. To be the last to see someone alive, to watch the light fade from their eyes, is like being admitted to the inner circle of a secret tribe After all, if anyone comes close to knowing the secrets of an afterlife, it might be these close witnesses, these classy women in beige. Mortals poised within eye and ear-shot of the precipice.

They have discussed it, these women, and likened it to seeing someone off on a very long journey – off to an unknown distant land, to war, to certain calamity. A departure that demands to be witnessed. Just as people tend to watch the trains, boats and planes that carry their loved ones away till they are completely out of sight, the dying are watched till the end. Sometimes it seems that the watching keeps them here – and the second that they are un-watched, they are loosened somehow, and slip away.

And even when the dying are done dying, and gone, it is hard to look away. Where the ship disappears over the horizon, where the last wisp of exhaust hovers, where there used to be light in someone's eyes. Even if it is not always sad, it is always moving. Both loved ones and strangers watch as if to look away would ruin something, or at least give cause for regret later. The spaces where people have been seen alive for the last time – these negatives, these absences, these empty chairs and beds and garden benches, are imbued with a kind of magic for a while; and sometimes, when there is a lot of love involved, a very long while. And then the survivors turn back to their world, now forever bereft of that particular set of shoulders, that laughter, that unique sense of humour.

It is a queer feeling, this last sight business.

Even for the volunteer staff in the hospice, who are more used to it than most. A fresh involuntary gasp is drawn each and every time. Last sight, last sigh. After all, as the Seneca Indians said, anyone can stop a man's life, but who can stop his death? It is the biggest thing there is. It's the ultimate brick wall. A brick wall doesn't give you a choice, it doesn't give anything away, and who knows what's behind it? It's solid brick. Even the mortar is brick.

Let's face it, a brick wall like this is downright scary. It commands respect. It says: Sit up! Dance! Be alive while you are alive! And if there is anything that these pampered women lack, it is this feeling of being alive. They are bored, bored, bored. It's the main side-effect of being good and classy. Especially, they're bored with their husbands, and the way that these men haven't changed in pleasing or surprising ways, but only predictable and fat ones. (Of course, they only see their own husbands in this unflattering light, and would assume vulture pose if by some chance any of these men were widowed. A single man of their generation doesn't stand a chance in hell of loneliness.)

'Where is Ismelda?' one woman asks.

'You didn't hear?' says another, in a smug important whisper. The women all stop drinking, and lean closer, breathe more shallowly. A piece of news! They almost smile.

'Hear what? Has she had another angina attack?'

'Are her veins playing up again?'

'She hasn't had another break-in, has she?' All anxious to have guessed the news before it emerges. To be wise, to be able to say – *I had a feeling, I just knew it.*

'Her husband, Tommy – you know he golfs?' They all nod, suck their breath in. 'Well, he had a heart attack on the course, Sunday. Just out of the blue.'

'No!'

'No!'

'No!'

But all their hearts are beating more quickly now; their eyes are brightening, muscles tensing. Shock can be very rejuvenating. Even sadness can rejuvenate, and it *is* quite sad to have one less potential widower. The numbers of their own generation are being decimated.

'And?'

'And,' she says, her hands uplifted in a helpless gesture that they all admire, 'he's gone. It was a massive coronary, apparently. One minute he was teeing up and saying how he couldn't wait to get home and into the pool, the next he was …'

'Oh, my. Poor poor Ismelda. And I was just having lunch with her on Saturday,' says one, to establish that although she has not heard the news, she is indeed a close friend of the now important Ismelda. Ismelda, who lost someone to the brick wall! Ismelda, who was visited by the brick wall outside the hospice!

'Yes, the poor woman. She'll be all alone now.'

'My, she'll miss him. After all these years, to be alone now.'

'I'll see if she needs some help organising things. Flowers. Ministers. Caterers.'

'I'll take her out to dinner one night, maybe keep her company.'

'Will you? I'll come too. She'll need a lot of support now. Oh, dear; quite a shock, isn't it? Makes you think.'

'I can't help imagining if it had been Gerry,' says one woman, of her husband.

'Or Harry.'

'Or John.'

'Or Sam.'

'Or Steve.'

'Poor poor Ismelda. All alone in her house.'

Then into the small silence that descends, all five women picture themselves widowed. The empty chair, the empty bed, the empty garden seat. Another moment passes while they have more thoughts. The clean toilet seat, the absence of certain smells, the extra food, money, quiet and calm. First choice in television programs and vacation destinations.

'Lucky bitch,' whispers one voice, so soft, so secretive that several women wonder if they have spoken out loud by accident.

The Truth

Real secrets never get told. People only tell the stories that don't make them look mean or selfish. Or they tell stories they've promised not to tell, in which other people are these bad things. Morag has never told anyone about her weddings.

She may be dying of three kinds of untreatable cancer and she may be living in a hospice and she may be a gold credit card criminal, but certain habits survive even these drastic changes. Brushing her teeth, keeping her room tidy, putting on clean socks and underwear every day, having a bedtime cup of tea. And tonight, she gets the old book out of her new sock drawer. (Her meticulous sock drawer, unlike her un-meticulous mind, which has countless odd socks and rotten bits of elastic.) This scrapbook is one of the few items to survive her regular culls of sentimental objects. It was one of the first things to be put in the suitcase to come here. It has remained hidden from each husband. Her proper photo albums have lived in legitimate places like bookshelves and coffee tables (and now garbage cans), but this book lives, has always lived, in dark secret places like the back of sock drawers or the tops of cupboards.

She slips on another brand new silk nightie (no need to launder, ever) sits on her bed, sips her tea and browses through her secret past. And there they are, more or less in order. The photographs recording each big day, the dried roses in a sandwich baggie, the invitations, the guest lists, the champagne cork wire covers, and several items that only she knows the significance of. The matchbook cover from *The Happy Hippo*, the envelope with a number scribbled on it, the Safeway's receipt for two avocados and a gallon of milk.

Keeping secrets is Morag's life-long condition. Well, it's everyone's life-long condition, if they are honest and have had half a life. But with Morag, keeping secrets has become a larger-than-average proportion of her self. She is unaware that other people do not carry such a burden inside, the same permanent holding back, the feeling of a soft object lodged in her digestive system. Morag has done bad things and swallowed them whole, and there they remain; sometimes in her belly, sometimes higher up in her throat, as if they are rising to make a break for it – to dash screaming out of her carelessly open mouth. And what terrible thing would they say? What has she done that is so bad? Broken laws, that's what. And broken hearts. But which laws? Which hearts?

Ah! That is the nub, because it depends on the perspective of the person judging. Morag is the victim of *relativo honestitus* – a rare condition believed to afflict three percent of the population, though by its nature it often goes undiagnosed and the true figure may be as high as ninety-three percent. Morag cannot be dishonest on one level, which regularly leads her into another kind of dishonesty. She is a chronic and honest liar. (Unlike the Snellings, who are chronic dishonest liars.)

She sits with her cup of tea, in puzzled judgement of herself yet again. Prepared to find allowances and release. So near the end, but how did it all begin?

Page one. School photograph of herself at thirteen. Inverness High School, 1964. Not a secret, nothing to be ashamed of, and yet there is something already clandestine in her eyes. Something duplicitous. It was snapped the year she began to get boyfriends. The boy year. The *boys* year, because she had never been able to choose just one. To say: this is the one, and to stop looking at other boys that way. And so she'd juggled them, all these nice boys, frequently very different from each other. Over the succeeding years there were athletes, sensitive chess players, homely boys with bad skin and glasses and tanned blond boys with Hollywood looks. She could not spare any of them, but sooner or later they objected to sharing her.

She hadn't been exceptionally pretty, or exceptionally anything. She looked like her sister, like many Inverness girls of her time – reddish hair in a bobbed pony-tail, short bangs, freckled skin and blue-grey eyes, green mascara-ed to death. Her school photos had lined up on her parents' sideboard, all uniformly plain. Her academic record had been better than she deserved.

Morag sitting still in church or a classroom was invisible. But Morag in motion – maybe that was it, she thinks, finishing her cooled tea. Because that's when it always happened; her men were always strangers, snared in transient unplanned moments. Running down the street to catch the bus once, she skipped by a boy holding a sign advertising teas for a shilling, looked right into his eyes and said, 'That's a good job.' As if she'd considered it in depth since the millisecond she'd spotted him. 'I want that job,' she said, and meant it. (Timothy lasted six months, his photo is on page ten, and still seems exciting.)

One young man, a museum guard in Glasgow, had been caught by her asking him, in passing and with no preamble, what a certain sculpture meant. What was the idea of a fat plane with miniature wings? He explained that it was to demonstrate the futility of all men's endeavours. The fragility of human hope. His face was serious, as if breaking some sad news to an innocent. 'Aren't human beings just wonderful?' she said. (Matthew had lasted five months. One of his letters is taped to page twelve, serious and wordy, full of pretension.)

Morag yawns, looks at the clock. She braces herself for guilt and turns the page to Ian.

'Will you eat that wee tiddler? If it's dead, you might as well,' she'd told a young fishermen sorting through his catch. He looked up to see a flash of red hair and pale legs flashing by on the pier.

'You have it if you like,' he called after her. 'I'm no needing it the day. Here, catch!' throwing the tiddler at her back, a wet satisfying thwack on her anorak.

'Better show me how to clean the poor wee thing then,' she'd countered, and sashayed back to him, a stroll that had the direct consequence of marriage eight months later.

Her wedding with Ian was in her local Church of Scotland. Everyone came, and her dress train dragged behind her like a cumbersome river. She remembered leaning forward to balance as she marched down the aisle to Ian. And handsome! How handsome he'd looked. Her heart had quite somersaulted, and looking at the photo now, it still did. With her forward tilt and her somersaulting heart she felt a little sea-sick, but thought nothing of it until it was time to kiss him and a sudden claustrophobic nausea descended. She had thought marriage would cure her of not being able to choose one man, but found to her great disappointment that it only made her restlessness more poignant and frustrating. Certainly, it made it less respectable. Married women were not supposed to think about those things. She woke up when she was twenty-six, looked over at her slumbering fisherman husband, breathed in his sour breath, observed his fine beard growth, and understood that she would never kiss another man in her entire one and only life; that, romantically speaking, her life was over. She studied Ian and found this restriction impossible to contemplate. To forever forgo other kisses. How could anyone settle for one set of lips, one pair of eyes, one set of shoulders? Saying no to possibilities was like embracing death.

Morag was doubtful about an after-life and she was frightened of getting the before-death bit wrong. Being a late walker, late at the toilet training, late talker, and general all-round late bloomer, she realised that this was a distinct possibility. That she'd lie on her death-bed one day and suddenly a light bulb would ping on above her. The answer to life's mysteries would appear forty years later than it did for most other people, and she'd croak, full of wasted wisdom.

She didn't cheat on Ian, and not only because no-one asked her. She didn't believe in disloyalty any more than she believed in an after-life. It was like voting Tory or going to church, you either did or you didn't. She simply wanted to try another life. And so she told no lies, had no arguments, took no lovers, did not say goodbye. Just left. The only scary part was buying the ferry ticket. Sitting in the noisy travel agents, handing over the money she'd been hoarding for months, made her dizzy. Like standing on a dangerous cliff-edge, eyes closed. After that, it was just a series of mundane events. First this, then that and that. Quite a lot of just waiting in mind-numbing queues. Eventually, she found herself with a small suitcase in Dublin, in a café near the Liffey, looking in the newspaper for jobs, circling flats for rent.

Morag turns the scrap-book page to reveal a man as red-haired as herself, beaming most winsomely at her. Desmond. Organic, wholesome, non-smoking atypically Irish Desmond came across her in a supermarket queue, having trouble with the bags. She couldn't open them; they'd sealed shut while being manufactured, but the cashier wasn't in the mood to slow up her business while Morag sorted them out. Desmond shoved all her things into his politically correct wicker shopping basket, and took her off for a coffee to Trinity where, surrounded by university students, she felt very different indeed. Desmond was not a student, but liked to associate with them. They gave him a certain intellectual respectability. Not amongst the students themselves, of course – he was their token working-class friend, to prove that they were classless. But to the outside world, who just observed them all as a lump, Desmond appeared to blend in and this was enough for him. And enough, it turned out, for Morag.

'Will we marry, then? I think we should, now. We should be at the marrying, you and me. What do you say, Morag?' asked Desmond one moonless night in Phoenix Park, in his usual half-mocking half-serious corny way. And what did Morag say? Did she explain that she would love to, but she was already married to Ian? Why, not a bit of it. 'No' would have been rude. Rude and hurtful, and a wordy conditional reply might have put him off altogether.

'Yes!' she cried, and Desmond swept her up into his arms and swung her around till she felt dizzy, and that was that. When he put her down she opened her mouth, then closed it again, fish-like. It was suddenly way too late.

Secret number one!

That first lie may have been quick, done for good manners, unpremeditated and monosyllabic – but that didn't stop it from leading to complications as heavy and criss-crossing as rusty iron railroad bridges. Once started, Morag could not stop.

She strokes the photographs of herself and Desmond in the church, and smiles. She could never resist a wedding, never. A big Catholic wedding, that one, with everyone getting plastered on home brew and rhubarb wine. One photo shows them shoving carrot cake into each other's mouths, faces indecently happy. Innocents, certainly, both of them. Desmond took her up to her thirtieth birthday, and she still can't eat steamed brown rice without thinking of him and his penchant for flavourless things. Morag apologetically kisses the air above Desmond's image, and turns the page.

A newspaper cutting from the jobs section, the day that she landed in Canada. Sitting in the airport reading the Star for jobs and apartments, while drinking tea made oddly from a Lipton's tea-bag and a pot of tepid water. It had come with a wedge of lemon and she'd had to ask for milk. The first of many queer customs. Morag sits on her hospice bed recalling her feeling when confronted with that innocuous cup of tea. As if the entire universe had just exploded.

Having never voiced her plans to anyone, they'd remained a little unreal even to herself. In fact, her whole self felt unreal. If she'd woken up to find herself in bed with Desmond, she wouldn't have been surprised in the least. In fact, she would have been relieved. A tiny bit.

But already, little spurts of excitement came shooting through her. This was *much* more exciting than the Oban to Dublin move. It was Dublin multiplied by a hundred. All the different accents, the different colours of people, the bigger everythings. Her path could lie in any direction, a multitude of lives awaited her like a rack of gloriously diverse outfits, all her size, or near enough. She knew no-one, and more importantly, *no-one knew her* and this fact unhinged her from her old self.

Once the freeing anonymity had worn off, in about a month, she'd been terrified, torn to shreds by immersion in an alien culture. Not much of Inverness Morag had been left. For survival, she'd answered some primal urge to emulate the natives, to not sightsee, to not stick out. She had not, after all, carried her home in her heart. Or in her hand. She had arrived in Toronto an empty vessel and let herself be filled to the brim. Which meant, ultimately, to have her bluff called. So it was not surprising that within a year, she had added to her criminal record.

Secret number two!

This time it was not a church wedding, but a registry office affair, attended by Teddy's parents and friends. She wore pink, despite her hair. A knee-length skirt and short jacket, with a collar-less white blouse. Very demure and feminine. And she did not experience any claustrophobia at all. Not for ages.

They lived in an apartment above a dry cleaners and shopped in little corner Italian grocery stores that had salamis and garlic and peppers hanging over counters. She wrote to her sister, of course. She said she was fine, just needed some time, and hoped everyone was well. She didn't tell her that she was married again, but she said she'd be back soon and she kept saying this for several years on Christmas and birthday cards, just in case things didn't work out in Toronto.

Morag stretches, yawns, gets more comfy and turns the pages of Toronto. It isn't taking long to go through all this – they are old memories, much perused, dog-eared.

Her third marriage was sufficiently different to let her think she'd done the right thing. Once, on a day-trip out to Galt, she was horrified to find a whole neighbourhood full of Scots. She cringed to hear her kinfolk speak. Really, she hoped she didn't sound like that. She wanted to be assimilated; to dissemble, efface herself. Of all reptiles she admired chameleons the most.

Babies were discussed, but they didn't materialise. She didn't mind until she got the film developed. She'd found a camera on a park bench and turned it into the police. When it wasn't claimed after three months, they phoned Morag and said it was hers if she wanted it. It had a roll of film half-shot, which she had developed, of course. Who could resist?

Maybe it held clues to the owner. Maybe the owner was murdered and the film would reveal incriminating evidence against some horribly ugly man! Or a lover! Or … or …or anything!

Morag opened the packet of prints and there they were – fourteen shots of a boy and girl of about two and four, playing in the park. She gave them names – Ross and Sarah. Nothing extraordinary, yet they filled her with such searing pain. Why? Perhaps because the tiny faces had looks of such careless love on them that it could only have been the mother who said 'smile.' And more – Morag could tell by the way they didn't bother posing – *they knew they were adored.* Just as they were. Morag hadn't thought of motherhood like that. She was missing out on all this mutual adoration, and for one bitter October afternoon in Toronto, she wept and wept till she looked frightening, and she had to tell her husband she had very bad flu and he was just to go away and leave her alone.

Teddy Tarantino was a good man; he went away and then came back, and cooked two steaks and never asked her about the state of her face. It had gone back to normal by then anyway. Silent – sullen even, at times – but a good solid man who plodded through his days at a reassuring pace. Only quickening slightly in winter, slowing in summer.

She should have seen it coming, but she didn't, and after nearly a decade of marriage she woke up one morning, considered her Teddy snoring away, and her heart plummeted. Oh no, she moaned. Oh God, no. But it was too late. She couldn't look at him again without thinking of death. Of the same thing over and over again till she died, no more surprises, no new man to explore, just Teddy.

She sighs as the sun goes down outside her hospice window. Sighs and tsks for the shame of it. Oh dear! She still feels very bad about Teddy. And mad at herself for throwing him away; now she has no-one. But how was she to know it would end up this way? How?

She remembers wondering why other people didn't see marriage in this morbid way. To want to get married was to want to know how you would die. With whom, anyway. If you knew this, you were as good as dead. She was too young to be dead. She absconded over the border on a Greyhound, with just a small bag full of essentials and small items of sentiment: among them this scrapbook. People say you can't run away, but they are wrong. Running away is the perfect cure for lots and lots of things. She left a little note. I am going away, it said. I will probably not come back. You did nothing wrong. I love you.

And that was the really maddening thing: she did love him, as she had loved Ian and Desmond. She loved them most of all when she left them. Loved them with a piercing, heart-breaking intensity. (It *is* a mysterious fact that the leaver loves more than the left. At least momentarily.) Morag wanted to hire someone to look after him when she was gone. Find another woman for him, but knew that was going too far.

Ah, life was complicated, and she could hardly fathom herself, just follow her deep compulsions. And when she got to the Buffalo bus station she felt alone in a most satisfactory way. Went into the restroom and looked at herself in the mirror. She looked her age. Only a little frantic around the eyes. She gave herself a quick version of her assured smile. Her 'everything's okay' exhalation of air, stretching of lips and tensing of cheek muscles. It worked; in the next second she didn't have to fake it.

It felt right to be alone and unknown again. She knew that it wouldn't last, this anonymity. She remembered this. The minute she stopped moving she would begin to talk to people, get a job, make friends, decorate a new nest, generally hem in her world. But she relished the dizzy nothingness, so she bought another bus ticket and headed south-west to California. I am alone and no-one knows me and I like this. These were truths, and important. It didn't mean that she liked herself a huge amount, but it meant that she knew herself a little bit, which was not quite the same thing, not a smiley smug kind of thing at all.

Husband number four followed. It was getting so easy now! She turns to the Harry page. Good old Harry.

Secret number three!

Her wedding to Harry had been in a hotel courtyard, shaded by eucalyptus trees and presided over by an Episcopalian priest. It was her nicest wedding so far. The food was barbecued and colourful and there was live music, a mariachi band in costume. Her dress was a long white cotton frock with antique lace at the neck. She had this photo enlarged – it takes up a whole page of her book – to remind herself of the one day when she looked absolutely beautiful. She settled with her plumber husband on Ben Nevis Crescent, and commenced to evolve a new life again. This took no time at all, with her practise. Time – huge shapeless chunks of it – passed, and she was quite amazed, shocked even, to find she was forty-seven one summery day when nothing else seemed to be going wrong. Just this. Forty-seven! So undeniably pre-menopausal and pre-ugly. What an age! Not that Harry, or anyone, knew how old she was.

Secret number four!

Age was definitely one of those flexible facts. Things she said had to ring true, and if they had no literal truth, well, this was unfortunate but not the end of the world. Her own birth year, for instance, was relative, and changed from day to day depending on who was asking and on her own mood. Once, asked to confirm her birth date by a teen cashier checking Morag's driving license, she refused on the grounds that there were people around who might hear, and declined the purchase.

Harry, like the others, had known nothing of Morag's previous, or concurrent, husbands. When he asked her if she had ever married, she said no. It felt, as always, like the truth. It's why she hangs on to her maiden name, even though she has husbands in most English-speaking countries.

Harry had been going along swimmingly. That is, he'd gone like the previous three – after a while she'd realised that she was still looking at other men to see if they could be the one. In fact, she'd even gone so far as to learn about Australian visas when he performed the incredible act of leaving her for the North Beach cheer-leader. She wasn't the one who was left, she was the leaver. It may be common in other women's lives, but for Morag it required a major re-think of her identity. He had made her a woman who was not preferred. Worse: she had been told why by Harry, who was far braver than herself.

'It's like you're not really here,' he said, throwing his clothes into suitcases.

'I'm always here.'

'That's not what I mean. I don't feel real with you. I feel like … like your idea of a husband.'

She had no answer for that, though he was over-simplifying as usual. He wasn't her idea of anything. His life felt more real than her own, but she had a difficult time imagining his thoughts. Perhaps she had a kind of autism. The feeling of jarring, as if she was the only person wearing purple on a street of green-clad crowds, persisted – not that she was in the wrong life, but that no life seemed to fit her. She was not life-compatible.

Morag puts the scrapbook away in the sock drawer, takes a pill, turns out the light and gets into bed. Looking at the scrapbook hasn't made her happier or sadder, but her internal sock drawer is marginally neater. Airing her secrets, even if just with herself, is calming. She is on the very precipice of sleep, and sends herself off with these sensible instructions, because she is a person who tries to do the right thing no matter what: Just keep doing it all. Get up in the morning, brush your teeth, take the pills, be nice to people, do everything the best you can do. Treat the days like spoiled over-sensitive children. Avoid eye contact so as to avert tantrums. Tip-toe. Breathe shallowly.

Oh dear.

Goodnight, Morag. Another day of your diminishing life is done.

Night at Gentle Valleys

While Morag tucks her scrapbook back into its hiding place and goes to bed, Fred Snelling gently snores down the hall and dreams of a dark-eyed woman. Well, a very young dark-eyed girl, to be precise. He cannot be judged for this, it is not perversion; in his dream he is only twelve, and the nine year-old girl playing doctors with him has skin the texture of silk and the colour of milk with not enough chocolate in it. Weak cocoa. They are in his closet, in the near dark, and he is dizzy with excitement. His bed trembles.

The hospice cleaners have gone home; so has the occupational therapist and the volunteers and cooks and the gardener. On duty, but hardly awake, is a nurse called Sally and an auxiliary in a pink striped dress. They sit in the dim lounge watching an old movie about World War One, and keep one ear out for whatever noise shouldn't be there. But not a very sharp ear, because there are only three residents – Morag, Fred and Connie. In the distance, a barn owl hoots in two descending notes, like it frequently does at this lonely hour of night. The women do not hear it consciously, but both sigh and suddenly feel a wave of sadness which they shrug off, as nurses and auxiliaries tend to do.

At the top of the house, someone else does hear the barn owl's mournful cry, and it doesn't make *her* sad. Connie, who has given up talking as too wasteful, sits wide awake on the window seat of the attic room, and looks out of the window to the starry night. Her face almost touches the glass. She peers, not at the sky, but at the dark garden – peers and smiles.

Connie, of course, has had another life; lots of other lives, in fact, like everyone who lives long enough. She has children, grandchildren, and at present, four great-grandchildren. Two of these people know she is at Gentle Valleys, but they are keeping their mouths shut. Which may not be necessary, since no-one has enquired as to her whereabouts in years. They are not that kind of family. Well, not every family is interested in things like great-grannies. Good folk, but not very … well, *attached.* These descendants are many things – hairdressers, home economics teachers, dental receptionists, down-and-outers on Market. Some are dead already, and one of these might have been a famous guitarist with a diminished number of digits.

Several of her relatives will in time get curious and ask about

Connie, but by then it will be too late, and their questions will remain unanswered. The two children, in their seventies, who do know her, who indeed left her on the hospice doorsteps one early spring dawn, only remember her as the spacey old lady who never spoke. They, so far, have not missed her one bit. In fact, they hardly remember her.

Is Connie interesting and important enough to remember? Of course. Everyone is.

Part Seven

I like to look at photographs of dead people too, Angelina. You can tell they were certain they'd never die. Not in their hearts. I feel kind of embarrassed for them, now they've been proved wrong. I blush for them. That forever look in their eyes. Do you see that in old photographs too? I also see their longing to be important and remembered. You know what I do? I talk to them, tell them things, ask them questions. Take them out of their frames or albums and air them, blow life into them. It feels like a duty, but one that I lovingly obey. Much better than praying. My name is Consuela, by the way. It means comfort. I would appreciate it if you will please remember me. Even though I won't know, it makes me feel better now, more calm. I would have done the same for you. Perhaps I have already.

Excerpt from *The Consuela Chronicles*, transcribed by Angelina Vietti, Fairfax, 1951.
Estimated age of Consuela: twenty-three.
Location of apparition: the window seat of Consuela's bedroom. She was sewing lace onto a long cream satin dress, assumed to be her wedding dress. This is not the last time she is sighted, but it is the oldest recorded Consuela. After her wedding day, she drove with her new husband to Stockton and was never heard from or seen again. Consuela is an unfinished story and hence the subject of at least two novels: *Girl Who Vanished* by S. Vance, and *Pilgrim Soul of Our Time* by Annie Smith.

Morag Decides to Sun Bathe

'Oh, hello, Dolores. How are you? Have you been waiting here for me?'

Dolores is in the Gentle Valleys reception area, perched on the only uncomfortable chair.

'Yes. Well, not long. Since seven-thirty. I told them not to disturb you, that I'd wait till you were up and about.'

'Seven-thirty? That was two hours ago. You've been waiting here all that time?' Concerned words, but Morag is frowning with irritation.

'Yes, well; I had nothing else to do, and I was really worried about you.'

'Were you? How kind.' Suddenly Morag feels a heaviness, dragged down by sympathy.

'Are you too tired standing up? Here, let me help you back to your room.'

Dolores takes Morag's arm and gently turns her around.

'No, no, Dolores. I'm fine, really.' She shakes her arm free and swivels around again, facing the open front door. Outside she sees a downpour of sun. There's a shimmering liquid pool of light on the driveway, and Morag has a sudden and unprecedented need to see the ocean.

'But Morag, you mustn't tire yourself. I came to read to you.'

'Ah. That's so, uh, so kind of you. But do you know what I've just remembered, Dolores? I have a doctor's appointment in half an hour.'

'Oh my, well, you mustn't be late. I can take you in my car.'

'And a taxi is taking me, Dolores. Thank you anyway.'

◆◆◆◆

There is no bus from Fairfax to Point Reyes beach. People that do not have a car and do not hitch-hike never go there. Despite the distance, about thirty miles, it is pretty much one road all the way, meandering through San Geronimo Valley and the golf course; Samuel P. Taylor State Park with its ancient mossy picnic tables and swimming holes; Olema, where you can stop for a cold beer if you want; Tomales Bay, where they farm good oysters and cook them in the shell on barbecues with garlic and butter; Inverness (*In*verness, unlike the Highland capital which is Inver*ness*) with its two competing coffee shops; Drake's beach, where Sir Frances Drake once landed, maybe. All the way to Point Reyes National Seashore, a twelve mile-long stretch of sand and treacherous surf, and a traditional white lighthouse with a good view of whales when they deign to come by. Which is hardly ever.

Although she has lived in Marin County for many years, Morag has never been here. She's been to Stinson Beach and once to McLaren's near the Golden Gate Bridge, both of which are on bus routes and are popular destinations on summer days. But not to Point Reyes. In her mind it has always been royal somehow – wild and lonely, an elite beach for car owners who do not care to swim.

Today she pays a taxi to take her from Gentle Valleys. It is very expensive – two hundred and seventy-three dollars – but well worth it. And besides, what is money now? With her gold card, money has taken on a whole new meaning. Have card will travel. She asks the driver to return in two hours, so she will be back in her room by the time Manuel comes for his evening visit. She is treating herself, and why not? She will be nurtured by this outing. She will mark, celebrate somehow, in a dignified way, her new status of dying person. It is a sunny day; sweltering in Fairfax, but not here. There is a briny breeze, and she is glad that she brought an over-shirt just in case. She swings her bag over her shoulder, waves off the taxi, and walks down to the shore. After a dozen paces, she stops to remove her shoes; places them in her bag. There is a steep incline where the waves suck the sand savagely back, like a labouring asthmatic. An undertow is illustrated in signs in the parking lot. They show a person being dragged upside down by green wavy waves.

She does not put her feet in the water. Morag is, despite her interesting life, a physically timid person. She stops inches from the furthest reaches of the foaming tide, closes her eyes for a moment and breathes deeply. Concentrates. I am here, she thinks. Yes, here I am, and the sea is also here, and it's a bit of sea I've not seen before and it's not seen me either. Time collapses and she almost falls asleep standing up, feels a delicious swoon of numbness travel down across her skin. Like sipping cool water when one is thirsty, eating when one is hungry: seductive, compulsive. And it takes some doing to stop. But she does, just as she feels herself swaying.

This is what dying is, and the cancer is giving me a wee preview. Well,

well. It's only a narcotic slumber, a drifting away, a letting go. She talks to her cancer, which she visualises as a small furry creature residing in her lower abdomen. Not vicious, because it is mindless, indifferent. Like the red fox who steals the pretty bantam hen, not because he hates hens and is blood thirsty, but because like Morag herself he has to eat, and his family must eat. Thus Morag owns her cancer and forgives it, even while regretting it.

Like a person told that their Coca-Cola has been spiked with acid when it has not, and they begin to hallucinate, Morag is beginning to interpret certain symptoms as further proof of her disease. She sees the absence of stomach-aches and headaches as the progression of the cancers. They have simply eaten up so much of her already, those bits are now impervious to pain; she is left limp and relaxed. Her weight loss is attributed to cancer, not to the bland hospice food or her new energetic bursts. Her body is a conquered country.

She feels light-headed when she opens her eyes. She puts on her new hundred-dollar sunglasses, which are identical to the week-old sunglasses sitting in her hospice room. (She left with nothing but her gold card, which led to a short shopping trip to buy sunglasses, sun cream, a three hundred-dollar camera, film, and two bottles of lemonade.) She puts these sunglasses on because she is in a public place and she is one of those self-conscious people who never know where to put their eyes in public places. A book usually does the job, but today, in the glaring sun, it will be the sunglasses. Keeping her eyes unseen seems to be a major reflex, but one she has never examined. She glances up at the parking lot; the taxi has gone, but it must have existed, otherwise how did she get here? Another wave crashes in front of her, green and grey, and some yellow in the froth; it pulls back a second before the next one gathers itself. The waves are quick here, much quicker than on the more sheltered beaches like Stinson. Hectic, relentless, masculine and most of all noisy. Like a hyperactive boy or an overpowering salesman who wins by sheer persistence.

She feels a sense of vertigo, as if the undertow has indeed reached her: not touching the water is not enough protection. She backs away up the incline, to a warmer dip in the sand, and suddenly notices that it is not such an empty beach after all. There are no folk in the distance on either side, but around her are about fifty bodies, all reclining. Why has she not seen them before? The cancer is affecting her powers of observation, giving her tunnel vision. Some couples, some loners, two family groups, about seven dogs. The sea is so loud, even here, that their barks cannot be heard, though they are racing about hysterically, chasing gulls, retrieving driftwood, rolling in seaweed. It is an exciting place to be. How can their owners just lie still as if they are dead?

She joins the other people, for a while. It is almost a primal need, confronted with wide-open spaces, to huddle with other beings, even if no eye contact is made. Primal, primitive, primates, us. And then, to further the impression, she notices that some of the bodies are almost naked. She has on her dark glasses, and so from her sitting-up cross-legged position, feels free to inspect this fascinating variation of bodies. Soft and milky skin, brown and tough skin, freckled and scabby and scarred skin. Skin that is like hide. Hairy chests, odd-shaped pelvic bones, bulging stomachs and shrivelled elbows. Asymmetrical breasts pointing away from each other. Bottoms that peek out of shorts – dappled, dimpled, tattooed, pimpled. And some bottoms, she notices jealously, are young and perfect. Revolting or beautiful, they are all poignant and a little too revealing.

What are we like, honestly! thinks Morag. There is just no getting away from bodily functions, when confronted with them like this. Clothed, it's easy to pretend we're more cerebral, somehow; in control. Clothes and conversation disguise the most essential obvious fact about us. We are animals. Animals with vulnerable bits on us. Animals without a single aspect that has not evolved to be functional. We function till we cease functioning, and that, in spite of all our fretting, is that. Back to dirt, air, water. Just this brief interlude when these elements join and we slip into a life and are aware of it.

Unless of course, the God-in-heaven stuff is true; she makes a mental note to investigate this hopeful possibility later. A church somewhere? A book? Hell, where does one get quick confirmation of an afterlife, and are late bookings accepted? Two-for-one confession and communion deals?

The sea roars in her ear. She opens a bottle of lemonade and drinks. Her fine hair already feels like it will need a bottle of conditioner before a comb will get through it, and this annoys her enough to forget her philosophising for now. And on top of that, two young women and a man walk too close to her, kicking sand in her eyes and somehow even into her lemonade, so that her teeth grit and grind. The lemonade is not sufficiently sweet, and not fizzy at all. Not like lemonade as she still expects it be. To make it worse, a wasp starts homing in on the sticky bottle, and Morag hates wasps more than anything. People! Beaches! Sour lemonade! Wasps! Nothing is like it used to be.

September 3rd, Sycamore House, Fairfax 1921

A wasp is chasing her and she runs clumsily. Not long ago, she never ran clumsily – she used to barely touch the ground, nimble enough to scale even the eucalyptus and palm trees. But something strange and terrible is happening, and it makes her clumsy. As if gravity is laughing at her, saying – ha! And you thought you could just do what you wanted forever.

'It's only your age, Consuelita,' says her mama, coming upon her daughter damp-faced and sad-eyed again. 'You are becoming a woman!' Her mama smiles proudly but secretively, as if becoming a woman is a great feat, but slightly naughty. 'It happens to every girl! One day you'll meet a wonderful man and marry, and have babies!'

Consuela glares. Not only is she clumsy now, with all the extra curves and bumps she must wear like a bulky cheap coat, but she is cranky all the time. Her mother suddenly brushes her hands down her apron, as if she'd like to wash them of her daughter's sulky expression.

'This is only what life is, my girl; there is not a thing you can do about it, so you can get that look off your face right now. Now go on out and fetch some milk from the ice-box please, there's a good girl.'

Consuela is a good girl, but almost against her will, like much of America, now that Prohibition is in full swing. Anyway, how can she be otherwise, living here with this kind of mother, and all these big kind hairy-faced Viettis running around and keeping an eye on her?

'Do you have enough money for your school party?' asks Rosamaria, offering her a quarter.

'Here, look what I found for your pretty hair, Consuela,' says Sophia, holding out some velvet hair ribbon.

'Come sit with me, Consuela, read me a story, please. No-one has such a fine voice,' says the great-Vietti-grandmother.

She is tired of being different and pays no attention at all to the dissolving ones, who seem to be deserting her in any case. She doesn't want to be different and she doesn't want to be the same. She is miserable and hates her life. She meets nobody interesting and goes nowhere interesting. It is the same thing every day, all day, and these late summer days are so very long, and not a single opportunity to stop being a good girl even for a minute.

She dawdles all the way downstairs and out the back to the screened porch to fetch a bottle of milk. Out of sheer boredom, and because her head feels too hot, she sticks her head right inside the ice box and licks some of the cold cream that has accumulated on the top of the milk bottle. It is a ridiculous thing to do, and not really enjoyable enough to warrant the stiff neck and humiliation when she hears the masculine voice behind her:

'You'll never fit in there, fatso. But I'll give you a shove in, if you like.'

She hits her head hard on the roof of the wooden ice-box.

'Get lost, Freddy,' she says. 'Nincompoop.'

They can hear Tommy Wong starting up the drive with the milk, cheese, butter and eggs. His two horses going a steady clip-cloppety-clip, despite the Vietti spaniels yipping at their hooves. Freddy grabs Consuela's arm and pulls her deeper into the shadowy porch. A drowsy blue-bottle fly buzzes into the screen and Consuela wants to open the screen to let it out. 'Let go of me.'

He does.

'Hey, today's my birthday, want to try something?'

She stops a moment before turning. If she takes his bait he wins. She's good at not taking his bait, usually.

'What? Try what?'

'Something real nice to celebrate with, from the *Italian Restaurant,'* he whispers with great emphasis, in case she doesn't get the code, Italian Restaurant meaning speakeasy. Meaning hooch, bathtub gin, booze.

'Sure; you're just showing off,' she says with contempt, but not before he has seen the flash of deep admiration in her eyes.

Out of the corner of her eye, in the middle of the perfect summer lawn, she suddenly glimpses different weather – fog, drizzle – and not only that, but a yellow car with two strangers swishing through puddles.

'Hey, whaddya looking at?'

'Nothing,' says Consuela, crankily. 'Not a durn thing, Fred. Just go get what you say you got.'

Fred's Day Out

Today is Fred's birthday! So his grandchildren, along with their friend Georgia-May, are taking him for a special day out. Rather, they are using this occasion as an excuse for an outing. (As if they need an excuse.) It is an especially beautiful day.

'Let's go to the beach and get stoned,' says Robbie. He's at the wheel.

'Yeah, cool,' agrees Carson.

'Stop it: act your age,' says Georgia-May scathingly from the back seat where she's sitting with their grandfather Fred. (Her husband is again absent, busy doing something. Probably working.) Age is an ironic topic for Georgia-May, given that she has felt about sixteen lately. Adam, or rather day-dreaming about Adam, has become addictive. His actual presence has graduated from a buzz in her nether regions, to almost unbearable over-stimulation. His absence is easier to bear. She is Adam-obsessed and, even now, seemingly her detached and sensible self, she cannot erase him. Is this how affairs begin? This kind of suspense, this tortured agitated negation?

She has left her daughters with her parents for a few hours and wonders how wise this is. Will they be forgotten, fed sherry chocolates from Moze's bowl, witness pretty bird carnage? Other mothers leave their children with their grandparents, so it must be an okay kind of thing to do, yet Georgia-May manages to worry about both Adam and her children. With great justification.

'Ah come on; we're not dead yet,' says Carson from the front seat. 'Anyway, it's Fred's birthday today, he deserves a special outing.'

'Let's go to Point Reyes for old times' sake, take a quick walk, then get Granddad back to the hospice in time for his afternoon nap. It's a great idea, Robbie: go for it.' Ever since the bus-money-from-June episode she's been feeling protective towards Robbie, as if to atone for the blow he must have suffered when she arrived first at work, ten dollars richer than him, proving both that she did not need him and that he was a wimp.

'No way,' says Georgia-May. 'And I hope you aren't still carrying joints around in your shirt pockets – it's so old hippie.'

'Party-pooper. I'm a young hippie, anyway. As young as they get. Average age of a hippie is forty-five these days. Isn't that right, Sis?

Tell her it's okay.' Robbie has been conciliatory towards Carson ever since the bus-money-from-June episode, because he realises he doesn't really like to take chances if chances can be avoided, and this newish inclination towards safety feels like a deep betrayal of Carson. Isn't danger to be shared? Chance-taking is their credo, but he is secretly learning new oaths of allegiance. Like 'I pledge allegiance to security and legality.' Oh, it feels naughty to be sitting so close to his sister and be having such conservative thoughts! But then, Robbie has always been the lazier one, and the straight road is the easiest to follow.

Robbie turns the car around and heads west.

'Jesus,' says Georgia-May.

'All *right,'* says Carson.

'Obolomio,' says Fred.

After Fairfax, on either side of the road, rise rounded golden dry hills. Arid and sensual, with the tang of eucalyptus on the air.

'You two are bad. Don't say I didn't tell you so if …'

'Naa, naa, nana naaa,' Robbie says in his best girl mimicry, finally eliciting a giggle from Georgia-May. Carson can't do this, but he can. It's a knack, like tickling with words. Not even words, it's his voice. Irreverent. And a willingness to look stupid.

In the back Fred is belted in and swaying to his own rhythm, eyes closed. Humming. Hands twitching, perhaps in expectation of Moze's saliva. Certainly some of his own saliva is drooling down his chin and dripping onto his trousers.

Of course, the sand is roasting and like a million sparkling gems; the sea is frightening and the waves are continuously crashing; the salt spray goes up their nose, turns hair sticky, coats their skin. They kick off their shoes, kick sand in some red-headed lady's lemonade, and let the Pacific greet their pale feet with green icy curling tongues. The water surges, riding up legs to knees, then sucks back, pulling the sand from under. Georgia-May's heart does a second's dance. But,

'Better head back; Fred will be roasting.'

'Left the windows open, didn't we?'

'Did we?'

'Don't ask me. Probably.'

'Still,' says Georgia-May.

'Yeah, okay.'

Robbie passes Carson a joint. It is probably the one thousand and eightieth joint he has passed her. She will never smoke pot with anyone else like she does with her brother. She sucks it in. The rolling paper is soggy and salty; the smoke is both sweet and harsh. It goes with the scenery, the dunes with their tufts of yellow hair. A grass joint is so much like ... well, grass. Georgia-May declines a puff and examines the sand for shells, of which there is a noticeable lack. Waves like these blast-destroy or suck back everything. Robbie and Carson blow smoke in her face till she gives in and has a few puffs.

'Right, better head back.'

'Right,' they say, but no-one moves.

They stand, smoking and getting soaked, then begin to walk down the beach. After the first hundred yards, there are no people. The marijuana has travelled from their lungs to their blood to their brains so that they now perceive a bubble around them; an old familiar bubble, the bubble almost of their childhood, where the adult world fell away soundlessly and they played their pottering meandering games with disjointed sentences and sighs. Three friends. Three kids. The dunes bake and beckon, and since the waves drown out their voices, that is where they head.

'Remember the time we saw the naked man down here?'

'Remember when you came down with your girlfriends?'

'I remember coming here and building a driftwood fire.'

'I remember driving here alone one New Year's Eve, at midnight, on speed.'

'You just wanted to be dramatic.'

'Well, duh.'

'Let's get naked.'

'Robbie, you are so gross. We should get going. Megan will be needing a feed; my boobs are killing me,' says Georgia-May, standing up. The marijuana has made her skin tingle, or is it Adam anticipation? Will she drive straight to his house? Cut to the bone?

'Man, it is so hot here out of the wind, I could go to sleep and die in this heat. Happily,' says Robbie.

Pets the Snellings Have Killed in Cars

1. Lady, who was left in Robbie's car while he took his new girlfriend down to the beach on a hot day to attempt third base. Yes, the window was down but only an inch because he was worried someone might steal his new tape player.
2. Heraldo the kitten, who had sneaked into the car for a nap on the sunny shelf behind the back seat, then been locked in for two days.
3. Spooks, the insecure mongrel pup who had followed them home one day from school and, frightened of being left behind, crept behind them into the car one day and was subsequently locked in it for twenty-four hours in July.
4. Missy, the golden retriever who couldn't bark for some neurotic reason. Had followed Carson out to her car one day, got in the back seat, then was sleeping so quietly in the back on the floor that Carson forgot all about her being there while she went to a three-day rock concert in the valley.

Fred is Dead

'Oh fuck, now you've blown it. My dad's going to kill you guys.'

'What do you mean – us?'

'I told you to take him back to the hospice hours ago.'

'Hold on,' says Carson, squinting in the glare of the sun. 'Is he really?'

'Definitely. Well, look at him! He's not about to burst into song now, is he? We fucking killed our own grandfather,' says Robbie.

'On his birthday!' adds Carson.

'Why isn't this surprising me?' asks Georgia-May under her breath. She is horrified, but also disgusted, yet again, with her choice of friends.

'Boy oh boy. This. Is. The. Worst,' says Robbie, looking the oldest he's ever looked, which is about twenty-nine. Fred is still sitting up but leans into the door now, his head lolling against the window, mouth open. His face is pink, but not sweating.

'Fuck! Shit!' says Carson, turning around to see if anyone in the parking lot has noticed.

'Poor Granddad.'

'Now what do we do with him?' wails Carson.

'Take him back, I guess.'

'To a hospital? Or a mortuary?'

'No,' says Robbie. 'This is what we do. This way we're not in trouble. There's nothing we can do to bring him back, but there's no need to take the rap. Joe would milk this story forever, imagine! Listen, I got it. Now listen up.'

He's thinking while he talks. Ideas forming with every utterance, in fact relying on utterance to exist. Robbie has never been able to think silently.

'I wonder what Fred's last thoughts were,' says Georgia-May.

Cynthia Rogerson

The Last Thoughts of Fred

He is a young man, and stripping off in the heat. Sweat pouring off him. No matter how many clothes he removes, he still feels too hot. Then he realises it's because he's in Santa Cruz, having a summer vacation with his mom and dad. Yes. Of course, and the sound of the waves, the beach where they always camped. He strides naked down to the water, a turquoise transparency, and is about to walk right in when he spots her. The girl with black eyes, the giggling girl who sells ice cream – helado – from her little beach shack. She is watching him. He remembers he's naked, and feels momentarily so hot with embarrassment that he almost melts; loses his breath, then magically she is naked too. Her demure red dress has slipped to the sands; it lies like a scarlet slash and she is walking – no, running – lightly towards him. Her breasts seem to grow, sway and swing, up and down and sideways; he feels dizzy watching the nipples gyrate. For a horrifying second he glimpses his dad coming from the tent area, frowning, a chore on the tip of his tongue, about to ask him what the hell he think he's doing, starkers on a public beach. Fred's body goes alarmingly hot again, then fades, as his dad also fades. He looks towards the black-eyed girl, and there she is right in front of him. She turns and gestures for him to follow, her brown buttocks twinkling. His heart fills with happiness, swells and swells so tight that he feels if he doesn't reach the water soon to cool off, he'll embarrass himself and she'll notice his giant erection. She's in the sea and the water is licking her knees, her thighs, then he is in the sea too. It feels numbing, like nothing, and he finds himself powerless, weak, he will drown, but he moves towards her in a kind of effortless lunge. She turns and gives him a radiant smile, her teeth so white in the sun that he has to squint. Her smile hurts him, she loves him, he has loved her all summer and now she loves him too; it feel so natural. And when the jelly-fish wraps its tentacles around his chest and stings like a fizzing electric shock, the pain is almost exquisite, before it is nothing. Hi Fred, says the girl. Kiss me quick.

A Minute's Silence in Memory of Fred.

Part Eight

You come from Ross? You look like a Ross person. Rich. I'm going to live in Ross one day, you watch. I'm not going to end up working at the French Laundry like Christina Tocchini: not me. I'm finding me a nice rich Ross boy to marry. A handsome nice one like Johnny the vegetable man, only rich. You look like you have a radio. Do you? I love the radio, and when I live in Ross I'm going to have ten radios: one in each room, including the bathroom. Then, wherever I am, I can do some dancing.

Excerpt from *The Consuela Chronicles*, transcribed by Kim Parnow, 1944, Ross.
Estimated age of Consuela: ten.
Location of apparition: under a table in the Vietti's dining room. Kim had come to attend a dinner party in honour of Luis Vietti, on the eve of his departure to fight in France.

Morag Finds Beauty

The ride home from Point Reyes is amusing. She is getting into the swing of things now. Getting her money's worth. On a whim, Morag asks the taxi driver to go past Ben Nevis, her old neighbourhood. Her old house, number thirty-seven, does not greet her with familiarity; in fact, it looks guilty and ignores her. The door is a different colour already and between strange new kitchen curtains she spots a woman's face over the sink. Fickle disloyal house! Several neighbours are out in their gardens but do not notice her, though she waves and calls to them through the open window. A taxi is not where they would expect to see her, and besides, they have already consigned her to the grave. So in one sense, it is bad manners to re-appear like this. Especially to the women who made such a fuss when she was diagnosed. (The casseroles! The self-healing books!)

'Keep going,' says Morag to the driver, whose name is Juan. They drive by the Golden Hills Mall, and she greets it as if it is a foreign country once visited but only carelessly; a country of good health barely visible from her new rocky island surrounded by brilliant icy sea. The Mall. Oh yeah, where I squandered my days.

Then she looks again and sucks in her breath. Swathed in freeway fumes, it is still flat-roofed, windowless and concrete-blocked, but now she notices something new. It is also, quite illogically, suddenly, *beautiful.* Strange and beautiful. Beautiful in its strangeness. And beauty makes her sad. These days, all beauty saddens her.

'Stop,' she says. 'Just stop here a minute, please.' She takes out her camera to record this strange beauty. The sun is dull, hazy – it is too far into summer for the sky to be true blue and the sun to be bright. But the light, being diffuse, takes the almost intentional ugliness of the building and makes of it something akin to a Turner watercolour. And why shouldn't the environs of ordinary people be seen as aesthetically pleasing? Why has she never seen it before? Golden Hills Mall, even with the eddies of broken Boone Farm wine bottles and Big Mac boxes, is the modern equivalent of an old European market place. Natives mingling, drinking coffee and wine, flirting, doing deals, buying, studying mirrors, snorting on mirrors. One day, she tells herself, people will buy postcards of this building and its clientele, and they'll call it picturesque. Some will even frame it to go above their mantelpieces or make posters of it. Above all, no-one will be able to believe it was once thought of as an eyesore, a functional retail outlet for the less wealthy. Individuals particularly given to nostalgia for times not their own will think of the phrase – going to the mall – as the epitome of a romantic line. There is pathos in a place not built for beauty, utilised by un-beautiful people. Like the black and white photos of the Gorbals and Harlem she has seen on walls lately. Lower class urban neighbourhoods always acquire poignancy in the end, why not middle class suburbs? Oh yes, their day will come. And about time, thinks Morag.

Morag clicks and clicks, then gets out of the taxi to walk closer and click some more. On the edge of her pleasure is a small nagging need to share this new view, this feeling. But Juan the driver feels a little nervous; he can handle drunks and junkies, but weirdoes give him the heebie-jeebies. He stares straight ahead at the hills.

Not far away, but not noticed, is Manuel. He sees Morag but she does not see him, even though she has just taken a picture of him. He is one of the distant shoppers caught in her lens; a blurred oblong holding a shopping bag. He recognises her immediately, despite the distance and the fact that she is out of context. He does not question this uncanny ability, this almost supernatural perception. If he did, he might notice a lot of other unexamined things about his life. But he is Manuel, so he does not.

He sees her, freezes, then begins to walk, and finally he drops his bag and runs towards her. He must tell her the truth right now! It is all so wrong, and he has the power to put it right. Why has he not seen the simplicity of it before?

When she gets in the taxi and leaves before he can reach her, he halts, panting. Knowing it can do no good at all, he calls her name and tells her the truth.

'Morag! You are not sick! I lied.'

The taxi is out of sight.

'I am a bad man,' says Manuel to the parking lot, to the freeway fumes, to the scattered cars. 'I am a very bad man.' Then he turns back to find his bag.

The Big Trick

The drive back to Fairfax is tense. The heat, the marijuana, the dead body. No-one looks at Fred, but out of the windows, or the rear-view mirror. They don't look at each other either. Robbie switches the radio on and off several times. Once, at a junction, Carson notices an old woman staring at Fred in the back seat. The woman looks disapproving. As if Fred is drunk. Carson shrugs, looks away. Robbie mentions that they are low on gas, and both girls tell him to keep driving anyway. When a police car drives behind them for a mile, they all make artificial conversation. But when a hearse crosses in front of them, they all shut up. Altogether a hellish drive.

Connie can see them all. She sees most things that go on around here. She sits in her window seat on the third floor, and watches them drive up. Her face does not change expression. Ever. She watches.

Carson, Robbie and Georgia-May all sit in the front and drive very slowly up the gravel driveway for delivery vans, leading to the back of Gentle Valleys. They stop and Robbie gets out and tiptoes up to see if the back door is open. It is, and he slips inside. A minute later, he is prancing back to them. He hasn't seen Connie's dark eyes peering down at him.

'The coast is clear. They're all eating lunch and Fred's room is empty.'

Robbie pulls Fred out of the back seat and props him between Carson and Georgia-May, who each take an arm very firmly by the elbow and lift his feet off the ground. Fred's head rolls forward till his chin is on his chest.

'Lucky thing he's a light-weight.'

'Even a light-weight's a dead weight. Shit. I want to go home. I want to read *Green Eggs and Ham* with Chloe under the yellow quilt,' whines Georgia-May, who has decided that she never wants to see Adam again, or do anything the least bit daring.

'Won't be long, Georgia-May. Come on.'

Robbie goes ahead and opens the door. Immediately, the air-conditioning hits them and their sweat dries and they feel perkier. Fred remains limp. The corridor is carpeted and the walls are soft lilac. From somewhere comes a radio playing KFOG. Manuel is in the office, back from Goldie Hills Mall, and hears them enter but assumes they are cleaners. Cleaners tend to use the rear entrance. He is scanning the Independent Journal for terminal cases and tragedies in general, but keeps turning to the comic page instead.

'Come on,' hisses Robbie. 'Quick.'

The girls have to keep moving because, with Fred's head tilted forwards, the momentum is terrible. They practically fall into his room, and dump Fred across the bed.

'Close the door,' says Carson.

'It's so cold in here,' says Georgia-May

'It's just so hot outside,' says Robbie.

'Let's get him undressed and into bed, quick, before anyone comes.'

They wiggle Fred's floppy limbs out of his clothes and into his pyjamas. It takes the three of them fifteen minutes. They haul the starched sheets up to his shoulders and arrange his head on the pillow.

'I wonder what his last words were?'

'I think his last words were about two years ago.'

'No, really. What was he saying in the car?'

'Nothing, just the bolomio song. O bolomio.'

'What's it mean?'

'Fucked if I know. Maybe it was from a cold cereal radio commercial from the thirties. A bowl of Mio! Yummy in your tummy. I wouldn't read too much significance into these things.'

'You never think anything is significant,' accuses Georgia-May, who, like Morag, suddenly considers re-discovering church. Confession. Absolution. Calmness.

'Shouldn't we do something about his eyes?' Carson wonders.

'Like what?'

'Well, like put coins over them. To pay the ferryman.'

'Jesus, where did you hear that?' Robbie snorts in contempt.

'Someone told me once, someone who knew a lot about these things,' Carson says defensively, because she's just realised she might have made it up. Always a problem with being an impulsive liar with a faulty memory.

'What ferry, anyway? The machine for the Larkspur ferry only takes dollar bills,' says Georgia-May.

'The ferry to Hades, moron. Besides, coins would keep his eyes nice and shut. No-one likes a dead person staring.'

'His eyes look pretty permanently shut, I'd say. He was asleep when he died. Anyway, we want it to look like he died here – let them deal with things like coins on eyes.' Robbie's voice ends on a squeak.

'Ah, Robbie: here's a Kleenex. I'll miss him too, but he was so old, you know.'

'This is ancient toilet paper. No, thanks. How old was he?'

'Since when were you fussy about toilet paper? I don't know how old. *Old* old. He had to go soon, and he probably hated this place anyway.'

'Yeah,' says Georgia-May. 'Like Moze hates the kennel, you know? She pines and pines. She always gets dog eczema. At least Fred died thinking he was just out for a ride with us.'

Then they all turn to look at Fred. He actually looks quite nice, in an old-guy way. The kind of man you'd think would have a laugh or two right now, if it wasn't him who was dead.

'Oh, shit. Now you've got me going too. Where's that toilet paper? Jesus, what'd you do, blow your brain on it?'

'Well, we'll get plenty of chances to cry in public soon; the funeral will probably be, uh, let's see, Wednesday?'

'What was that noise?'

'What noise? Listen, just try and keep a surprised look for when they tell you he's kicked the bucket, right?'

A low emission from under Fred's sheet. A series of small pops.

'Oh, puke, disgusting.'

'Oh!'

'He's worse than Moze.'

'Let's get out of here.'

'Open the window first. No, just go.'

The three compose themselves, and peek out of the door before leaving. No-one. They let themselves into the sterile corridor and begin tiptoeing towards the exit door.

'Paras! Wrong way! The go-out door is this way,' says a young Latino woman whose plastic name tag says *Hi! My name is Maria! Can I help you?* She's new and doesn't know them.

'Oh, right; silly us.'

'Muchas gracias,' says Carson, never one to pass up an opportunity for social interaction, especially with the classes who should feel grateful for her patronage and wouldn't dare snub her. No snob, she. She is a liberal Marinite, born and bred, after all. Carson could no more ignore this cleaner than she could ignore donuts.

'*De nada; hasta luego*,' says Maria, giving Carson the reward of a shy smile which might or might not disguise her contempt. She is inscrutable.

They walk slowly to the front door, with exaggerated nonchalance. No-one, of course, notices, except Morag who is sitting on her bed with her door wide open and is fascinated to see a tall young man with sweat running down his face, saying, 'Just act normal', and two shorter young women beside him, one saying, 'God, will you stop talking like that. You make it worse.' They disappear and Morag smiles, feeling the pull of strangers' lives and a faint feeling that she has seen them somewhere before, and recently. (She has. The beach.)

Once outside, the heat hits the three villains like a wall, and walking becomes a kind of swimming. The summer air is a substance, a glutinous, odour-filled substance which conspires with gravity to make movement slow. By the time they are in the car, they are all yawning.

'Better get home,' says Robbie. 'Before the shit hits the fan.'

'You always put things so succinctly.'

'I do it for you. Make your life simple – hey, I look after you two, right?'

'Yeah, right,' says Carson, and simultaneously thinks – now Fred is dead, she can accelerate her escape plans. She can slip away between the cracks of the broken routine.

Cynthia Rogerson

Two Volunteers in Fred's Room

'Phew, what a stink. Should I open the window?'

'No, not with the air-conditioning, dear. I'll get the aerosol air freshener. Alpine Meadows'll do the trick.'

Morag Writes her Heart Out

'Excuse me?' Morag almost whispers this.

'Yes?' says the receptionist, looking up from her magazine.

'I wonder if you could do me a favour.'

'Oh, certainly, Miss McTavish. What can I do for you?'

'Has that Dolores woman gone home?'

'Why yes, she left half an hour ago.'

'I see. I wonder if you could please tell her I am not up to any more visits? Next time she comes, I mean.'

'Oh, I see. Are you unwell?'

Aside from dying, you mean? Morag almost says, then remembers the etiquette.

'Oh, no, I'm fine. It's just, with time so short . . .' Morag pauses while a sudden wave of guilt surges through her. Poor Dolores – she'll be so hurt. And besides, it isn't as if Morag has so many friends that she can go tossing them away. 'Oh never mind, don't tell Dolores anything. She can visit any time; I'm up for as many visits as she wants.' She gives a slightly hysterical giggle. 'She can move in with me, if she wants!'

'Oh, I understand, don't worry. Mixed feelings and all that. She seems a lovely person, and quite genuinely concerned. I won't say a thing.'

'Thank you.'

'Any time at all. But you do know that Dolores is now a volunteer here at Gentle Valleys. Don't you?'

'A volunteer?'

'Oh yes. She attended the induction meeting last night, and starts tomorrow. Very keen, she seems. Especially curious about the Consuela phenomenon. But no reason at all why you should ever see her. We volunteers mostly stay in our lounge.'

'Who is Consuela?'

'Oh, nobody; nobody at all. Just a ghost, but you don't believe in ghosts, do you? I certainly don't.'

The receptionist smiles and makes a mental note to tell the occupational therapist that Miss McTavish seems to be having social adjustment problems. Maybe she needs a little sing-song therapy. Maybe a little poetry therapy from that loopy poetess who keeps offering to inflict verses on the bed-ridden. Yes, Morag looks the sensitive type; a little culture might be just the ticket.

◈◈◈◈

Deciding to be kind to Dolores makes Morag feel good. In fact, it is almost intoxicating. She sweeps the most recent UPS packages, yet unopened, off her chair and sits down. There is a rushing in her ears which she fancies is the surf of Point Reyes, echoing. There was something so hectic about that beach. She has a feeling it might be too young for her; that she might have matched its pace better, earlier in her life. Now she fancies smaller waves, and lapping – not crashing. What was that poem about raging against the dying of the light? She bets a young man wrote that. A man in his restless thirties. Not a forty-nine year-old woman. Rage was a waste of good emotion, and took too much energy. Rage would be too busy to notice the halo over Golden Hills Mall, and incidentally, over the entire world. Morag doesn't know this, but her pupils and pores have actually dilated since the Mall experience, as if her physiological response to this opening of her mind has been to literally open everything. Her eyes look limpid and dreamy, a little opiumy, and her skin is moist and soft. Wisdom, from whatever source, physically suits her. She opens a can of Diet Coke and finds a pen and some paper. It's time. Letters from my death-bed, she whispers to the room.

Sept. 3rd
Dear Aggie,

It's me, your long-lost sister. I phoned a while back, but you were out. Did your daughter mention it? It's been a long time. Let me see now, six years? How bad of me, how silly and lazy. Well, how are you? Despite what I said last time on the phone, I do hope you are well and life is being kind to you. It feels like that was someone else who said those things; I honestly don't feel like the same person. But I must be. I mean, who else would remember those words but you and me? They were nasty words, not true, and I hope you have banished them to a distant place where they can't hurt you, or better yet, put them in the bin. If you still hate me, it's only what I deserve, so don't feel guilty if you do. I probably would too. I mean, what's the point of going around forgiving people? They'll only step on your feelings again. (By the way, do you ever see Ian? Is he all right and has he found himself another wife yet?) But then again, who else knows the stories of our growing up, but us? Not a single person. You and me, lass, we were there. Betty's secret about her baby and who the father was; Mark's lawnmower that he stole from Eddie because he was mad about the football Eddie borrowed and lost. What happened to Izzy's hamster the day of the school picnic at Dornoch. No-one else knows.

And who cares if we don't see eye to eye any more, Aggie, and you vote Tory and I never voted at all, to mention one thing. Who cares, isn't our shared past more important? We connect each other back to the beginning. Dad with his coal bucket. Mum in her pinny, hanging out the washing. Sunday night baths. That picture of Bonnie Prince Charlie above the mantel, with our Highland dance medals hanging from the frame.

So listen, Aggie; just in case you are still listening, and haven't thrown this away, in case you have opened the envelope, I just wanted to say I love you and you are not all those things I said you were, not by a long shot. I'm sorry for not being a better sister, I am ashamed, and hope with all my heart you are happy.

Life here in California is fine. A little too hot, but otherwise fine. Can't complain. Harry is working hard, and we might put on a deck next spring, if the pennies add up. That's it for now,

Love, Morag

P.S. By the way, I am thinking seriously of coming back to Inverness.

This letter goes in an envelope, addressed and sealed. Then she picks up another paper, humming. Happy. This is fun; why hasn't she tried it before? Instant relief for the cost of a stamp.

Late Summer

Dear Ian,

(Oh dear, oh damn! says Morag, pen poised. How to say it, what to say …) *It's been a long time. I can't even count the years, it's been that many. Did you ever think we'd get to this age? And yet here we are already. Life is so short. Life. Is. So. Short.*

It's me, your first wife who ran off and left you with no warning, and certainly no reason. I am writing this long-overdue letter just to say that I want to picture you happy and unharmed by me and my behaviour. I hate what I did, HATE IT. I am so sorry. I hope you still have the Margaret Isabel, or if you don't, that your new boat is twice as big and shining, and the fishing has been good to you. You probably let others take it out now, do you? I hope you have kept your health, as I have kept mine.

That's all I have to say, really. I wish you well, Ian. I wish you so very well. I hope you have a dozen grandchildren at least, all with your dark eyes and dimples.

Regards, Morag

P.S. Not only is life short, but you only get one! Isn't it extraordinary?

Morag sits back, sighs, closes her eyes a moment. Imagines she can feel the cancer, her little furry creature, sapping her strength. This both frightens her and urges her to finish; to get things straight quickly. She sits up, folds the letter to Ian, slips it gently inside an envelope and reaches for more paper.

Afternoon, Calif.
Dearest Desmond,

Hi there, old friend. It's me, that terrible woman you rescued in the Safeway's queue. Yes, ME! I often think of you, I do. Oh yes, I really, really do, Desmond. I have even missed you on many occasions, but never thought it was a fair thing to tell you, in case it gave you hope. And I was never going back to Dublin, so I never saw the point of getting your hopes up. But then, I'm sure you hate me enough now so it's not a risk anymore. Probably you have got another wife and family. And I hope you do, Desmond; you deserve a lot better than I gave you.

I am in another world altogether over here in California, and I have got tell you that some days Ireland seems unreal to me, as does Scotland. But other days I look around, and this place seems even more unreal to me, and I think I might have made a big mistake somewhere along the line to end up in such a strange place as this. Foreign countries are fine when things are going fine, but when they are not, the foreignness just feels unfriendly, scary even. Stay cosy at home, Desmond.

Love to all the veg, and yourself,
Morag

P.S. Didn't we have fun?

September 3rd, very hot day
Dear Doris,

It's me, Morag. Your old neighbour from Darren Drive. Do you remember me? I know it's been a long time. Way too long, but that's why I wanted to write. (I hope you are still at this address.) For many years, I have been wanting to write to say that you were right about the Buick. I don't know why I let such a stupid thing as a scratch on a silly old car matter so much. I mean, it was dumb and I see that now, and I just hope that you are all right in your life, and that you can forgive me. I was immature, screaming at you like that. Did it cost much to get that window fixed? Tell me, and I'll reimburse you, no problem. I hope you don't hate me anymore.

Meanwhile, life here in California is fine. I have become used to living here, and it is still a thrill to be able to take a bus into San Francisco and ride the cable cars, even if I am not a tourist anymore.

Love, Morag

P.S. Do you ever see my Ted?

Morag crosses out the postscript about Ted, then cuts it off with nail scissors, because crossing out has not been sufficient. Puts this letter in an envelope and reaches for more paper.

Way too late
Dear Teddy,

My dear Ted, this is such a hard letter to write, and so long overdue. I have often thought about you. Did you get my letter, way back when I left? Actually, there were two letters – the note I left on the fridge and the letter I posted from Buffalo. I hope you got both, but I know it wasn't enough and I did badly by you. At least I should have sent you my new address and kept in touch and given you a chance to ask questions. I know you must've wanted to ask questions. Maybe I was waiting till I had some answers, I don't know, but there is no excuse and I am sorry. I hope that you got over me leaving in a short time and decided I was not worth it, and found yourself someone else. A much nicer, more normal woman. A nice Canadian girl. You are a lovely man, and certainly did nothing to deserve the way I treated you. I mean it – the reason I left was nothing to do with you at all! You were a fine husband. I had a problem with being married, that was all. I would have left you no matter who you were; no matter how rich or poor, or funny or stupid or sloppy or slow or fast you were. I liked you a lot. Especially I liked the way you made Sunday breakfast, and the way you would disappear when friends like Doris came round so we could have a good old chat, and the way you never flirted with them. And that powder-blue checked shirt you used to wear on weekends just about broke my heart when I left. I almost stole it, I loved seeing you in it so much.

I believe I loved you a great deal, but not enough to change my strange ways. I was, I am, nothing but a no-good fickle fly-by-night, and you were well rid of me.

I have a life here in California and it is an all right kind of life – not fantastic, but not horrible either. It putts along, the days fly by like I never believed they would. Well, maybe you know, we are the same age. Again, I hope you can find it in your heart to forgive an old idiot who treated you like, well 'like shit', I can hear you say, and you're right. But I am sorry. Enjoy your life. If you have not done so, find someone to love right away.

From someone who will always remember your garlic steaks,

Morag

This is what Morag's taxi ride to the beach she'd always wondered about did for her:

It showed her the beauty of Golden Hills Mall.

It made her feel kindly to Dolores.

And it produced these five letters, which now lie in a neat pile on her desk. Five paper packets of words, seemingly honest words yet omitting a big truth. Soon to be despatched to foreign places, to be opened by unsuspecting people, who will or will not have given her a second thought in decades. At least one will have moved and not receive their letter at all, but its purpose has already been fulfilled.

Morag smiles, sighs, yawns, stretches. Feels as if she has just returned from a party with all her dearest and long lost friends and past loves. If all this virtual communicating is so good for her, why doesn't she socialise more? But the actual presence of friends can be too stimulating, too tiring. Manuel, for some reason, does not tire her, and though he makes her cranky she can bear his presence indefinitely. She spends some time pondering her immunity to Manuel. He is, after all, a person, and a very irritating one at that.

Much later – this day has lasted almost five years – she goes to bed, warm and full-stomached, and marvels that she has lived forty-nine years and so far has managed to ensure that every night she is in a warm bed with her stomach full. Not everyone can accomplish this. How has she acquired these survival skills without trying? Even now, dying of three kinds of rare cancer, she is looked-after, pampered, safe.

Lucky. Undeservedly lucky.

Part Nine

The opposite of happiness is not sadness. Happiness and sadness are both good. They're feelings, silly. The opposite of happiness and the opposite of sadness is emptiness. Emptiness is to be avoided. Emptiness. You know – days and weeks and years that you don't remember because you haven't been paying attention. For whatever reason, and you might have a real good reason, Diego. Maybe your life is painful and you don't want to pay attention. Maybe you have already had an exciting time; maybe you've been in a war, or in love, and nothing since touches you. I don't know, it's your one and only life, you tell me. You look solid enough, but are you really alive? Are you?

Excerpt from *The Consuela Chronicles*, written by Diego Ferrero, 1973.
Estimated age of Consuela: twenty.
Location of apparition: Diego's bedroom closet, which was originally an alcove in Sycamore House. He was a Vietnam vet who lost both his legs in Penang, and spent a lot of time in his bedroom.

Joe Johnson asks Manuel that Question Again

'What do you mean, *dead*?'

'Dead. As in not very alive anymore.'

'Fred? Impossible.'

'No, very extremely possible. In fact entirely likely, given that his heart and lungs are no longer functioning.'

'No, no, this is too much. Why me?'

'You shouldn't get so attached to the clients, señor. Though it is heart-warming to see you so moved.'

'What?'

'*Nada*. Do you want my hankie?' He pulls out the one that Morag gave him.

'I want some dying people, damn it; dead are no use to me. Jesus Christ! You can get them here, but can you keep them alive? Useless imbecile!'

'Morag McTavish is still alive. Very, very alive. But this guy, Fred Snelling, is way beyond my help. Or anyone's.'

'This is terrible, terrible. Fred! Of all people. I was counting on him to tide us over.' He puts his head in his hands. 'I'm cursed; this is a disaster. A hospice with everything but patients! We're doomed. If the board gets wind of this, I'll have to sell. Unless ...'

'Unless what?'

'Unless of course we manage to delay it.'

'Delay what?'

'Unless we, say, pretend Fred hasn't snuffed it.'

Manuel smiles, thinking his boss has a sense of humour after all.

'No, I mean it. Just till things start looking up. A few days. Bound to be some more by then. If you do your job.'

'I don't know ...'

'Or you might not have a job any more.'

Manuel sighs, loses his smile. El Sombrero is not an option, but how many false diagnoses did he have in him? 'And what will we do?'

'Oh, just leave old Fred. No need to notify anyone. Tell the staff he has his own private carers, and they must leave the room alone. Not even change the sheets, understand?'

'But what if his grandchildren come to visit? They were here earlier. In fact, they took him for a drive. Maybe it was the drive that did it.

Then again, the guy was just plain ancient.'

'Jesus, fucking families. Listen, just come and tell me if Carson and Robbie come.'

'But . . .'

'No buts. Where there's a will, there's a way.'

'Is a will involved?'

'Shut up, Manuel. God, did I ask for stupid jokes when I hired you? Do I look like I require them? You belong back in the kitchen, washing pots.'

'They did pay me every Friday, at least. Maybe you are right.'

'Just kidding, Manuel. Look, here's twenty to keep you going. Now get out there and find sickness. Why should a little lack of death get in the way of perfectly successful business?'

'*Sí, sí,* señor.'

'And Manuel?'

'What?'

'Put Smelly's air-conditioning on the highest it will go.'

Manuel leaves, but he doesn't go out seeking sick people to give fake diagnoses to again. He hasn't the stomach for it any more. And yet the impulse to tell Morag the truth has faded. Telling her might make her hate him. Probably she would kill him. And after giving the matter careful consideration, he has decided that a friendly, deceived Morag is preferable to a hostile, undeceived Morag. But he will tell her one day, one day when he can figure out how to deflect the blame so she does not hate him. He does not know how he knows, but he seems to know that her scorn would fatally wound him, and he is not in the least bit suicidal.

So he takes a walk into town instead. Breaks Joe's twenty to buy a beer in a cool tavern. Reads *The Chronicle,* and later orders a pastrami sandwich on rye.

No News

She knows she should stay home, safely away from the scene of the crime, but after several hours of fretting to the background noise of Barney videos and toddler chatter, Georgia-May is unable to restrain herself. After dinner she straps both children in, tells her husband to go play golf or the equivalent, and zooms down the road.

Home. Fairfax. San Anselmo still doesn't feel quite as home-like.

'Hi Mom, what's up?' says Georgia-May. Opens the fridge, helps herself to a scoop of peanut butter, eats it off the spoon. Drinks juice from the carton.

'Georgia-May! I wish you wouldn't do that, it's so unsanitary.'

'Sorry, Mom,' off-hand. She can hear her baby getting restless in the living room – little baby grunts. Another minute, then the day is pretty much shot. Well, it's shot already. She's helped murder a harmless old man – Fred, a man she's known her entire life. And worse, she's plotted to get away with it. Not to mention all those hours having a virtual affair. Georgia-May! A wholesome mother of two and bread-baker and rememberer of birthdays! Scooting up and down roads with corpses and babies, while philandering in her mind!

The phone rings. Georgia-May's hand carrying more peanut butter to her mouth freezes.

'Hello? Oh, hello Joe, where are you? You haven't been in the garage all day. I've missed you, honey,' says June. 'The hospice still? Honey, don't you think you should come home now? Oh, no. Oh dear. Oh dear, dear, dear. Well, never mind. No, don't worry about it. It can't be helped. All right. Yes, I understand. No problem. Me too. Goodbye.'

She hangs up the phone, looks worried for a second, then gets out a head of lettuce and begins to wash it in the sink. Georgia-May, who has read articles about denial and displacement activities, puts an arm around her mother and says,

'It's all right, Mom; it's all right. Let go. Cry. I'm here.'

June, repulsed by another woman touching her, flinches.

'Let what go, Georgia-May?'

'Your grief, Mom. Cry. Go on, you'll feel better.'

'What are you talking about?'

'Mom, Mom. Look at me. What was the phone call about? You can tell me. Talk to me.'

'What phone call?'

'Exactly. You're hiding your pain, Mom. Let it out into the light, then we can begin to make it better.'

'Stop it, Georgia-May. You are so weird sometimes. Isn't that the line from *Hey Jude*?'

'You're blocking, Mom. The phone call. Think back.' Letting go her embrace.

'Oh, that phone call.'

Georgia-May gets her smug look and says, 'Good girl, Mom.'

'That was just your dad. He said Edna can't have us over for bridge this week because Albert has the flu.'

Georgia-May's smile falters. 'Oh! Well, that's too bad, isn't it? Very inconvenient. Any of that mint ice-cream left?'

'Maybe you should have a nap, honey. I could watch the girls. You know how you get when you're over-tired.'

'I am not over-tired.'

'You always say that when you're over-tired. Honey.'

Georgia-May is about to deliver a scathing retort when she is distracted by something passing close outside the kitchen window. A dark girl in a green dress.

'Wait,' she says, and goes to see. But there is nobody, and nothing at all.

She turns around to her mother, hands on hips, puzzled frown.

'Did you, uh, see something just now, Mom? Like a girl, kind of running by the window?'

'In a green dress?'

'Oh, thank God. You saw it too.'

'Well, no, I didn't see her this time. But I know who you mean. I think it must be that Consuela they go on about. You know who. I often see that green dress flash by. Well, this used to be part of their garden, I suppose. Sycamore House.'

'So. You see ghosts.'

'I didn't say that. I don't give it any thought at all.'

'Well, I didn't see Consuela. I saw a girl who must be very fast, and was gone when I went to look. Okay?'

'Oh yes, honey. I'm sure you're right.'

Back in her own house, Georgia-May puts her toddler to bed, while her baby is scooped in her arms. Georgia-May is tired. When she sits on her bed to read a story, her eyelids feel sticky, and when she shuts them a minute, the glue cements and she sinks down. It is the normal tiredness, with Adam and Fred guilt on top. Georgia-May is used to guilt; she is a mother and she sucks it up better than the Snellings.

'Wake up, Mommy. Wake up.'

'Why?'

'Because you're squashing me.'

'Oh. All right. Look, it's too late for stories tonight. Two books tomorrow, okay?'

Something about her tone of voice and haggard face quietens her daughter, and very uncharacteristically she does not reproach her with past broken promises.

'Night-night, my poor old Mommy.'

'Night-night, my angel pie.'

Then she stands up, still holding her infant. Georgia-May cannot remember a time when she was not carrying around a baby in her arms. She knows there *was* a time, and not that long ago, but still she cannot recall what it felt like. Did she have any muscles in her arms at all, pre-baby? Over the last three years there has been an infant body in her womb or arms (and usually attached orally to one of her nipples), for four thousand, eight hundred and seventy-six hours. Despite the way her skin reacts to Adam, she has been touched to death. She goes into the marital bedroom, where her husband is reading motorbike magazines.

'Don't put her in here with us,' he complains.

'Shut up. Unless you're getting up to nurse her tonight, that is. Are you?'

'Just let her cry, honey; you're spoiling her. You know what my mother says. If you feed her at night, it's like a reward for crying and she'll never stop.'

'Screw your mother.' She considers leaving her husband, for whom she is too tired to summon even a small vestige of her former affection. But then remembers that Patsy from her mother-toddler group has just left *her* husband for someone else's husband, thereby making it impossible for any other mother to quit their hubby for a while without risking the copy-cat label. It would be as tacky as wearing the same dress to a party. A girl has to have some originality, and Georgia-May is way too proud to give anyone an opportunity to lump her in with the

Patsys. No, no, no. And so her marriage is given yet another reprieve.

She curls up under the quilt and arranges her infant's mouth so she can pop her right nipple in while sleeping. Soon there is just the sound of Georgia-May's deep breathing and the baby sucking. A sigh from her husband, whose night will be broken anyway. He will be kicked by his baby on and off all night, and the quilt will gradually slip off him and get tucked in around his wife and daughter. Then his face changes, noticing Georgia-May's enlarged breast wetly flopping out the top of her nightie.

Georgia-May is not asleep, despite the deep breathing. She is trying to assimilate the day's events. A century-long day, full of concealment. What does it remind her of? Lots of things that include strain, pain, confusion, and that almost giddy sense of anarchy when she spends too much time with Robbie and Carson Snelling. She can't shake the impression she is the elder one by twenty years, the mature sensible one. Something to do with being a mother; she has left them far behind in the maturity stakes. But they all did something really bad today, and it makes her slightly nauseous. Especially, it makes her un-amorous.

'Georgia-May?' In that voice. The encroaching hand on thigh.

'Forget it.'

'Ah, we never do it any more. You'll love it, once we get started.'

'Fuck off.'

'Yes, then?'

'Touch me and you die.'

'Just checking.'

◆◆◆◆

Robbie, who has spent the evening selling carrot cake and cappuccinos at Café Ole, flops onto the living room sofa.

'So. How did they break it to you?'

'They didn't,' says Carson.

'What do you mean?'

'I mean, no-one has phoned with the bad news. I've been home all afternoon, rehearsing a shocked sad face in the mirror, but nothing.'

Robbie sits down. Frowns.

'Bizarre. It's ten o'clock. He's been, you know, for half a day now.'

'Maybe they don't do breathing checks on patients that often.'

'I can't believe it.'

'It gets weirder. Get this. June phoned earlier wondering if I wanted to come with her to take Fred his birthday cake tomorrow, as she forgot to do it today.'

'Christ. What did you say?'

'I said okay. What else could I say?'

'Well, I can't go; I'm working all day tomorrow. You've got the four-to-eleven shift, by the way. You go and check out old Fred. We need to know what's going on.'

He puts on a David Grey CD, the first non-hippie CD he's ever bought. Carson looks up, startled. Good music, but no Snelling nostalgia attached to it. New, blank-slate stuff. Robbie feels guilty. He's forgotten how little he's told Carson about his university plans, about Elizabeth, so of course the CD will make no sense to her. Carson studies her brother, her little brother that she has loved more than anyone, and sees how ignorant he is of her thoughts, her plans for independence, her solo forays. He seems both more loveable and vulnerable. Naive. How will he live without her?

Plus, there's the Fred fact for both of them. Guilt, guilt, guilt, a substance neither Snelling has experience of. No matter how bad they've been in the past, they have never felt guilty. Worried about getting caught, sure, but no guilt. It's a new food and they don't like it. It tastes *terrible*. It tastes so terrible, it is possible neither one will ever be bad again.

◆◆◆◆

Elsewhere, on this final day of Fred's life:

Joe is asleep, not dreaming about Fred, but football. His hands are twitching. June is wandering around the house, turning lights on and off. Moze has fallen asleep with her mouth still chewing Joe's slipper.

Manuel is also awake, drinking coffee and plotting how to find another dying person without lying to a healthy one; and into his thoughts, unbidden, comes the smell of home – tortillas, chilli, fried shredded beef, sweat, hot earth, dust in his nostrils. Music. And the sound of waves, for his house had been right near the shore. He stares at his Nescafé, wondering if the coffee smell awoke this memory, since it was always Nescafé they drank at home. Nescafé and tinned condensed milk, since there was no refrigerator. Milk that was thick and sweet, but somehow he never thinks of buying it here. It wouldn't taste right. With the memory has come a certain feeling – the way he always felt at home. Mildly lazy and calm, bored. Himself. Moving up the social ladder is not relaxing. The perfect solution, of course, would be to cross a life in Baja with lots of money.

Morag can't sleep. Or, rather, she has fallen asleep already, after the taxi ride to Point Reyes, the epiphany at Golden Hill's Mall, and the cathartic letter writing. She has fallen like a stone dropping into a pond, a deep dreamless slumber. And then woken up before midnight, completely clear-headed and muscles twitching to be up and about. She tries tricking herself back to sleep, to no avail. Finally gets up and with a blanket wrapped round her shoulders, sits in the chair by the window and draws the curtains open. At first she thinks she sees a young girl, maybe ten, hiding an Easter egg in one of the planter boxes. But she blinks her eyes and the girl is gone, just a shadow. Silly, probably a side effect of the cancer. Cancer*s*. She looks up at the sky.

And there they all are. No clouds, just a sliver of a moon low on the horizon. Hello stars, she says in her mind. Tell me again. How small my problems are, how less than nothing is my life. How endless the universe. She takes slow deep breaths. Tell me you shine over everyone, even my sister and my Ian in Oban, and my Teddy in Toronto, and my Desmond in Dublin, but not stupid old Harry, and probably they don't see you because the sun is outshining you in those places, but you see them anyway. Am I right? Tell me again.

But this time there is no answer. The stars do not answer, nor the moon. And as if to confirm her suspicions, a fog she hasn't noticed drifts in, muffling the astral bodies, making them seem uncommitted somehow; anonymous and indifferent. It feels demoralising. The stars and moon have not demoralised her before. She has never minded feeling insignificant or humble; in fact, it has often been her consolation – how could her crimes be very bad when her life was so unimportant? But never has she felt truly unperceived. The night sky has, in a way, been her ally all her life. Her personal ally. What has happened? She shivers, tells herself to grow up before it's too late. Of course, it was always only the world, and why should the world take special notice of her, or anyone in particular? It's always just been her childish fancy that she was viewed tenderly, even preferred. Because she fancied that she understood the nature of the world, and more – fancied the world rewarded her for this, like a cosmic guardian angel.

Wake up, she tells herself now. The sky never, ever, not even once, noticed you. There have been no celestial thank-yous. No echoes.

And yet.

When she rises and turns with a deep sigh to go back to her bed, she has to resist the temptation to turn around. She feels a sensation at her back. As if there are eyes on her.

Meanwhile, just visible in the garden of Gentle Valleys, in fact right in the middle of a huge patch of irises, plays the little girl spotted by Morag. She is all by herself, but doesn't seem lonely. She knows she has half an hour before chores, and kicks her ball around and whistles, and waits for her mamacita to call. Also just visible, but only from the corner of a careful looker's eyes, is a teenage Consuela. In fact, the place is littered with Consuelas, once you start looking. She lived here from her birth till the age of twenty-three. There is hardly an inch that is not covered by her feet or hands, or seen by her eyes. She is picking some berries in the part of the garden that is now a gravel driveway. Her hand reaches into the shadows and retrieves ripe red berries, which she tucks into her gingham apron. By the sweat on her brow and her rolled up sleeves, she seems to be in a hot day. You have to look really quickly to see her. But at the same time, not focus on her. Catch a glimpse while swivelling your head to see something else, something more solid. She might catch a glimpse of you, and not think anything about it. Just accept you, maybe talk a bit. When she sees herself, her different selves, she just nods, sometimes smiles.

Don't forget Fred! Dear old Fred, who lived for a lifetime on one block, who had given up fear as too energetic and time-consuming. He is all right now. Definitely all right, beyond noticing anything; it didn't take long for Fred. The Fred that could have been measured as an electronic blip has joined all the other blips. Up, out and away. And the rest – the Fred that has weight and volume but no consciousness, that Fred waits in a terribly cool room in Gentle Valleys. Why? He waits because his presence, breathing or not, is still required.

And Connie. She is Connie and she is not Connie. Like most elderly folk, she has already been many different people, as unconnected to each other as distant relatives. Her body has completely changed cellular structure hundreds of times, and she has lived long enough to contain eighteen lives. Nineteen, if you count the time her youngest went off to school and before she got the job at the grocery store, a strangely agonising ellipse of time. Twenty, if you count the life she is in now – the empty days of gazing out of windows, listening for the laughter of children long grown-up, or the whistles of steam trains. These lives, each one of them, lives on in her memories. But this day, September 3rd in consecutive time, has finally bitten the dust. Thump!

Part Ten
September 4th

Can you get out of my way, please? I'm busy. I'm looking for my puppy. Petey! Have you seen him? Petey! Where is he? I'm worried about him. He has no road sense, and those Vietti boys are crazy drivers, just plumb crazy! Me and Mama are going to the city and Petey's got to be inside the house. Train leaves in twenty minutes to catch the ferry, and look at this fog! Oh, I guess by your sunglasses you're not in a fog place. Well, it's foggy here, all right, and we'll probably be stuck out on the bay for ages. Oh, look; here he is. Come here, boy. Look at that mud, you bad boy!

Excerpt from *The Consuela Chronicles*, transcribed by Mrs. Roberta James of Fairfax, 1961.
Estimated age of Consuela: nineteen.
Location of apparition: partially inside Mrs. James's parked car, on a piece of road which used to be the back section of the Sycamore House garden.

The Cleaners

'Wow, he looks dead already.'

'Old age takes some white folk that way.'

'Hey, you two,' says a nurse. 'Get out of there, that room's reserved. Private, special, um, er … private.'

'*Sí, sí,* we are going; we forgot about this room.'

'Can't you read?'

'*Sí, naturalmente,* we can read.'

Silence.

'What does it say, then?'

'What you say?'

'Read this.'

'*No se.* We read *solamente Español.*'

◆◆◆◆

'Honestly. Cleaners!' says one middle-aged nurse to another, munching her way through some date nut loaf.

'At least they have their own staff room.'

'Do they?'

'I think so.'

'That closet on the top floor? Oh well, I guess it's what they're used to. They've got it easy, anyway, this is an easy place to clean – I mean how much mess can three patients make?' she asks as she shakes cake crumbs from her skirt onto the chair.

'Exactly. In fact, I wonder if they're here as part of some charitable employment scheme. You know, a keep-them-off-the-welfare type thing,' says the other, as she spills her coffee on the carpet and moves her shoe to cover up the dark stain.

'Probably. Still, it must be better than where they come from, it must feel like heaven on earth here. I'm glad they're able to get jobs and stuff.'

'Oh, I totally agree. Totally. I know, let's have another quick coffee before we do the rounds.'

'Do you think we have time? There's always so much to do here, I never know whether I'm coming or going. We've got all these forms to fill in, too.'

'Oh, I know, that's why I love it here. Bustle, bustle, bustle. We're just busy bees.'

And they bustle down the hall, bristling with contentment. Nothing like the proximity of people like Connie and Fred to cheer you up when you're twice the age of your bank manager.

Meanwhile, the cleaners scoot silently in while the nurses are gone, sweep up the cake crumbs, wipe surfaces, wash coffee cups. Chatter softly away about TV soaps and garage sales and recipes that don't put on the fat. Connie hears them from her darkened room, their Hispanic voices like running water, barely intelligible but nourishing just the same. She opens her mouth and joins them, all alone, a rich river of silence. Connie is alive. She does not require responses.

Morag Finds and Loses God

Morag begins to explore her new territory. Not just the halls and rooms and garden, as she is encouraged to, but the wider more forbidden world outside the hospice grounds. She puts on her new Jimmy Choo shoes and begins by sneaking out the hedge, and so is not spotted. She feels fine; in fact she feels great. Young, energetic, bouncy. She cannot get over how life just keeps happening, how day follows day and things happen in every one. She walks north for half an hour, with no goal in mind but to have an adventure, to see what she has not seen before. This part of Fairfax is all new to her, she is sightseeing. And there, at the end of a narrow leafy lane, as if it has been calling her all along, is Our Lady of Happiness. *Nuestra Señora de Felicidad.*

It seems to fill a wrinkle in the hills. A slash of white in the deep green, the sparkle of it looks like nothing so much as a benevolent wink. Founded almost a hundred and fifty years ago by a rogue and rebel Catalan priest, it was named after the small church he'd left behind in Barcelona. For refusing to give it a Saint's name, he was sent back to Spain and never saw Our Lady of Happiness again. It being the time in history it is, and the fact the neighbourhood has few Hispanics, the church is never well-attended and Father Reilly, the Irish priest, has taken to whisky in a big way. Not a popular venue, but important still. Carson and Robbie Snelling's parents' funeral was here. Joe and June Johnson married here, and had a secret long smooch under the baptismal font on their fortieth wedding anniversary. Connie keeps trying to get here, but keeps falling. (She has a problem with walking in the house, steps down too hard, loses her balance.) Georgia-May Johnson will consider divorce, while sitting here. Fred Snelling was baptised here. Manuel went to confession once here, in a futile attempt to regain his faith. Consuela helped do the flowers here once. Maybe twice.

It shines in the midday sun, gleams whitely and the door is open, its dark cool interior beckoning. Morag enters, on tip-toes. She is Scottish, from a background that makes entering a Catholic church feel slightly wicked. And so she enters quickly, relishing the naughtiness. She even dips her hot fingers in the holy water and crosses herself as she has seen Catholics do. Forehead, belly button, left shoulder, right. Oooh, she shivers with the irreverence of it. It takes a minute for her eyes to adjust to the dimness. There is not much here, not the gaudy gilded Catholic display she'd hoped for. A wooden crucifix on the altar, four stained-glass windows, but no gold anywhere. A faint whiff of incense, like cinnamon or memory. A dark-curtained closet, presumably a confessional, at the rear. About twenty short pews, on either side of the mid-aisle. At one side, in a little alcove, is a black wrought iron device for holding candles, some of which are lit.

Morag smiles. This is fun. This is magic. Church-raised, she has never actually given religion a real shot and prayed. Gone through the motions, sure, but real prayer about real souls – it suddenly seems like a miracle that she is here, right here in a soul shop, so to speak. She must act at once to utilise the magic, and she must act in the right sequence, with sincerity in her heart. Never mind that it's not her particular soul shop: it'll do. She looks around, and yes, she is alone. The only sound is the insects humming in the heat outside. A few birds, jays and finches.

She goes to the candle-holder and kneels down on the padded cushion. Digs in her pockets till she comes up with a twenty; puts it in the box. Finds some matches and lights one of the little white candles in red glass cups. First one, then she goes whole hog and lights all the remaining candles, till she is bathed and roasting in an inferno of candles. She feels a little deranged, attributes this to the cancer. Forgives herself and begins to pray.

This feels different, new; by fluke chance, she has found a loophole! The miracle clause! She is talking. Asking. Begging. And she finds that religious fervour, in her, brings out profanities, albeit amateur profanities.

'Listen, you,' she says. 'This is crap, and you've got to fix it, right? I mean, get rid of the sick stuff, okay? I am not ready, not one bit bastarding ready to fuck off. So bloody fix it, okay? I am here, and I totally one fucking hundred percent believe you can do this, because you are, you know, who you are. The big man. You own all the Monopoly properties. You get to play with whatever the hell marker you want. The silver slipper, the bloody choochoo. So, I'm playing by the rules, right, I am paying my two fuck-a-duck hundred to pass go, I am here and I lit all the bleeding candles, look at them! So please, show me you're not crap and let me the fucking hell go. And you will, won't you? Yes, I do believe you will. I do I do I do.'

She closes her eyes, scrunches up her face, and concentrates all her yearning in her heart and sends it shooting out. If it was visible it would be an aurora borealis, radiating out above Fairfax. She may be new at this wish business, but boy, Morag is good.

'Great,' she says, finishing, sweating slightly, light-headed. 'Okay. That's great. Ta very much. Sorry about the swears.'

Then she hears a car pull up, quickly blows all the candles out, hurriedly re-lights two, which she hopes is the original number, then scampers out to the sunshine. An atheist hot-tailing it.

It lasts a while. After a few blocks, she still feels hopeful. But by the time she gets within sight of the hospice, she feels silly and sighs as it all drains out of her. She can actually see her hope wafting away in the wavering hot air, like a steamy mirage. Look – there it goes. All yellowish and smelling of panic. Poof. Gone.

Visiting Fred

'May I help you, please?' asks the conservatively coifed receptionist in brown leggings.

'It's me, June Johnson.' June puts her boxed cake on the desk.

'I'm so glad to meet you. My name is Dolores.'

'My husband owns this place. In fact, *I* own Gentle Valleys,' she whispers, blushing. She is, in fact, June Goldwater, and has always supported Joe's myriad, often ill-fated, projects. Joe likes to moan about her credit card bills, but he has never once paid them.

'You must be new.' June extends her hand. 'We're here to visit Fred Snelling. This is his granddaughter, Carson. Now, where has she gone? Honestly, that girl. Always dawdling. Isn't that a wonderful word? Sort of the walking equivalent of doodling. Well, you know, aimless, and that pretty much sums up Carson. Do you have any dawdlers, Dolores?'

'Uh, well, no. I'll buzz the doctor, and he'll be right down.'

'No need, I know which room Fred's in.'

'Yes, but I have instructions to notify the doctor before anyone sees him. You don't mind waiting a minute, do you?'

'I wonder why? No, no, I don't mind at all. Carson, why are you hiding behind that fern?'

'I'm not hiding, June; don't be ridiculous.'

'You look terrible. Are you two eating enough?'

'Yeah. I mean, no. Not a lot, lately. Look, June, do you mind if I skip this and take a little walk around the garden? I feel faint. I'll meet you outside.'

'All right, dear. You do look very white. Go and sit in the sun, I won't be long.'

Carson departs and June settles onto the creamy leather sofa. Notices the well-leafed copy of *The Consuela Chronicles* displayed prominently on the coffee table, makes a mental note to replace it. Consuela cultists were a nuisance, though it is still hoped they might choose to die here.

'Any Consuela hunters lately, Dolores?'

'No, not lately, Mrs. Johnson. There was a big crowd from Alabama last month, I believe. Before my time.'

'Oh, well; when it rains it pours. Did they buy any copies? Or just read this one?'

'We sold a few dozen, I think. I could check. Will I check?'

'Yes, would you?'

Dolores disappears behind her desk, presumably to dig out receipts, while June sits and reads a glossy magazine about gardens and how to have a pond in a deck. On the wall behind the reception desk are two framed photo-collages of all the faces who have worked here. The largest of the two contains the faces and pink-dressed shoulders of eighty-four women, all smiling. The words underneath read: *Gentle Valleys Volunteers, 1994.* The smaller picture has a beaming Joe Johnson, three smiling nurses, five cleaners, two occupational therapists, an aromatherapist, a beautician, and a manicurist.

'I do like those photos,' says June, who has looked up from her magazine. 'So many people working here, it's hard to believe. I leave it all to Joe, of course; I haven't got the brain for any kind of business. But I am so impressed. Look at all those faces!'

'Oh, my; there's more than that, Mrs. Johnson,' flushed from the exertion of not finding any receipts for *The Consuela Chronicles.* Joe has pocketed them and the cash, but June has forgotten all about them; Dolores is off the hook. She can tell by June's intense stare that she is one of those in-the-moment people, like a four year-old. 'There's the cooks, Mrs. Johnson. Also the gardener. We're an enormous happy family.'

'How many patients are there, these days?'

'Patients?'

'Yes, residents, sick people, whatever you call them.'

'Ah! Here is Dr. Mendoza now.' She beams flirtatiously at Manuel. 'He'll take you to see Mr. Snelling.'

'Mrs. Johnson, nice to meet you.' Manuel extends his hand.

'Oh! You're new too. Joe never tells me anything. Very nice to meet you, doctor. Are you really a doctor? So nice to see you Hispanics rising up the ladder. It's the American way!'

Some people can get away with this, and June is one. Manuel smiles warmly, and they begin the walk down the hall.

'Now, Mrs. Johnson.'

'Oh, just call me June. Say, do you know what? I feel like I've seen you somewhere before. Outside church one Sunday?'

'Yes? It is possible, but I don't think so. Lots of men look like me. Mrs., uh, June.'

'Don't be nervous,' she says on impulse, which startles Manuel. Her hand is on his sleeve. Does he look nervous? Guilty? He takes a surreptitious sniff of himself.

'Just because I'm the boss's wife, I mean. Relax.'

'Well, yes, all right, June. Thank you. About Mr. Snelling. I just peeked in and I'm afraid he's sound asleep. He had a bad night last night.'

'Oh, poor old Fred. Did he wake up and sing all night? Or was he out having a wander? What a man for wandering! Like his granddaughter.'

'Ah. Yes. Something like that.'

'I'll just be very quiet. I just wanted to say happy birthday. I'll leave his cake at reception. It was yesterday, September 3rd. If he's sound asleep, I'll leave him to his dreams.'

His birthday? Manuel, even Manuel, has to pause and reflect on irony; and then he has to reflect on its purposelessness. This, especially, pleases him.

Ladies in the Garden

I, Morag Angusina McTavish, of sound mind and body – of sound mind, anyway – do hereby will all my material possessions to ... to ...

Who the hell to?
Does she love anyone? Really love?
Does anyone love her?
Is she, in fact, a loved individual or not?

◆◆◆◆

Morag weeps in the hospice garden. There she is, on the bench by the rose bushes. She has kicked off her Jimmy Choo shoes in her abandon.

Not loud weeping; in fact, very gentle weeping. Like a lady. Clean hanky to hand, she has organised this quiet time in the garden precisely to weep. A scheduled cry. Not just because she has been to Our Lady of Happiness and come away unhappy. And not just because she is dying either. She is unhappy because she is the age she is, and she is not truly intimate with anyone. Her imminent absence will leave the tiniest of ripples, which will rapidly disperse. She has neglected to make contact, and no life will be the poorer for her passing. Her one and only life has been spent – no, squandered – avoiding closeness. Shallow cowardly woman!

But here comes an unwitting witness. Carson is not a typical woman. This is demonstrated to her time and time again, with worrying frequency. When she sees another woman sitting in the hospice garden, head bowed, weeping quietly, she can not rush up, put her arms around her and say:

Tell me what the matter is. What can I do for you? I've got problems too, you know, mostly to do with being a bad and infantile person. I just killed my own grandfather. Oh, and it gets worse. I sneaked his corpse back here, and am about to be publicly confronted with this fact by a woman who will never trust me again. But tell me, why are you crying?

She does not say any of this, even though she thinks that this is what some women do, it's what women are good at. Spontaneous sympathy. Confidences.

No, she feels shy, and wary of being intrusive. She is without her brother, her buffer. If he was there, she would take one look at Morag's neatly-ironed blouse and ultra-feminine shoes and snigger. Alone, she gains humility, and embraces it even as she finds it unpleasant. She lights a cigarette, circles around Morag, bends to look at flowers, sticks her nose in some roses, pretends not to hear or see anything unusual. But Morag becomes aware of her. Straightens up, blows her nose, and says:

'Lovely, aren't they? I don't know how they blossom in all this heat.'

'Oh!' says Carson, startled, not just by Morag's voice, but by her face, which is familiar. Where has she seen it? It could be an older version of her own. Both women have the same shape, the same fair skin, the same thin fly-away hair. In Morag's case, the shape is slightly thickened, the skin looser, the hair thinner and a different colour. Altogether more washed-out and blurred, but essentially the same. It could be that they share some common genetic stock, even share a great-great-grandparent. In fact, it wouldn't be so very unlikely. Snellings, like a lot of Marinites, originate from Scotland, after all. Or perhaps not; perhaps they are just two women newly inclined to look for reflections of themselves in others, and so in that sense, they have met themselves. Twins in self-absorption.

Carson's eyes meet Morag's; four pale blue eyes shyly gaze. Scenting the whiff of possible rapport, and maybe, just maybe, the key to their own puzzling natures.

'You look familiar; have we met somewhere?'

'Possibly,' says Morag. 'Do you ever eat in El Sombrero? I worked there till last month. In the kitchen, mostly, but sometimes I waitressed. You look familiar too, but from somewhere more recent. I can't think where, though ...'

'Small world, I guess. You sound English; are you English?'

'No, not at all, my goodness, I'm Scottish. English!'

'Sorry. I'm not very good with accents.'

'Ach, it doesn't matter at all. I'm hardly anything any more, anyway. Been away more years than I was ever there. Maybe I'm not so Scottish any more.'

'I love Scotland. I'd love to go there, I mean. I don't know. I've never been, but I think I should go,' she finishes weakly, feeling like an idiot. What nonsense! Where is it all coming from?

'Oh, aye, and why's that?'

Carson sits down on the chair next to Morag's bench. Puts out her cigarette, looks at the trees and says, 'Well, I guess because ... I want to go somewhere, and Scotland is ... a place, for instance, where they speak English, at least.'

Morag can't think of a reply, but lifts her eyebrows in an encouraging way.

'And also because maybe I should try living away from my brother. Right away. As in another world away. Before we both fossilise into some kind of weird unattractive arrested development. We've never sort of ... *left home*, so to speak.' Carson blushes, confessing this, but feels good. Maybe she is a typical woman after all! Only three minutes into the acquaintance, and she's already spilled the beans. 'I'm starting to not like us very much,' she adds, in order to complete her confession.

This does the trick – one taste of a stranger's intimacy and Morag's sadness has fled. Morag is, above all, an observer. Manuel is a helper, Joe is an opportunist, June is a dreamer, Georgia-May is a philosopher, Robbie is a hedonist, and Carson is a – well, even Carson doesn't know what Carson is yet, besides generally bad. Carson is in the cocoon still, though an unfocused light is piercing the membrane.

'Does your brother feel the same way?'

'I don't know. Who knows? But probably not; he's pretty content with the way things are. He'll probably be devastated. I worry, imagining him on his own. And I don't know how to tell him I'm leaving. I love him so much.'

The word *love* brushes by Morag like a breeze, strokes her chest and throat – so much power in such a clichéd word! She can't account for it, and swallows hard.

'I feel like I'm asking for a divorce, but what exactly is the protocol for brothers and sisters?'

'I've no idea,' says Morag, thinking that she doesn't even know this young woman's name. 'I have to admit, I find that even the protocol of divorce is way beyond me. I mean, how does one tell people things that will certainly hurt them? To their face? When they've done nothing wrong? I've sometimes wondered if there's a physical object in my throat that seizes up around words like goodbye. A real coward, me.'

'Yeah, well, that's about it for me too. I've been thinking about leaving, having big adventures on my own for a year now. It's starting to keep me awake at night. Trouble is, I know exactly what Robbie will say when I tell him. He'll say – Cool, when do we leave? And I'll have to explain I need to go alone, or I'll never notice anything. Being with him kind of blurs everything.'

Morag nods, engrossed. Aren't people just wonderful? she keeps asking herself.

'Right now,' continues Carson, 'my mind doesn't have to work very hard. I'm here, this is home, and Robbie and me, well … the scenery is almost invisible.'

'Ah, but look around you. How could it be invisible? This place is paradise.' Morag indicates the red and pink roses, the sycamores, the blue-jays, the blue sky, the magnolia house sitting in quiet splendour.

Carson looks. Sighs. Can't feel it. Says:

'You know how people feel they might be in the wrong sex body? Well, I think I'm in the wrong country. This place is not me. You must think I'm crazy,' she says. 'My name's Carson, by the way. I, we, live just down the road in the house where we grew up with our granddad Fred, he raised us, really he … oh!' God damn it, she thinks, and blows her nose.

'Is he inside the hospice now, dear? I'm so sorry, but you shouldn't be upset. It's perfectly comfortable in there. And he's probably enjoying himself, spoiled to death right now by all these nurses and volunteers.' Morag wonders for a second, as she speaks, if it is her gender that is to blame for their reluctance to bring her cups of tea – every single staff member, bar Manuel, is a woman. Would they tend a man with more enthusiasm? Is Manuel like the cock of the brood? And Fred, their baby?

'My granddad Fred? Yes, he's inside.' She looks stricken.

'Is he now? I've not met him yet, but no doubt I will. My name is Morag McTavish, by the way,' says Morag, and extends her age-speckled hand. 'I'm a patient here. And I don't think you're crazy at all, dear. Not at all. Listen, I'm having the same thoughts myself, lately.'

Carson, momentarily insane with guilt, wonders if Morag has also murdered her grandfather. Then regains balance.

'What thoughts? That you're not grown up?'

'No, no,' says Morag, laughing. 'Well, quite possibly I haven't grown up, but it's more the worry that I might be in the wrong place that upsets me. That I've tried to have both places, be a sort of geographical bigamist. But maybe life doesn't work that way. Maybe you have to choose one, and blood is thicker than water. Your birth place is like your family.'

'Is that why you were, you know, crying earlier? Are you homesick?'

'Exactly, but exactly. That's it in a nut-shell. Not very complicated after all. And I thought it was my imminent departure, but it's only a wee bout of homesickness.' Morag shudders as if she's finally finished her crying bout, and smiles weakly.

'Well, you know the cure for homesickness,' says Carson. She wonders if she should ask about the imminent departure, but it seems too private a question; and maybe she doesn't really want to know the answer. Especially since she is beginning to identify with the woman rather strongly. The last thing she needs is to come out in sympathetic symptoms.

'Aye, I do indeed,' says Morag. 'I'm just thinking on ways to accomplish it.'

'How long have you been away from Scotland?'

'Oh, now that's a question. Let me see. Since I was twenty-six, and that was … twenty-three years ago. Too long. I've been back for visits and such, but my, my, too long altogether since I lived there.'

'Are your parents still alive?'

'No, but I've a sister, Aggie, and all her bairns, and her bairn's bairns.'

Carson's face is blank, as she pictures this sister Aggie with dozens of big barns and little barns. 'Five daughters, and twelve grand-children already!' adds Morag, and Carson's barns dissolve.

'Do you have any children yourself, Morag?'

She holds her breath for the answer, as if Morag is telling Carson's own future. Will I or won't I?

'No, none at all.'

'Oh.' Carson sighs.

'I don't know how it happened, but the time slipped and then it was too late. It doesn't matter too much. If I'd wanted them badly enough, I imagine I would have them. What's for you will no go by you.'

'What?'

'Just like, oh, *que sera sera*.'

'Doris Day? Didn't she have babies?'

'Never mind. Now, listen. Tell me about your name. It's so unusual.'

'I know. My pretentious literary parents. Carson McCullers was my mom's favourite writer when she was pregnant with me. Mom and Dad were a bit like that, always finding old things and people to pick up and adopt. Giving me the writer's name was supposed to make it up to poor old under-appreciated Carson. They were the kind of hippies who really believed in the peace and love stuff. I remember them teaching me and Robs how to make the peace sign.'

Carson demonstrates this.

'And they were nostalgic about anything older than the fifties. Mom used to dress in long skirts and silky dresses with lots of little flowers, and Dad used to wear suspenders and these long-sleeved T-shirts with a row of tiny buttons at the neck. They loved going to flea markets and picking up old junk. That's mostly what I remember about them. Getting up early every Sunday to hit the Sausalito flea market. Hot dogs for breakfast.'

A small pause, while both women recover from the tangible longing that Carson has just issued into the air. Carson is surprised; Morag is not.

'They sound such wonderful people. Dead, are they?'

'Pretty much. Yeah. Long time ago.'

'No wonder you and your brother lean on each other so much. It can't be a bad thing. Imagine if you didn't have him? Or he, you?'

'I'd probably be a grown-up.' Oh! The twinges of betrayal she feels saying this out loud!

'I think you'll probably find maturity is a wee bit over-rated. Ask your granddad.'

'Oh, Fred. Poor old Fred.' Oh! Oh! More and more twinges of betrayal, a whole sharp-edged series of them. Jab jab jab.

'I'm sure he's happy here. It's a fine place, four-star hotel. In fact all of Fairfax is lovely. It's ... what's the word ... funky? Like it never really figured out what to be – posh or artsy or ordinary, so it's got that nice loose undecided feeling. I like the way there are no malls and the roads have ruts and the creek always floods in winter and the whole place never feels anything but sleepy.'

'Do you?'

'Oh yes. I never minded taking two buses a day to come out here to work. It was worth it, just to smell the trees.'

'But you want to leave it and go back to Scotland, Morag.'

'But not because it isn't lovely, Carson.' She says the name with the full rolling 'r' in the middle, giving Carson an instant urge to be in a place where everyone says her name that way. 'I love being here,' continues Morag. 'I love it, I do. Only, it's not mine. *It's not mine*. Maybe it's as simple as that. My ears want to hear voices like my own. Maybe I'm needing a cup of tea made with Highland water, too.'

'Yeah, I can understand that,' says Carson. But she can't. Not at all.

Pause, while each woman contemplates their situation. Morag slips her shoes back on, makes as if to reluctantly leave. Too much rapport is starting to feel like a rich meal, and she wants quiet now. Also, her problem, her furry animal, her imminent departure, has come creeping back, drawn by the sound of her carefree laughter; it needs attention again. Dark is right, dark is true, it says. All laughter is impotent. All intimacy powerless.

'Maybe we'll meet again,' says Carson hopefully.

'Perhaps, though I'd rather like to go home. *Home* home. Inverness. Well, good luck, Carson. It's been rather, well, *extraordinary* meeting you.' Morag extends her hand, grasps Carson's.

'And good luck to you, Morag. Good luck to us. Ladies on the move. Hopefully.'

They stand and hold each other's hands, serious now. They look at their hands, hold on.

'We would be doing the right thing, I'm sure,' whispers Carson.

'Oh aye. And not before time.'

And then, out of the sun-soaked air, THE IDEA materialises.

◆◆◆◆

Later, when Morag is back in her room excited by THE IDEA, Carson is still standing in the garden wondering why June is taking so long. Has June found a corpse, or is Fred in there slobbering over his shirt and not dead at all? Carson's eyes are not focussed on anything, thinking these worrying thoughts, so she is quite startled to suddenly note a quick movement low to the ground near her feet. She looks down and there is a little girl, sitting on the ground, pulling carrots. Carrots? This is a manicured lawn, where did the carrots come from? And where did this mysteriously-dressed dark little girl come from? Carson takes a step back, feeling dizzy, and the girl looks up and smiles.

The Big Moment

'Here we are,' says Manuel, after his lengthy spiel about the current fund-raising events and the state of the roof and the party planned by the volunteers, to which June is most welcome, if she brings something to barbecue. It's all just one happy family at Gentle Valleys. The Waltons at heaven's gate.

'I wouldn't go too close in case you disturb him, Mrs … I mean, June.'

Fred is lying on his side, his face away from the door, so all they see is the back of his head.

'He seems very sound asleep, indeed,' says June. 'Dead to the world, bless his heart.'

'Oh no, not at all, he's perfectly fine,' says Manuel.

'I didn't mean … oh, never mind. When he wakes, will you tell him I came to wish him happy birthday?'

'Oh yes, of course.'

'Well, thank you Dr … .'

'Manuel. Please.'

They leave Fred. Manuel walks to the door with June, whom he likes very much, shakes her hand and says goodbye, then double backs to Fred's door again. Makes a mental note to tell Joe that the odour is getting worse. Goes to open the window against all rules, but surely in Fred's case it is imperative. Sees Morag down in the garden, laughing with a young woman. This is what he looks like, watching them:

Morag is rocking with her laughter, intoxicated with it, and it carries up to him, and this is the moment he knows he is in trouble. Look at the picture again. Look hard. Do you see it? Cupid's arrow flying up from the rose garden, in through the window. It is not the first arrow, but the first to hit home in a fatal way. Manuel gasps, puts his hand to his chest where the arrow is embedded. First she is another woman he loves, then pow, zap, ouch, he is in love, which is very different. Which is the opposite in many ways. Here is what Manuel's face looks like in love:

You're right. Not as cute. Being in love is a terrible, demoralising and unflattering state to be in.

Meanwhile, June has forgotten about Carson waiting in the garden. She goes home. Pours herself a glass of iced tea, wanders through to the living room, has a daydream about Joe, then remembers and hurries back. Carson is leaning against a tree, looking nervous.

'How about some lunch, Carson? Sorry I took so long with your granddad. Are you all right? You look like you've seen a ghost.'

'Oh, well, I'm okay. I'm fine, June. How was Granddad, by the way?'

'Fred? Oh, right as rain. He's always fine.' June dusts her hands together.

Carson takes a deep breath. Lets it out. Takes a deep breath again.

June notices – June always notices things that really matter (and Fred's non-existence doesn't really matter, believe or not) – but doesn't say anything. Carson's forehead has its *Private Property – Do Not Trespass* sign.

Part Eleven

Life is unfulfilled yearning; the state of want. And if you're lucky and live long enough to wish for death, then life ends with a dream come true.

Excerpt from *The Consuela Chronicles*, transcribed by Cathy Cuneo of Santa Fe, who was a visitor in Sycamore House, January 1942. One of the more popular quotes that has been incorporated into posters, cards and bumper stickers that say: **I live in the State of Want!**
Estimated age of Consuela: seventeen.
Location of apparition: the bottom step of the staircase.

Ways in which Manuel loves Morag

He has seen her laughing in the garden, a condemned woman who laughs anyway. He loves what he sees in her eyes and he knows he has never been in love before. Never. Which means, he realises, that if he hadn't met Morag – in fact, if he hadn't lied to Morag and created this new laughing glowing defiantly open Morag – he might have gone the rest of his life having never really fallen in love. It's a thought. Especially for a man who considers himself a great lover.

What does he love about her? Not the touch of her skin. Though that might be heaven, he would love her untouched just the same. He loves the way she makes him think about things. Things like life and death and what bodies are and what souls are. Manuel loves Morag's questing soul, like Yeats loved Maude Gonne's pilgrim soul. The same lost restlessness, the same honesty and courage and endless seeking. William Butler Yeats and Manuel Mendoza. Both captured by what could not be captured, one only slightly more eloquent than the other. Both poets – oh yes, Manuel is definitely a poet, in a never-written-a-poem way. And both in love with souls. Souls they would still love in aged bodies, if given the chance. And even more, if not given the chance.

Morag has not been loved in this way before. Her soul has gone unnoticed for the most part, and she has been loved for her willingness to be married. That, and her freckles and carrot cake. Her naked soul is virgin territory.

When Manuel looks at Morag's eyes these changed days, when he brings her a cup of tea or listens to her, he cannot help but see: Morag is so full of *not body*. She makes him spiritual. And this is what he decides souls must be: All the intangible and unique parts of a person. Life urges and personality. A soul is what moves a body to dance even when there is no dance floor or dance band or dance partner. Manuel's soul is what persuades him to whistle some days; to whistle his own particular whistle, even down lonely dark lanes, wet trouser cuffs flapping through puddles, drawn curtains twitching. A soul doesn't seem to notice that it has no cause to dance or whistle, and that is the saving grace of a soul. It saves without cause. Morag lives and laughs and searches, with no hope of respite, no escape from the brick wall. (As do we all.)

Manuel watches Morag from a distance. She walks alone, stepping lightly, softly smiling, and the watching-Manuel tells himself that he is a different person now. This fills him with a delicious melancholy. Loving Morag's soul has chastened him.

Nothing needs to happen between them. So much has already happened.

Part Twelve

Love Letters from my Death-bed

Flora, you know what? Sometimes I think everything I ever do or say is so's I won't feel alone. But I'm not, silly me. For one thing, there's always been myself, at all my ages, keeping company with my current self. You're not alone either, Flora, though you probably find this hard to believe. Love yourself, all your selves. Laugh at your own jokes. I know you have a sense of humour, Flora, and I guess you need it, going around on your ankles like that.

Excerpt from *The Consuela Chronicles.* Transcribed by Flora O'Brien, San Francisco, 1976. Flora saw Consuela twice. The first time Flora was in the room that used to be the Vietti kitchen, doing her tai chi. The other time she was sitting on the toilet reading a magazine, and suddenly Consuela was there looking in the mirror, combing her hair. Honoured by Consuela's visits, she dedicated her first novel to her.
Estimated age of Consuela: twenty-two.
Location of apparition: Sycamore House downstairs bathroom.

Reality Slips Several Cogs

'Hey, mister. Spare five bucks for a large latte?'

'Get a job, loser.'

Robbie is in a bad mood. It's been a day of fussy vegans, anorexic coke-heads and obese joggers. At one point he had to be a bouncer, a rare necessity in a Café Ole. All this on top of the stress of being an uncaught murderer. He weaves through the spare changers, strides past all the cappuccino outlets and health clubs, finds his car and drives home. Hears Carson in the shower. Switches on the answering machine and braces himself for the bad news. Joe's or June's hysterical voice – what words would they find for Fred snuffing it?

And there it is: June's weak hesitant voice crackling through the air:

'Robbie? Do I talk now? This is June speaking, it is Monday afternoon and the time is 3:34. It was your grandfather's birthday yesterday. Just reminding you, in case you forgot. Me and your sister went to see him today. Had a great lunch at Waco Taco. Have a nice day.' Click.

Carson, damp and smelling of talcum powder, comes in the room and flops on the sofa. Moans loudly, head in hand.

'Carson, what's going on?'

'Robbie, you will not believe this. Fred is not, like, dead. June visited him today. At the hospice. I was there. If he'd been dead, she would have noticed. Even June would have noticed that, Rob.'

'Impossible. He was definitely completely dead.' Whispering.

'Well, duh. But. Spooky, huh? Do you think this is what they meant by the long-term effects of marijuana?'

'What? Carson, you are losing it.'

'Okay, you're right, though it's a tempting theory. How do you explain Fred not being dead?'

'I can't.'

'My head hurts. I hate it when a week starts out all normal and then goes unreal on me. What if Georgia-May phones up and she says we never went to Point Reyes?'

'Then I'll look into the long-term usage theory more deeply.'

The phone rings and Carson answers it. Robbie grabs the extension to listen.

'Hey, Carson,' says Georgia-May. 'What's going on? My parents haven't said anything about Fred, and I think they would have, right away. After all, I've known him all my life. What is going on?'

'Oh, thank God.'

'What do you mean?'

'Look Georgia-May, something very strange is going on. If Fred is dead. Actually something even stranger is going on if he's not.'

'What do you mean if …'

'Listen, the hospice and your dad and mom … well, they don't seem to think he's dead. Your mom and me went to visit him, and he doesn't appear to actually be very dead at all.'

'Oh, thank goodness. We didn't kill him then. He was probably just asleep. Oops, Chloe's fallen in the toilet again, gotta dash.'

Carson and Robbie hang up the phones. Robbie turns on the radio and opens a beer.

'So,' says Robbie. 'We fabricated the whole scenario, kind of a mutual illusion, because we like making things up so much. Makes more sense that way.' Takes a long swig.

'Haven't we already had that theory?'

'Have we? I thought we just had the long-term drug use theory. How about the idea of mass hypnosis, only it's just you, me and Georgia-May?'

'Okay. I'll buy that theory. I want to buy that theory. It's less scary. It means we can keep smoking.'

'Want a beer?' burping loudly.

'Jesus, look at you. You're more and more Homer Simpson-ish every day.'

'He's my hero.'

'You moron, you've got it all wrong – you're supposed to be Bart. Joe's Homer, and I get to be smart sane Lisa.'

'Not fair. Not to mention totally inaccurate.'

'Tough. Give me a beer. Got any chips?'

'Nah, have a chocolate donut instead. Anyway, so who is Georgia-May in Simpson-speak? Maggie?'

'Dunno. Maggie's too young to tell. But Georgia-May did suck on that dummy thing till she started school. Remember how her dog used to chew it up and she'd put it right back in her mouth?'

'Not really.'

The alcohol and sugar hits Carson's blood stream and she thinks *why not now.*

'Robbie, I've been thinking.'

'Yeah?'

'Yeah, I've been thinking. I might do a bit of travelling. Maybe Scotland.'

'Yeah, brilliant, hit the road before the shit does. But I'll have to renew my passport first.'

'No, I mean, like I'd try going on my own.'

'As in *without me*?'

'Well, pretty much. Yeah.'

'Sure, hey, fine, great. It's a big scary world out there, but hey – you don't need me, you'll be fine. Leave me to pay the piper.'

'Like you would anyway.'

'Hey, more than you would anyway. So go! Have fun! You'll do fine without me.'

'Oh, Robs. I may not be fine. But I think I should try. Have a look, anyway.'

'Are you sure this isn't just mid-life crisis stuff?' Thinking back to their birthday two weeks ago, which they had celebrated by stealing a Sarah Lee chocolate cheesecake from the Seven-Eleven, and eating entirely by themselves on the beach, followed by three massive joints.

'Thirty is hardly mid-life, Robs.'

'Depends on how long you live,' says Robbie with a snort of laughter, despite his sudden urge to cry, which he will not even come close to giving into. 'Anyway, thirty is one of those ages where people do weird things. It throws lots of people, Carson. Some people get married and mortgaged at twenty-five just to avoid depression on their thirtieth birthday.'

'Yeah, well, hopefully I'll be too busy having a European adventure to worry about that.'

'Are you sure it'll be fun?' He sighs and swallows hard to get rid of the lump. 'Who knows you over there? No-one. No-one knows you over there.'

'Exactly.'

'There's no-one there with, like, the same frame of reference. Who's going to get your jokes? Fix food the way you like? You'll end up one of those ladies talking to themselves.'

'I know, I know. And I'll leave you all alone, mumbling to yourself in donut land.' Carson is not looking at Robbie at all, she has to keep her eyes fixed on the refrigerator, has to concentrate to keep her voice steady and light. Why have they never learned how to be any other way with each other? They've no emotional practice.

'Stop. I drool just thinking about it."

'Maybe you are Homer after all.'

A pause, while Robbie rounds up his troops.

'Actually, Carson, to tell you the truth, sis: I'm only a fake Homer.'

'What? Don't belittle yourself, Robbie.'

'I mean it, I hate to tell you like this, sort of shocking to say, but seeing as how you're planning to desert me anyway, I can tell you. About Elizabeth. And the engineering course at Berkeley I'm applying for.'

'Yeah, sure.' Carson is giddy, her eyes bright, her voice high-pitched. 'And you've got a suit too, right? You are such a sad bastard, Robbie. Maybe I should take you with me after all.'

Silence, till they finally meet eyes over the dirty sink.

'Actually, Carson, about the suit?'

Wandering Morag

Looks in every doorway, till – eureka! Her own room again! She runs to her bed, hugs pillow, hugs teddy, hugs diamond necklace. I'll never leave home again, Toto. Especially, I will never take those pills again. This place is a bloody maze. Sits on her bed, rocking. A volunteer comes in, looks startled to see Morag.

'Excuse me, do you work here?' asks Morag.

'Well, technically yes. I'm a volunteer.'

'I wonder if you could clean my window? It's needing a good clean.'

'The cleaners could, but it's their break time. They'll all be in their staff lounge.'

'Where is that?'

'Top floor.'

'Big place, isn't it?'

'Well is has to be, with all the staff.'

'Lucky patients, then.'

'Oh, I don't know any of them,' she smiles modestly. 'It's not my business. I do funding and flowers. Mondays and Thursdays. My husband says it gets me out of the house.'

'That's, uh, nice of you.'

'Oh, I don't mind at all. It's a wonderful place. I love it here. Great atmosphere. Everyone's happy, you know?'

'Hmmm. Good. That's good.'

'Oh yes, it's a happy place.'

'Right.' Pause. 'But isn't this a place for people who are dying?' Morag *really* shouldn't have taken those pills, she is forgetting her manners. No saying the D word!

'Oh!' she laughs. 'It's not about death, it's about life. That's what they tell us at induction meetings. The hospice is definitely not about death. *Life.*'

'Aye, life … I'm so thirsty … a cup of tea … I wonder if …'

'Yes, well, I have to go, now. I'll tell the refreshment volunteers you want a cup of tea. Don't you worry about a thing! Have a nice day!'

Morag takes the bottle of pills that Manuel gave her and flushes them down the toilet. Drugs were never her thing, she shouldn't have let him persuade her to try them again. Then she sets about cleaning her already clean room, folding clothes and straightening out her bed, and finds it soothing. It is Morag's eleventh day in Gentle Valleys, her fifteenth day of knowing she is going to die. Her three-hundred-and-ninety-second day of not knowing that she desires Manuel, but only her fifteenth day of not knowing that she is in love with Manuel. Manuel the doctor, the strong modest smart handsome doctor, has plunged her physical desire into much deeper waters. She is well water-logged now.

Despite this, her appearance has improved a great deal since her move to Gentle Valleys. She gets manicured, massaged, and aromatherapied daily. Between the hours of ten and three, there are professionals lined up to bestow their gifts and services on her, and she is a queen. A tiara would be a nice touch, she tells herself, and pictures her gold credit card, still sitting snugly in her bag. A gold glittery over-the-top tiara. Must be a catalogue with such things. Checks the yellow pages under *T*.

Manuel visits her every morning just after breakfast, and again, just after dinner. She has all meals in her room. There is a dining room, but she hasn't seen it yet because Joe prefers to hide the fact that he has only one other patient. Only one other breathing patient. Fred lies not far from Morag, taking up space but not air.

When Manuel comes to see her, the room suddenly contains enough electricity to power the entire town. It could be measured by a curious researcher, if one existed nearby, investigating the amount of electrical discharge emanating from couples who have not yet consummated their passion. A lucrative book could be produced on the findings. *Domestic Uses for Pre-Coital Energy*.

Of course, neither Morag or Manuel care. They are too far gone and are way too stupid. They have no idea what to do. They move with difficulty around each other through air charged with their own longing. They bruise their lips against the absence of lips. They have boring conversations; it has to be said that their conversations pre-lust were a lot livelier. Longing has stupified them.

'How are you today, Moragita?'

'Oh, much better, Manuel.'

'You're looking fine.'

'Thank you. Is it another hot day outside?'

And so on. All their thoughts are encoded in their body language, which does not go unnoticed by staff, and Manuel gets a ribbing from the nurses and from Joe Johnson.

'Hey buddy, hoping for a mention in the will?'

and

'Watch it Doc, there's a word for people like you, and it starts with 'n' and rhymes with becrophiliac.'

Manuel ignores the crass comments without any difficulty because he is completely suffused with Morag thoughts. And what happens? Not a thing. True romance is in that place where *nothing has happened yet.* Of course, the inaction feeds the infatuation. Morag's days have fallen into a pattern. Mornings of lusty thoughts unfocused on anyone, days of pampering, evenings of lusty thoughts likewise without focus, with interludes of a strange beautiful loneliness while she wanders lost in the corridors or looks out the window at the night or sits weeping in the garden, as Carson found her. She is sublime sublimation. Not that pure lust is ever wasted – it improves circulation, the view, the way cotton feels on bare skin, the temperature of the bath, the taste of red wine: everything. But it also diffuses; turns thoughts to mush.

Nevertheless, her plans to go to home to Inverness are slowly solidifying. From a vague feeling in her heart, they have taken up clear residence in her mind. The logistics are being worked out in her lonely interludes. Steps are being taken. She and Carson are going to the travel agents tomorrow afternoon.

And where does Manuel come into this plan? He does not. Her lust exists only because of the impossibility of its being satisfied. In fact, thinking about leaving nourishes her yearning. Distance and self-ignorance, in Morag's book, are essential for true love. Morag, the cerebral idiot.

Georgia-May, the Frustrated Writer

Georgia-May pulls out her folder entitled *Great Novel* because she's had another brainstorm while breast-feeding. Something about the milk draining out, her captive state and her strong desire to escape her environment, sends her into deep creative mode. If only she could finish this! She settles the infant down, slides in another video for her older child, and turns on her computer.

When she momentarily pauses, fingers poised over keys, she begins to think of the Fred problem instead. She sighs. She doesn't need this complication. This is writing time, not Fred-fretting time. Guilt is so draining. Anyway, he wasn't *her* granddad. Carson and Robbie have always got her into trouble. She should really drop them, leave them behind completely. Losers. But then a memory rises up with all the surreal clarity that chronic sleep deprivation can bestow, and she gets that same jolt in her belly that she got watching them drive away from her parents' the other night. She closes her eyes.

She is seventeen and it is morning recess at school. She's hanging out with the friend she always hangs out with when the Snellings aren't around, which is a lot in their senior year. Another only child, nerdy Nancy. Carson and Robbie appear at the school gates. They are supposed to be home, sick with a bug, but it seems normal to see them. Georgia-May leaves nerdy Nancy to meet them at the gate. Carson is beautiful, so beautiful, her hair like pale wheat, her eyes like pale sky. And Robbie – he is so tall and his frizzy long hair is in a pony-tail. He has a beard. They don't look like high school kids suddenly, which makes Georgia-May feel even younger than she is. Plus, she cannot ignore the fact they are glowing. Even on this bright May afternoon, there it is – a brighter shining ring of light. And on their shoulders are back-packs.

'We just came to say goodbye, Georgia-May. We're off to Mexico.'

'But it's not vacation time yet.' Georgia-May remembers this part best – her sudden panic at being left behind.

'No, well. It is for us.'

'What about graduation? Will you be back for that?'

'Probably. Maybe.'

'What about your granddad?'

'We told him. He said "see you later alligators."'

'Oh.' Pause. 'Can I come? I'll come with you, just wait.'

'Not this time, Georgia-May. You know. Your mom and dad would never let you, and besides, we really need to get going now. We'll send a card, okay?'

'Yeah, okay. See you, guys.' She watches them leave a few seconds, then calls, 'Hey, when are you coming back?'

But they have begun to hitch already, and a blue station wagon pulls up. They get in and are gone, into a sea of strangers, people who don't know them, don't know about their parents' car accident, or Fred, or their funny yellow house, or how they did on their SATs or what shows they like to watch on television or what they eat with fries. Georgia-May feels dizzy as the indifferent world swallows her friends; shudders and steps back as if she too might slip into oblivion.

Damn.

The baby has woken, the video has finished, and life rushes back in to fill the tiny whirl-pooling hole that the memory has left. Life, which still has the Fred crisis at its heart. Guilt and anxiety come pouring in and milk suddenly refills her aching breasts. Poor Georgia-May is almost too bloated to pick up her baby.

And where does Adam fit in now? Have they kissed finally? Tested the waters of their passion? Or have they denied themselves each other in a selfless act of sacrifice for their families? Have they had a tearful heart-breaking scene to be re-played many years hence, whenever a certain nursery song is played? Will they occasionally come across each other at cocktail parties and with cool maturity exchange knowing looks over the olives?

None of these things. Georgia-May sees Adam almost daily in the course of neighbourhood toddler social life, but there is a mysterious lack of fizz when they meet now. Nothing has happened, nothing has been resolved or even discussed. The crush has fizzled out so completely that Georgia-May has to wonder at her own sanity – had she made the entire thing up? Or was it just a virus that she now has the antibodies for?

Cynthia Rogerson

Joe's Day

'Hey, Joe. Check it out.'

Fred's right arm goes up and down.

'Excellent, Manuel. So lifelike.'

'There's more.' He turns on a tape of snoring, and an old man voice saying 'Howya doin', guys!'

'Hmm, not so good. A little suspicious.'

'Oh.'

'But keep the arm thing. I like that.'

'You do?'

'Oh, yeah. You have a real talent.'

'For what?'

'For, for you know. Making dead people look not dead.'

'Gee, thanks, boss. *Gracias.*'

'No prob. Now get back to work.'

Joe heads back home to find June asleep in her chair as usual, with her D.H. Lawrence upside down.

'Are you asleep, honey?'

'Of course not, Joe. What a silly question.'

They eye each other a moment, as if checking for ripeness.

'In the mood for a swim?'

'Oh Joe, you know I'm always in the mood for a swim with you. Silly boy. Come here, let's get those clothes off.'

A UPS delivery man pauses outside their house on his way elsewhere, and listens to the shrieks and splashes. The protestations of June and her dissolving into girlish giggles – and Joe's roaring good humour as he whoops and dives. The delivery man smiles, and thinks to himself – kids! As if he has never been young himself. And he hasn't, not quite in that way.

Part Thirteen

Would you agree that people's hopes and fears, all their emotions and instincts, might in fact be distilled into the molecules of their flesh and bones and blood? Stranger things are true. Birds and fish with minuscule brains can nevertheless carry the memory of their species, not their experiences, of where to migrate. Abstract things like geographical directions can embed into molecules of grey brain cells. Well, is it so strange then, to wonder if peoples' cells might carry their lifes' experiences? And that these cells disintegrate and eventually rejoin the soil, adding their unique history as well as nitrogen and other fertilising chemicals? And that this soil could become farmland, and nourish the food we buy from our markets and cook and eat, and allow to become part of our living bodies? People have lived and died on the earth for very long time. By now, a sizeable part of our soil might be decomposed human and animal remains. The potato, for instance, that you baked tonight for your dinner, might in fact owe fifteen percent of its substance to previous humans.

How could this be discounted in any view of man's emotional evolution? We are not only what we eat, but perhaps who we eat. Every morsel of nourishment is tainted with pain and loss, joy and hope. We eat and breathe our ancestor's failed expectations and illusions, their explosions of love. We have evolved, are evolving, into increasingly tender receptacles of heartache.

Excerpt from the essay *Scientific Proof of Emotional Evolution* by Alex Cumingsky, 1949. Alex was a great fan of the Consuela cult, and was president of the Consuela Chronicles Club from 1940 to 1952, when it dissolved due to disinterest. Although he only saw Consuela once, his theory is in large part due to her strong influence. Consuela cultists at that time believed that her vivid emotions allowed her to defy physics, and foresaw a time when everyone would have this ability.
Estimated age of Consuela: fourteen.
Location of apparition: next to Alex Cumingsky on the Sycamore House garage work bench. Apparently she didn't say much, just asked him if he was related to the Perry family.

The Plan

Georgia-May, Robbie and Carson, at Café Ole at the corner table in the shadows. Three café lattes half-drunk in front of them, the crumbs of some muffins. Georgia-May's daughters are asleep in her car, just visible from this table, and Georgia-May keeps flicking her eyes that way.

'We break in and see for ourselves,' says Robbie.

'Don't be so ridiculous, Robbie,' says Georgia-May. 'You always have to make things more dangerous than they need to be. Just go in the day-time, say you want to see Fred. Be normal.'

'Ah, Georgia-May, you always spoil my fun.'

'You're such a baby, Robbie,' says Carson, who still feels aggrieved that she'd not been the only one with secrets. Who feels, illogically, rejected. Who has seen the suit for her own eyes, and flinched.

'Is that why you want to take off without me?'

'One of the millions of reasons. Did I tell you, Georgia-May? I'm taking off on my own for a while pretty soon. Scotland.'

'Oh my God, Carson. On your own! Wow. Will you need someone to cut the cord when you go? I can sterilise my scissors.'

'Of course, I'll definitely need your scissors. Think I'd trust him to let go? Also, you could check his water bowl from time to time while I'm gone. Maybe crack a window too.'

'No problem. 'Bout time you two tried the world solo. Though I don't suppose Robbie will be solo for longer than a minute or two.'

'Oh yeah? Got some of your friends in mind for me? Send 'em on over. They can line up.'

'In your dreams, loser.'

'He's already got someone, Georgia-May. Elizabeth the law student.' She says this with true Snelling snide-ness, never before directed at a fellow Snelling. Robbie can't help but shiver. 'Ah Carson, don't be jealous,' he says. 'Let's get back to the Fred thing. So. What do you think, a day-time above-board visit? Or a thrill-seeking scary night-time break-in?'

Carson sighs. Georgia-May checks her girls, sighs harder, and blows all the muffin crumbs off the table onto the sticky tile floor. She's feeling wise and world-weary, as married women do who have just finished an entire affair from first passionate kiss to zilch buzz, all in their head.

'Goodie, we'll break in then,' says Robbie.

'Might as well have a few last days of fun before we grow up, hey?' says Carson.

'Look, there're good reasons.'

'Not to grow up?'

'For sneaking in. If there's some kind of cover-up, they're not likely to let us too close to him in the day, are they? We need to do our own … investigation.'

'Jesus,' says Georgia-May. 'You'll be wasting your time.'

'How do you know?'

'Because I went there yesterday.'

'You did?' say both Carson and Robbie.

'Of course I did. Not that I doubted Mom and Carson, but I wanted to check it out too.'

'And?'

'Fred lives, guys.'

'How could you tell?'

'The usual give-away signs of life. I said "hi" and he responded. Kind of.'

'How?'

'He moved his arm. Like this.'

'No fucking way. What else?'

'Jesus, what do you want, him doing aerobics? He was never that energetic to begin with. A wave is something.'

'Did he say anything, sing anything?' whispers Carson.

'Well, not exactly. No, actually.'

'No obolomio?'

'No obolomio.'

'Ah.'

'Ah ha.'

Snellings Sneak Around

Robbie and Carson crouch in the dark. The sound of breathing, slightly phlegmy. The closet fills with their daydreams. Shopping lists, flirtation memories, fantasised romances.

'That's it, then.'

'Try the door. Slowly.'

They creep out into the hall.

'This place is dead.'

'Which way?'

'Not that way, Robbie. This way.'

'Shhh, the other patients will hear you.'

'Which door?'

'This door.'

'Whoops, wrong door.' Robbie shuts it before Morag sees him.

'Hello? Who's there?' asks Morag. 'Is anyone there? I can hear you. Could you please bring me some water? I am so thirsty, I am dying of thirst. Tonic would do, and a slice of lemon. Please don't go away. Come back, come back! I need you!' she says before collapsing back onto her pillow. A gin bottle, half empty on the table, shines in the moonlight.

'Here it is. This is the room.'

'Right, slip in behind me then.'

'Yup, there he is.'

'Christ, this place is like the North Pole.'

'Stinks like shit. What is that smell?'

'Pine trees and road kill? Offhand.'

'Shh, don't wake him.'

'As if.'

'Sit over here a sec.'

Quiet.

'Wow, that is one dead granddad.'

'I know, I can hardly hear him breathing.'

'No, I mean *dead* dead.'

'Oh wow, gross. How can you tell?'

'His chest. Look. No movement.'

'Maybe he's so sound asleep that he's breathing really shallowly.'

'Okay. Okay. We'll have to get closer, touch him.'

'No way. What if he wakes? We'll give him a heart attack.'

'Look moron, the whole point is, he can't wake. We killed him, remember? Baked him, boiled him, fried the old geezer to a crisp.'

'Oh yeah.' Pause. Carson starts singing, low. *'Oh to be home again, down in West Virginnie.'*

'You're getting like him. Like Fred. It's scary.'

'Take that back. I am not.'

'Are, I'm afraid Sis.'

'Not.'

'Are.'

'Wow, total regression. I feel like I've been in a sensory deprivation chamber and floated back to my adolescence.'

'Shut up, Carson. You're an adult, a fully functioning twenty-nine, I mean thirty year-old who brushes her teeth twice a day and has no police record. Yet. Repeat it to yourself.'

'I am thirteen. I hate my brother.'

'No no no. You weren't listening.'

'I am six. I have peed on myself.'

'Carson, stop it.'

'Shh.'

'Okay. Look, we've got to find out for sure. I'm going to touch him.'

'Go on then,' Carson dares him.

'Well, you do it too.'

'No way am I touching a dead person. Cooties. Corpse cooties.'

'Jesus, how are we going to know he's dead unless we touch him?'

'I've seen it on TV, Robs. You just feel the pulse on their neck and wrist.'

'Go on then, do it.'

'But that's touching him. I can't. Look at him. Dead Fred. He's been dead for days. It doesn't really suit him. He looks all caved-in.'

'Look, let's count to three, I'll do the wrist thing and you do the neck thing.'

'Oh all right.'

'One. Two. Three. Go.'

They extend their hands, but jerk back the instant they make contact, and squeal, falling back on the floor.

'Oh gross gross gross, he's a fucking stiff.'

'I've touched a dead man.'

Silence, while they reverse back to the chairs.

'He's not just any stiff, Carson. He's our Fred. Gramps.'

'I know. Good old Granddad. Shit. I kept waiting and waiting for him to be dead; didn't he seem to take an awfully long time about it?'

'Ages and ages. I can't remember when he wasn't ready to croak.'

'How old was he?'

'*I* don't know, Robbie,' as if accused.

"Well, how old was dad when you were born?'

'Thirty.'

'So, thirty plus thirty is sixty.'

'And Fred was thirty-five when Dad was born.'

'So Fred must be at least …'

'Wow. At least ninety-five.'

'No wonder he expired in the car.'

'Why didn't we know how old he was? That's such an incredible age. I should have paid more attention.' Pause. 'I can't believe I'm thirty now. That is so sad.'

'Get a grip, Carson, you're in the presence of your dead grandfather.'

'I know, but well, that's kind of it, too. I mean, life is just going. I hate time just pouring away. It's the thing I hate more than anything.'

'Oh, you're just doing that old hippie thing again, like you have to be really young forever.'

'I am really young.'

'You're immature at times, Carson, but really young you are not.'

'What do you mean? Have I got wrinkles?'

'Yes.'

'Where? I do not. I do not look my age.'

'Jesus, what's it matter, what are we going to do about this?'

'About what? Oh, Fred. Nothing, I guess. What can we do?'

'Tell people he's dead.'

'Why do you think the hospice aren't telling us?'

'Yes, why!'

'Wow, do you think Joe will bill us for this week, then announce he's snuffed it?'

'But we don't pay anything, it's a charity. Fuck knows why they're not telling us, but this place gives me the creeps. Let's go.'

Carson and Robbie begin to creep out, then they both return to Fred's bed and have similar thoughts about their new grandfather-less state. Hard to say where the difference is, since Fred has not played an active role in their lives for a decade. Nevertheless, he has always been there. Now they come to think of it, he has been their only tie to their infancy and childhood. Fred soaked up their shock and panic when disaster left them orphans, while simultaneously dealing with a grief of his own that they have not yet considered. What they notice now, in their silence, is a gap where an ignored piece of old furniture stood. An old comfy lopsided sofa, perhaps. With a particular smell and squeak when you sat on it. Pretty much non-functional, but a familiar part of the room. They both feel a draft, shiver slightly in the absence of Fred in Fred. It is a little annoying.

'Goodbye, dear old man,' says Carson solemnly. 'The air will be forever absent of Obolomio.'

'Thanks, Granddad. For my existence,' whispers Robbie.

'Loved you.'

'Yeah, I did too. Still do. Love you.'

'But we're not kissing you. You are way too dead for that.'

'That's right, too dead, too smelly. No touching.'

And they arrange the blankets around him, tuck them in, smooth them over.

Suddenly Fred's arm rises and waves.

Morag Not Asleep

Morag, who spent her formative years in a flat above her father's drapers shop on Church Street, Inverness, and who is more and more tenderly looking back on those days, has a hard time sleeping. Her room is luxurious, the temperature stays at a steady sixty-five, the bed is soft and she has enough pillows to pamper every angle of her neck. But still she cannot sleep, even after the gin, which tonight has reversed its usual role and made her sober. Perhaps it is too quiet. Perhaps it was that interruption earlier when someone opened her door, then quickly shut it without apology. She sits up in bed and looks at her glowing clock. 2:30.

To hell with this, she mumbles. Her furry animal is still there, but she doesn't feel too bad. She swings out of bed and turns her light on. She paces a little, looking out the window, then at the walls of her room. Suddenly realises the problem. I am bored. I am so bored. I have never been so bored. Dying is the most boring business in the world. You just have to bide your time till it's over. Wait and do nothing but boring things. If that daft lady asks me once more if I wouldn't be happier weaving a tapestry or writing a bloody poem, I'll wring her scrawny wee neck, so I will. (Her old accent comes to the forefront, this early hour.)

'Oh, this is ridiculous!' she says out loud. 'I canna wait for Scotland!'

No more waiting, not a single second of waiting. Checks for her gold card, puts a coat on over her new satin nightie, slips shoes on but no socks. Has a dim plan to find a taxi to the city, catch a late-night show somewhere, maybe even a bar. Do sleazy late-night things. Neck with a stranger in a restaurant booth. Get outrageously drunk. Take illegal drugs, for a change. She considers brushing her teeth for this adventure. Was it worth brushing teeth that would out-live you? Was it worth doing anything good for yourself at all? Eating broccoli? Not smoking? Creaming your face with anti-wrinkle lotions? Was it worth getting changed out of your new satin nightie?

Suddenly she hears small shrieks. She opens her door and sees two dark figures, one mysteriously Carson-like, race within inches of her. They do not notice her, which makes her wonder for a minute if she is indeed dead already. Is she now a ghost, like in *Ghost*, where the dead are slow to pick up on the fact they are goners? She can smell their fear; they leave behind a kind of sour whiff, reminds her of puppy pee, or daffodils. *Was* that girl Carson? Impossible. Carson is an honest day-time sort of person. No, they must be the same people who opened and shut her door earlier, when she'd been so thirsty. Before she'd used the bathroom tap water.

'Heavens,' she says, brushing some of their panic off herself. 'Heavens above, what is all that about?'

Then wonders if she has just witnessed a dastardly deed, a mugging in the hospice. Now who would credit it? But the world is a strange place these days. Her escape plan can wait a minute, while she does the heroine bit. She teeters down the hall towards the reception, calling out feebly, 'Hello, anyone there? Hello? It's me again, only I don't want a drink this time. I think there's been a robbery. Or something.'

No answer, but the distant sound of laughter as the night staff play scrabble in a room upstairs where Morag cannot climb, not because her knees are knackered, but because there is a cord across the bottom of the stairs and a sign that says employees only. (Connie is the only resident allowed a room upstairs, and only because she kept crawling up the stairs to get there and kept rolling back down, so Joe gave up and let her stay there.)

Morag decides to investigate by herself. Creeps bravely back down the hall on tiptoe to Fred's room.

Snellings at Home

They've discussed Fred's life and confirmed death, despite his bizarre moving arm. They've eaten two bowls each of Frosted Flakes. Dawn is around the corner.

'Don't go to Scotland, Carson. It's too far. You should stay here. It's not like I'm marrying this Elizabeth anyway, she's just like another girl,' he lies. 'And the suit, well, I've spilled cranberry juice on it already.'

'Shit, Robs, that wouldn't make any difference. I want you to find someone. And you'll look great in a suit. Anyway, wherever I end up, you can always visit.'

'I know, but don't you get it? Visiting is not the same as living with. I hate visiting. No offence, but it's exhausting and, and, and *artificial.* And you know me, I probably just won't visit because it would require, well, you know. Effort.'

'You're so lazy.'

'You say that like it's a bad thing to be. Anyway, would you bother visiting me if I suddenly took it into my head to move to Timbuktu?

'Sure.'

'Well, I want you in the background. Here.'

'Oh, thanks very much.'

'I mean, if I'm in the mood we can go see a movie, get a few beers. On impulse. Scotland is beyond impulse visits.'

'True. I'm going anyway. Roll a joint, Robbie. Maybe we should try a nap before work.'

'And what about Fred?' Robbie starts rolling.

'Fred's dead. What about him?'

'I'm going to tell Joe we know. I'll tell him everything. It's too weird, him thinking we buy that fake moving-arm stuff.'

'Hey. Good luck. You always were the play-it-safe kid, underneath. You spent June's money on a bus.'

'Thanks.'

'It wasn't a put-down. You are. You know when to be honest.'

'Maybe, but you got there quicker and cheaper.'

'That was luck.'

'Well, I was jealous you beat me and still had the ten bucks,' says Robbie, passing her the joint.

He flicks through his CDs, puts on a KFOG compilation. Joan

Osborne's 'One of Us' oozes out of the speakers. *What would you ask, if you had just one question,* they both sing loudly.

'Do you think we'll remember any of this?' asks Carson. 'All these kinds of times. Us just sitting around, singing, getting stoned.'

'Dunno. You know what all this business about Fred feels like?'

'A bad acid trip?'

'No, I mean the fact only we seem to know the truth, or whatever, and we've been bad. It feels like one of our adventures. Fred might be the last adventure we have together.'

'Hardly an adventure.'

'It is. It'll become one of those memories we keep harking back to, and changing, and arguing about. You'll probably have a totally different version.'

'Naturally. I'll be the heroine in my version. You'll be the idiot kid brother.'

'My version will be the truth.'

'Like there can be an objective version.'

The CD goes into "Cry Love", and both listen for a minute. Pass the joint back and forth.

'We've got to tell Joe. You're right,' says Carson, holding on to a lung-full then exhaling.

'How do you think he'll feel about it?"

'Don't know. Mad if he's known all along and we blow it for him. Depressed, otherwise.'

'Shit, now you mention it, this whole thing is depressing. It makes me feel kind of, like …' Robbie struggles to find the word.

'Older?'

'Yeah. That's the word, all right. We're not grandchildren anymore, Carson,' he says woefully.

'I guess Fred kind of shoved us up the ladder.'

'Huh?'

'You know, the ladder you don't want to reach the top of, but some jerk's always dying and making more room for you whether you like it or not.' Carson puts out the joint, yawns. 'Got to admit it, Bro, time is moving right along.'

The music speeds up, as if to illustrate.

'Stop it, it's too sad,' says Robbie.

'Want to borrow my wrinkle cream?'

Still the jokes, but when they head off for their sleep at sunrise, both faces are slack and older-looking and their eyes are inward and serious. Foretelling of their middle-aged selves.

Carson has a bad dream. It is confusing where she is, but clearly it is the wrong place. She has made a wrong decision, and the decision is irreversible. The wrong place. Wrong wrong wrong. Oh no, she whispers in her sleep. Oh no – her brother has died. That's why it's wrong. Robbie is dead. Oh! God, it hurts. It creates a huge white burning space.

Then, as if she senses her own limits for pain, she pulls herself out of this dream. It takes so much strength, and the dream has so drained her, that she lies in the dim light more than half-ready to sink back into sleep. But she forces her limbs to move, to complete the waking process, to leave the dream safely behind. She has recognised her room, knows she is still here. *Still home.* The tickets have been bought, but there is no law that says she has to use her ticket. The relief is intense. She smiles.

Finally, she snuggles back down, down, down into a dreamless slumber, the limbo of the uncommitted. The decision, meanwhile, is banished to a safe distance. Hangs in the air above her head. The known or unknown. Stay or leave. Which?

One thing for sure. Fred is dead.

September 6th, Sycamore House, Fairfax, 1929

Fred might as well be dead, for all the letters he writes. Consuela hates the mailman, hates him. So what does she do, after her chores and when she is finished hating the mailman every day? She turns up the radio and dances in the kitchen. Today, she dances to Dardanella. She is finally graceful again. Around and around she goes. She has always loved to dance; she lets her feet smile for her. A small puppy scrambles into the kitchen. Petey! she says, and she sweeps him up into her arms and carries on dancing. Petey squirms and makes high-pitched yearning noises.

The music drowns out the man's knock, so he watches her through the screen door for a while. When the song ends, he stamps his feet as if he has just arrived and knocks very loudly. She jumps.

'Oh! Can I help you?' She puts Petey down. The puppy runs straight for the man, and starts tugging at his trouser cuff. The man doesn't seem to notice or care. In fact, there is a dead look in his eyes. A dead, past-humiliation, past-shyness, bone-tired look. Another song begins, a slow happy one with a woman singing about loving some man.

'Why, yes; I hope you can,' he says, taking his hat off. 'I was just passing by and thought someone here might need some jobs done. I can do all sorts-a things. Digging, picking, hammering, sawing, chopping, you name it. Got any work at all, then, Miss?'

While he talks, Consuela tries not to breathe his odour too deeply, and notices that he is a young man, despite his dead look. A young man who, she guesses by looking at his wet shoes, has just hopped off the freight train where it slows down by the creek.

'Well now, work's pretty scarce around here,' she says kindly, 'but tell me, where are you headed?'

This is always the hardest part. *Don't give them money*, she's been told by the Viettis. They can sleep in the shed and have a bite to eat, but there is no work here at Sycamore House any more. No spare jobs at all. They'd had to let Fred go last year, it's that bad. Viettis are bankers, and the bankers are getting hit bad, especially since they never once imagined this situation.

'Headed up Seattle way, heard there's some apple picking soon.'

'I heard Washington's real pretty in the fall.'

'Don't worry about not giving me no job, Miss. I understand. Things are real tight everywhere you go these days.'

'Yes. I'm sorry. Wait here.'

The man crouches, his felt hat in his hands, and he keeps turning it round and round as if it drives something. His bag sits on dusty ground, a small cracked leather suitcase held together with twine. Consuela brings him a tall glass of milk and a plate with four slices of bread spread with dripping, and two boiled eggs and some home-made tomato chutney.

'Thank you kindly, Miss,' smiling thinly. 'This looks real good.' He looks uncomfortable, and Consuela realises he is proud and is waiting for her to leave so that he can eat alone. The music changes to another fast dance tune. It looks too sad, him sitting there on the ground, a full grown young man, down on his luck like that.

'I've got a better place for you to eat that. Come here,' she says. He follows her round to the front of the house, to her favourite place: a sturdy bench and small table under a completely symmetrical oak tree.

'Are you sure no-one in there minds me sitting here?'

Consuela looks towards the big house, notices the old woman in the upstairs window seat as usual. She is staring at Consuela and this young man. Petey chases a butterfly and the young man belches discretely.

'Nah,' she says. 'No-one's home right now; they won't be back till dinner time.'

The young man's eyes look marginally less dead when she says this.

Cynthia Rogerson

Morag McTavish has a Conversation with a Dead Man

Tip-toe tip-toe, down the dim corridor, no noise from anywhere, just the muted hum of the air conditioner, sucking in and regurgitating old breath. She peeks around the open door to Fred's room and sucks in her own breath. Shivers in the cold blast of air, wonders how he manages to sleep in such a cold room.

'Sorry, sorry,' she whispers. 'I just wondered if everything was all right in here.'

Silence.

'Hello? I heard a noise, thought you might need help. No? I guess not. Guess it didn't disturb you. Sorry.'

Starts to sidle out the room, but retraces her steps.

'Listen, I know it's the middle of the night. I don't want to alarm you, but do you mind if I just sit in your room a minute? I haven't actually talked to anyone for hours. This place – great food, but the company stinks, if you know what I mean. Well, except for one man. The doctor, actually; you must know him. He's all right.' Actually, you stink quite a bit too, she thinks but does not say.

She sits in the chair in the corner. Shivers again, pulls her coat closer. Thinks to herself how unused to the cold she is now, how unpleasant, no – painful, she finds the sensation. Especially her hands. And how depressing to be in a cold country, where even in August it might be possible to not feel truly warm through and through. No: she has complained of the heat in California, but her yearning for fresh cold Highland air has surely been sentimental. To think that she might be speeding to the airport in a week, headed for Scotland. She must be insane. She can leave this place without having to go six thousand miles to freeze. Anyway, didn't someone say you couldn't go home again? Some clever old guy. She looks at Fred.

'Wow, you are some sleeper. Better this way. You can't interrupt, and I won't be embarrassed tomorrow if we see each other.'

Morag surveys the room – much like her own, only colder. And smellier. Also, more personal belongings – in fact, it looks as if he's lived here for a long time.

'So, what are you in for, I wonder? Me, I've got a whole host of cancers and this is where they stuck me instead of my own house. So I can be looked after properly; given occupations to take my mind off things like pain and morbidity. You know. But hey, it reminds me of a waiting room. Like an airport lounge or a modern train station. Clean, tasteful, impersonal, and so boring that tonight I feel like I'm going berserk. Know what I mean?

'I mean I hate this bloody place. I'd rather be dead already.

'Sorry about the bloody. All the old words keep cropping up; it's my age. I'm regressing. Soon I'll be telling you all about my sister when we were bairns and her whingeing and the dreich weather I used to hate and now think I yearn for, but I don't really. Not really. Though the weather here is a bit too one-sized. Either long blocks of heat, or pouring rain. I think, after all, I prefer my weather in bits and pieces. You know, a bit of rain, then an hour later a bit of sun. And less of the summer heat altogether, it can wear me down. I'm knackered. Another old, slightly rude, word.'

Silence for five minutes. Tick-tock tick-tock.

'You don't even snore. I like that in a man. Just peaceful, hey? Good for you. My first husband was a bittie like that. He'd curl up and still be like that when he woke.

'Were you a husband, I wonder? I bet you were. I bet you were a good husband. Maybe you still are. Is there a wifey alone in her bed not far from here, keeping to her side of the bed, wishing you were there? Keeping your pillow plumped up. Hearing noises in the night, and going to nudge you awake, then remembering?'

Another small slice of time slides by. The conditioner hums. Outside, an owl terrifies a field mouse, and sounds apologetic about it. Morag sighs and says,

'I wonder what all that commotion earlier was about? Maybe just some staff hanky-pankeying. Oh, I've got the American slang too, a right hybrid I am.

'My name is Morag, by the way.

'Sounds strange to me sometimes these days, that my name is still the same, when I don't feel even remotely like myself anymore. No, that's wrong; what I mean to say is, I don't look like myself anymore. The Morag I have always been has lovely long reddish-brown hair. Oh, you wouldn't believe how lovely. Thick and wavy. Morag has freckles and gets sunburned and has a complexion like fresh cream. Morag loves to dance, and sing. And now Morag seems to be imprisoned in this other body. This completely useless and falling-apart body.

'Do you ever feel like that?

'Can't tell you how nice it is to just talk like this. I don't know why I don't try it more often. Not very many good listeners in my life these days, I suspect. Well, there's Manny, he's quite nice. But somehow I don't tell him much.

'Have all your friends popped off? My friends haven't all popped off, but I live so far from most of them that they might as well be dead. It's a weird, lonely feeling, isn't it? I mean, I feel as if there's no-one who remembers what I remember; it's as if my past hardly exists, it's so close to evaporating altogether. All their lives and mine; nothing left at all. It makes me feel half-dead already. As if I'm fading.'

She examines her own hands.

'But no, I can see fine. I'm still solid.

'And I've had a good life. No regrets. Or maybe one. One wee one.

'What's that? Oh, you'll laugh. Or you would if you were awake. But then, I'd never tell you if you were awake. Funny – sleeping men can feel like diaries. Okay. My one regret. It's a big one, and it makes me so sad some days, like I blew a big chunk out of my life, but it'll seem small to you.'

Morag whispers especially low:

'I wish I'd married a man who made me laugh. Really laugh. But none of them did after a while, none of them. There's been a great dearth of belly-laughs in my life.

'There. Doesn't sound like much does it? And yet, saying it out loud hurts so much, you wouldn't believe. Like I made a really quite big mistake.

'Aye, so it does. Ach, well.' Sighs. Giggles.

'Better leave you now. Thanks so much, you've been ever such good company. The best I've had in ages, I feel so much better now.'

She stands by the end of his bed, smiles wistfully.

'You're dead sweet, so you are.'

A Cleaner Discovers the Truth

Maria, the new cleaner, is changing sheets in Morag's room after breakfast. Morag sits at her desk and writes a letter. Pauses.

'There's a lovely quiet man in the room down the corridor; do you know his name?'

'*Quien? Donde?*'

'Man. In nearby room. What is his name?'

'Ah! Señor Smellon! *El es muy riche.* Has own nurses and maids; we no see Señor Smelling. We no allowed open door, even.' She giggles, eyes midnight-black.

'Is that so? A millionaire, is he? Well, it makes no difference in the end; you can't take it with you.'

Writes "Mr. Smellon" on an envelope, puts a letter inside and licks it shut.

'Will you please give this to him, anyway?'

'Oh, no Señora, I cannot. We are told never go near door Mr. Smellon.'

'Oh, surely he won't mind a letter, look here.' Finds money in her purse – two hundred bills.

'Oh! Señora! This is *mucho dinero.*'

'Well, I'm rich too. Will you manage to give him the letter?'

'Oh *Sí, sí* señora, I will do it now while no-one else is here. *Uno segundo. Por favor.*'

'Por whatever you like, lass. Off you go, then.'

Maria takes the letter and leaves. Morag hears a scream, then running feet, and Maria's voice.

'*Esta muerte! Esta muerte! Dios*!'

Not again, is Morag's first reaction. What is it with that corridor and door?

Then other footsteps come rushing, at least a dozen of them, the nurses, the volunteers, the cleaners, the kitchen workers. Where were they all when I wanted a glass of water? thinks Morag. Then, thundering down the hall, come Joe and Manuel.

'Out of the way, out of the goddamn way! Jesus, let me through,' says Joe.

'Yes, Mr. Johnson. Maria Gonzalez found Mr. Snelling has, has, passed away sir,' says a nurse. 'It's her first death, and she lost her head a bit.'

The crowd gives out satisfied murmurs, which bounce softy around the hall. Phrases like: Yes, I remember my first time, dreadful shock it was. And: Ah, I had a feeling, I just knew there was something about today.

'When?' asks Joe, whose angry voice and face puzzle the staff. He's obviously forgotten his role, and all those things he told them at the induction meeting. He should have on his sad-but-resigned face.

'Why, just now, doctor.'

'What was she doing in there? I gave explicit instructions.'

'She said she thought it was another room; she was confused. It was an accident.'

'Fire her.'

'She's quit, sir'.

'Fire her anyway. Right, leave this to us, everyone. Just, just, just, go away, can't you. Find things to do.'

They all just stare at him.

'But sir, there is nothing to do. That is the problem,' whispers the nurse in Joe's ear.

'Well, I'm doing the best I can,' whispers Joe, exasperation in his restrained tone. 'I'm aware it's a slow time and everyone's been depressed but I'm doing my best. It's not my fault everyone's so goddamn healthy here. Where I come from, snuffing it is as common as sneezing.'

'Yes sir,' says the nurse loudly, having decided that being the receptacle of Joe's confidences probably isn't all it's cracked up to be. 'Go on, everyone; shoo,' she says sweetly and the crowd disperses. She takes one more look at Joe and Manuel, then turns to follow the crowd. The staff room will be a fun place just now, they'll brew up the best coffee and order a cake from La Salle. Joe and Manuel go into the room. Look at Fred. Manuel crosses himself. Joe looks irritated, then regretful.

'Well, that's blown it. Never mind, he had to go in another day or two, anyway.'

Manuel is mumbling prayers.

'Why are you carrying on like that? The man's been dead for three days.'

'It's a stage of bereavement. I'm only just now accepting it.'

'Oh, shut up.'

'Sí, sí.'

Manuel leaves the room; pops his head guiltily into Morag's room. And there she is, sitting on her bed, pale and trembling. *She knows,* he thinks. Then realises it's just Fred's death that she knows. There she sits, surrounded by pretence and lies. Healthy bodies purported to be ill, corpses pretending to be alive. What has he said to her that is the truth?

'Moragita,' he whispers, from the depths of self-loathing.

'He's dead, isn't he? The man in the room down the hall.'

'Yes. That man, he died. Sadly.'

'Am I really dying too, Manny? Is this really happening? I thought I really believed it, but I guess not, because now I feel so, so frightened. I feel like hell, Manny. Am I really and truly dying? Tell me the truth.'

He enters the room and shuts the door. Before he can move towards her, she is up and around him. Her hands go all over his chest and back, rove like hungry beasts, then settle in for a tight stranglehold around his middle, while she presses her face onto his shoulder. For a first contact, it is surprisingly un-erotic. He stands and lets her take what she wants. Comfort, solidity, safety? She's not wanting sex, that much is abundantly clear.

'Am I dying?' she whimpers. 'I can't be. I can't be. Am I, Manny?'

Then his hands and arms go around her, stroke the back of her head, the small of her back.

'Shh, shh,' he says.

'Tell me.'

'Hush hush.'

She gives a little yelp and seems to swoon, so he has to hold tighter, and slopes her over to the bed. Lays her down, covers her up, while she weeps silently, surrenders in every pore to her imminent demise.

'I will be back later, Moragita. I have to do a few things, then I will be back. Ay, caramba!'

'Kiss me,' she says, or thinks she says; he makes no sign that he hears.

But later, waking from the sleep that she has cried herself into, she does not open her eyes and think – oh my God, I am still dying. She thinks – *not dead yet.* And this seems so lucky, such a relief, so amazing, that she laughs out loud. It is waking up from a bad dream, multiplied by a hundred. Meanwhile, deep in her psyche, a different defeat is being conceded. The news has travelled back from all her muscles and skin;

contact with Manuel is not repulsive. It is not repulsive. Not even one little bit repulsive.

June Sits with her Penguin

She is on the bit where the mother and son get physical – Lawrencian style. All flowers and currents running. Industrial England wafts off the page – coal and dampness and fecundity. She reads the same sentence over and over and frowns. The phone begins to ring and she gets up to answer, gladly letting the book slide off the table. Stupid story, anyway. No connection to reality. Mothers never feel that way about their sons. Absolutely ridiculous.

'Hello? Joe? You sound funny. Have I forgotten something? Did you pick up your peanut butter sandwich?

'What?

'Fred? Oh dear. Are you sure? Well, I suppose he had a long life. Still … nothing will be the same now. There's always been Fred, hasn't there?

'What, Joe?

'Sure, I can tell Robbie and Carson. I'll just pop over now. Poor things, they'll really miss him.'

June takes Moze with her, or Moze takes June. They both amble over the road to the Snelling house. There is no sign of life, aside from all the bird racket and the very distant hum of traffic. A little breeze keeps the heat from being unpleasant and June, as is her wont, lifts her face and half-shuts her eyes to catch the full pleasantness of the moment. She may be sixty-six years old, but nothing in her body tells her this. Her step has life in it, her mind registers no aches or pains, or even fatigue. June, as ever, floats. But then, she is living a soporific life. She is rich, her husband loves her, her house was bought pre-Proposition 13.

'Hello! Yoo-hoo! Anybody home?'

'Oh, hi June; come on in,' calls Robbie from the shadowy interior.

June enters, timid now because she has just realised that she hasn't been inside this house in more than ten years. She has always been the visited, not the visitor.

'How are you, June? Anything up? You look a little puzzled,' says Carson, still in her old tartan robe.

'I'm fine, kids, honestly. I like how you, uh, changed this room.'

The room is a murky yellow, obviously unpainted for years, but she feels the need to explain her staring.

'Well, thanks, June. I guess we got fed up with the new painted look, so now we're going for neglect. It seems so much less formal.'

'Oh Robbie, you are so funny.'

'I know. Do you want to sit down?'

'No, that's okay.' She yawns. 'I guess I'd better get going.'

'Taking Moze for a walk today, are you?'

'Yes, Joe's just so busy. You know life at Gentle Valleys.' Another yawn. 'Oh!'

'What is it?'

'Ah. I have some very sad news, I'm afraid. Joe didn't want to tell you on the phone, so here I am. Do you think you should sit down?'

'That's okay. What is it, June?' Robbie winks at Carson, discreetly.

'Well, you can stand if you want, though sitting down's mostly what I think you should do. But you're not kids any more, really, and you must do what you like. I like young people to have minds of their own. It's a good sign. Stand away, I say!'

'Okay, okay, we're sitting now.'

'Good. That feels right. I knew you'd come to the right decision.'

'So, June: tell us.'

'Right.' She gathers her hands together in a prayer position. 'I'm very sorry to tell you, your grandfather has – well, he's passed away. Gone. Did you hear me? I bet you're glad you're sitting down now. See? You're in shock. Just breathe, cry, whatever, I'm sure I've got a book at home on what to do. If you just wait here, I'll run and get it.'

'No, listen, that's all right, June. I just can't think what to say. You take Moze for a walk. Thanks for telling us.'

'Yes,' says Carson. 'It's all right, we're all right, don't worry. Thanks.'

And June re-enters the placid Marin day having completed her mission, slobbering Moze in tow. Well, that's done, she thinks. The space in her mind where Fred dwells will not shrink for months, hence warding off re-adjustment shocks. One of June's secrets, even secret from her, is to say no to unpleasant thoughts until they are palatable or old news. (Think of a lock gate in a canal. The boat waits for the level of water to rise before venturing further, hence maximising stability.) And so she continues on her walk, her mind filling with dinner ingredients and television prospects. *Are You Being Served*, 7:30. Tortellinis and salad. *Antiques Roadshow*, 8:30. Rocky road ice cream.

Part Fourteen

I'm not haunting you. Does that relieve you? I'm still alive. This is me; I'm sixteen right now and I'm still happening, the day I'm in is still bright, though it looks like it's raining in yours. Is it? Why is your face wet? I haven't died yet, but I promise you, Father, after I do you will never ever hear from a dead me. Dead is dead. I won't look anything like a person, and I certainly won't be doing any talking to anyone. I'll be air, soil, sunsets and storms. All souls are air, soil, sunsets and storms. I'll be kindness and crankiness and poignancy distilled a million times, released slowly for centuries, till I'm no longer separate from an apple core, a dog's hair, a sea breeze. But this is not the tragedy, Father. Here I am always, and every moment of my life is always happening, and if you can hang on to this kind of eternity, the rest doesn't matter. The tragedy would be having the kind of life you don't want to keep happening. Don't worry, Father; maybe you're only dreaming me. On the other hand, maybe I'm dreaming you. In which case you'd better hope I never wake up, because you'll be dust then. Less than dust. Dust that was never dust. A pocket of wind.

Excerpt from *The Consuela Chronicles*, transcribed by Father Carlos, 1947, Lagunitas. This is the last entry transcribed by Father Carlos. It is thought that her teasing sense of humour and her references to the absence of a spiritual after-life caused him to cease to encourage her. It is well documented that, despite being baptised and confirmed in the Catholic Church, Consuela refused to attend mass after the age of fifteen.

Estimated age of Consuela: sixteen.

Location of apparition: Our Lady of Happiness Church, Fairfax.

Burying Time

June stands by the kitchen window drinking water, and sees cats fighting near the bird feeder again. She hates it, but not enough to go outside; clap her hands to shoo the cats and warn the birds. When she remembers she nags Joe to get rid of the bird feeder and he says he will, but there it still stands. On the other hand Joe, who is still combing his hair in the bathroom, always purposefully fills the bird feeder – not to be a carnage spectator but to encourage nature, give it a little nudge. Just as he buys goldfish for the pond to feed the racoons. It is the arbitrary cruelty of nature that he vicariously enjoys.

June holds her breath, frozen, as a fluffy Persian freezes in pounce position under a blue-tit. Joe comes into the kitchen, startles her.

'Joe! Can't you wear shoes instead of sneaking around in your socks?'

'How could I surprise you then, honey?' goosing her and cackling when she squeals.

'Joe!'

A car horn toots. 'Who's that?'

'Just Carson, in our car.'

'Why?'

Joe sighs. 'I've told you, June. Me and Carson are going to the funeral home early to confirm arrangements.'

'Why is it called a funeral home? I mean, why would a funeral even need a home? Or is it someone's home, used for funerals?'

'What? I don't know, June; will you please pay attention? Robbie will pick you up around ten.'

'Oh good, I'm glad,' looking like she's just been invited on a double date and she got her first choice of man. 'You go off now and have fun and drive carefully.'

'Okay, see you there.'

'Aren't you forgetting something, honey?'

'My wallet? Have you been playing games again?'

'No.'

'The keys?'

'Nope. Here's a hint.' She puckers up her mouth, a wrinkled soft squishy suction organ.

Joe kisses her hard, then soft and long. The car horn toots again.

'No wonder all the girls chase you.'

'Used to chase, you mean.'

'Have they stopped,' she asks, genuinely interested. 'When did they stop?'

Joe leaves and June goes into the bathroom to do her makeup and hair. She stares at her face in the mirror. Just looks for two seconds, in disbelief, then shrugs and concentrates on her eyes. Smoothes a little blue shadow on her lids. Some concealer under her eyes. Avoids other parts of her face, but rests her eyes on her eyes, where she is still recognisably herself. Then looks in her closet for some funeral clothes. She has done this quite a few times before, but not enough to feel she's got the complete hang of it. Her grey floral Laura Ashley, or her cream linen suit? Pauses in front of her closet door, then hears a noise. A small scuffling noise.

'Fred? Is that you, you naughty boy, wandering off all the time like that? I'll be there in a minute.'

A brave day-time racoon slips through the garden, dragging some of her garbage, and she realises that the house is empty, truly and permanently Fred-free. Her words, having no other ears to lodge in, seem to linger on the air. The word Fred is absorbed into the summer air and walls of the house, and finally the remains get swallowed by June, who has to nod her head several times to do this. After some time of staring and sighing, she chooses the Laura Ashley. Classy but not too sombre. Then she sits in her chair and picks up her Penguin to wait for her true love.

A Snelling Funeral at Our Lady of Happiness

'Whoaa there, Father, you're bogarting.'

'Sorry, Robbie,' says Father Reilly in the high-pitched voice of someone holding their breath. He passes the joint to Robbie. Robbie sucks it in. They are in the shade, leaning against the pale cool walls at the back of Our Lady of Happiness. The glaring day has driven them to it. That and the job ahead – the seeing-off of Fred Snelling.

'I don't feel anything,' complains Father Reilly, who has never tried marijuana before but has convinced himself it could be a legitimate alternative to the booze. *If* it works. 'I should've stuck to the whisky.'

'It'll hit you in a few minutes. Just wait.'

'Roll another one, it isn't working.'

'Well, okay; sure, Father. If you're sure.'

'Just roll it; the mass starts in about five minutes.'

Robbie does so, quickly, and lights it. Has one puff, then gives it to the red-faced priest.

'Keep it, Father. Hope it does the job.'

'Hey,' whispers Robbie as he slides into the pew behind Joe, Carson, Georgia-May and a relative he only vaguely recognises. Fred had been a great family man, only not with his own family. They turn around and acknowledge Robbie proudly with their public grieving faces as if to say: no-one can say that we don't know how to grieve! But then most people have an unerring instinct for such matters, and Robbie is not impressed. Behind are two dozen well-dressed sombre mourners. Robbie frowns at them. Who are they, extras in the cast? Or a service provided by the funeral home at a small supplementary cost? Which reminds him – exactly who is paying for all this?

The priest begins to walk up the aisle with a very slight smile tucked into his belly, and Robbie whispers to Joe,

'Where's June?'

'What do you mean, where's June? Didn't you pick her up?' Joe mentally refers to his list of things Robbie has forgotten: times he's been late or not turned up. This gives him more pleasure than he'd admit to.

'No.'

'I told you we had to go early, and I asked you to give her a lift,' hisses Joe.

Father Reilly removes some red satin vestments and clears his throat. Experiences a strange lightness, feels as if his head is trying to lift off his neck. It alarms him that this does not alarm him. Robbie blushes angrily. Joe has no right to speak to him like this. He goes too far.

'Joe, I'm afraid you did not.'

'Did.'

'When?'

'Yesterday, I left a message on your …'

'Well that was pretty asinine,' raising his voice here, and becoming the focus of the congregation nearest. 'What *on earth* makes you think I listen to my machine? What kind of sad bastard listens to their fucking messages? The whole idea is to avoid communicating. Christ, Joe.'

The organ music begins. After a nudge from an altar boy the priest indicates to the other two altar boys that their slow dance can commence. Incense wafts, joints creak and the congregation rises. Joe turns his angry righteous face away, so no-one sees his suddenly worried and sad face. He is imagining June home alone, waiting and waiting, maybe getting worried, and reflects that the main problem with being mean to someone a lot is that you end up feeling sorry for them the rest of the time. Then he remembers – and this is a very rare remembrance indeed, his secret – that he never once felt handsome until June went out with him, and he never felt loveable till June agreed to marry him. Joe has not always been this Joe. June created the strong cocky Joe, who blames Robbie for most things.

'This is so totally fucked,' mouths Robbie to Carson and the church in general.

'I know,' she says.

But a smile creeps out in Carson's eyes, oh yes it does. She loves her brother. It hits her like a barrage, a tidal wave; she adores him unreservedly. Joe and Georgia-May are there in the swooning swamp too, definitely an integral part, and June would be if she was here.

◆◆◆◆

June's head drops and her mouth drools slightly. The hairs on her chin and upper lip quiver with her breath. When her book drops, she jerks awake.

'Joe? Robbie?'

She tsks, feeling the edges of crankiness now. They'll be late if they don't hurry up. She looks at her watch, then looks again. Then she does the things she always does when suddenly doubtful. A June reality check. Checks the newspaper. Yup – right date. Wednesday – funeral day. It is marked on her calendar in the kitchen, but she checks that too, just in case. So where is everyone? The funeral will soon be over. In her hurry to go to the front door to see if a car is outside, she trips over Moze.

'Moze!' she says, exasperated. 'Move, you big lump.'

But the old dog does not move. In fact, not one part of her seems to be moving. She has slipped into the slipstream of Fred's departure.

◆◆◆◆

After what seems an unusually long time of just staring at the congregation as if waiting for them to speak, the priest puts his sheets of paper down and begins his sermon.

'Some people, some people … well, some people are the refrigerator noise you don't notice till the fridge stops working and your beer is warm.'

Great opening line; everyone perks up.

'Some folk are clocks that tick quietly, precisely, and we – the world of flawed creatures – we imagine that we need these folk as background in our lives; we function better because they are ticking away, humming away, and do not require attention. They are reliable. Then one day their battery is flat, and we do not wake to their alarm ringing; we sleep in and our day is disordered.'

Pause.

'Frederick Snelling was around a very long time. A very very ... very long time. He had probably become absorbed into the background of a few folk's lives. Most people here will have known him their entire lives.' He peers at the congregation. 'Indeed, I'm sure none of you knew a time when Fred did not exist. Frederick *overlapped* us all. And like the fridge that finally hums its last hum, one of those curved heavy fifties jobs that never break down, it will be a while before this fact really sinks in. Before the, uh, cold beer is missed.'

He pauses, looks dreamy, seems to forget where he is. Nice cold beer, his eyes are saying. 'And when it does, it, I mean he, will be really, uh, really missed.' He looks at his notes and continues in a monotone. 'Frederick will live on in God's kingdom, or in the world around you, however you perceive immortality. Dust to dust, ashes to ashes.'

Here he pauses, gauges the congregation. Or the air above the congregation. Continues with a disarming friendly tone.

'But let's face it, when you get right down to it, dust just isn't the same. Is it? I mean, does dust offer you a drink? Does dust laugh at your jokes? Fred will be missed. Possibly some of you will be wanting to tell him, right now, about this event. And my feeble, er, humble attempt to honour him.'

An altar boy farts like they do, discreetly, in the pause. Father Reilly feels a giggle fit swelling up, turns and coughs into his hands, clenches his fists till his fingernails cause pain, and by some physiological displacement his suppressed giggles turn into tears and a runny nose. An altar boy sniggers, which threatens to infect the other altar boys. For a second the entire altar troupe teeters on the edge of hysteria. They all want to shriek with laughter till they pee in their pants. In a way, being stoned helps here, because Father Reilly senses all this supernaturally fast and manfully grabs control. Wipes his face, blows his nose, turns back to face the church.

'Excuse me. I'm sorry.' Blows his nose again. 'But it is such a hard thing to say goodbye. So many sombre emotions ... '

This works for twenty-seven seconds, until he looks up and makes eye contact with Robbie Snelling, who has the serious expression that he habitually reserves for concealing being stoned. Father Reilly is not aware that he is about to laugh; the marijuana may make him sensitive to atmosphere, but it has played havoc with the mouth-to-brain messages that normally alert his brain about things like laughter. Which is why, when the air explodes out of his mouth in a braying wheezy bleat, it is almost like projectile vomiting. He has salivated more than usual, and he sprays most of the front row. Joe wipes his face with a tissue.

By some great good fortune, after the initial shocked silence during which Father Reilly is almost doubled over and on the verge of suffocation, his strange laugh is interpreted by the congregation as some kind of nervous affliction, or even illness. It is too bizarre, too silent and painful, to be anything else. One of the ladies who normally does the flowers, appears next to him and offers him a bottle of spring water along with an expression of extreme concern. He drinks the water. Clears his voice. His stomach aches.

'I'm better now. Thank you, thank you for your patience.' He pauses while he feels another mood take hold. His voice lowers, somehow acquires a slightly southern accent. 'The Lord moves in mysterious ways. And he causes some mysterious things to grow on this mysterious earth. Feel the mystery. Open your hearts and minds and souls, and love the Lord!'

He looks around, perhaps hoping for some raised hands, some evangelical responses. *Yeah I feel it, you've got the stuff, Father; praise the Lord!* Finding nothing but bemused expressions and dry eyes, his Pentecostal mood fades and he refers to his notes and reads in a solemn tone, his standard agnostic funeral piece, partially lifted from *The Consuela Chronicles*:

'Life, like love, like the earth and all the planets and stars, exists separately from us. This is hard to comprehend, in our daily busy lives. We are born where we are and who we are by some miraculous combination of biology and chance, and we plug into all this life floating around as if it is ours. As if it does not pre-exist us. Then one day, one calm resigned or violently sudden day, we slip out of the world and it is never again witnessed by us. It can be hard to bear, this indifference.

'My advice to grieving people is to re-visit their lost ones in the places they lived their deepest selves. Not the place of their death, but the hill-top where they loved to picnic, the fireside chair where they sat reading, the coastal road they loved to drive. Close your eyes and listen. Unfurl your heart and breathe deeply. These lost *missed* souls will still be there somewhere. Their voices will echo. Perhaps your missing will summon them. Time may not be linear, though life is finite.

'Mainly, do not stop loving the person who has died. Not because that person will know, but because the state of loving will make you more open to life. Much more open than the state of hardened defensive loss. Keep your heart unfurled.' Pause, while he looks at the air above the heads of the congregation. 'I kinda like that word, don't you? Unfurled.'

Father Reilly stops talking again and mimes a flag unfurling with his hands, a dopey smile on his gentle face. Several of the congregation imitate his hand motions unconsciously.

'Remember that one day someone may wish to get another glimpse of *you*. Make sure it is a happy glimpse. Be thankful that you have found a way to live and love, blindly, with or without the help of a god. It is with great and fortuitous good luck you are here.'

He looks up and smiles. He loves this part. He has them, he drinks in their attention, he should have been an actor, goddamn it. He looks heavenward and smiles.

'Frederick Snelling, we will remember you with joy and delight. Thank you for your life.'

◆◆◆◆

Morag stands at the back of the church. It has taken some doing to get out of the hospice and walk down here, but she's made it, and she doesn't feel in the least danger of collapsing. The furry animal has taken a rest. This is where she wants to be this sunny day, saying goodbye to Fred, though she hadn't even known his name till a few days ago. Her middle-of-the-night talk with him opened a few windows and she is grateful, and is not going to quibble with the ethical issues of being grateful to a corpse. One takes solace where one can.

She recognises Carson sitting in one of the front pews alongside Joe Johnson, the hospice owner. They seem a bit agitated, but that's only natural. Probably they are restraining their tears; that's what shaking shoulders usually means. She tries to imagine her own offspring, had she had them – the boy named Ross and the girl named Sarah: the laughing children in the park photographs, the shadow-ghosts who have followed her across the continent. Ross and Sarah at their mother's funeral brings a tear to her eye. But her imagination is too vivid, and she suddenly feels their acute resentment that she'd spent all their inheritance with her new gold credit card. Maybe they wouldn't be crying but whispering in the pews, telling each other to look out for receipts so they could return some of the new stuff, try to recoup their loses. After all the times she had oatmeal cookies waiting for them when they came home from school on cold winter days! Well okay, but there would have been at least one day like that. That must count for something in the end. One genuine tear shed, anyway. Ungrateful bairns!

Oh, to hell with it; she might as well have a good cry now, since there was no guarantee there'd be any real tears at her own funeral.

Morag goes to town with crying. She's had so much practise now that no-one would believe she'd been a novice crier as recently as three weeks ago. She cries uninhibitedly for herself and for the loss of her listener, Fred. Crying feels good, and very like laughing.

Father Reilly looks up to see who is actually crying for old Fred, and assumes she is an old flame. Not as old as Fred by a long shot; maybe she is even an illegitimate daughter … she is really giving it all she's got. Oh, well; good to know old Fred had had it in him, one way or another.

Not another eye is wet. The girls are mostly checking out the boys, the women are checking out the other women's dresses, and the men are thinking about football teams that might beat the team most Snellings support. The religious among them – well, the only religious Snelling, a cousin called Millicent from the valley who keeps eleven cats – is praying, but keeps getting side-tracked by all the souls in purgatory, her favourite location to aim prayers. She keeps having to shake herself, grip her prayers, which feel like a slow flowing river emanating from her upper chest, and divert them towards her mental picture of Fred. But maybe that's the problem. When she had really looked at him last he'd been half-drunk and snoring on her couch, twenty-five years ago at her own daughter's wedding. Fred had smelled of garlic and bourbon, and burped loudly in his slumber.

Behind Bernadette are an old man and a young woman – Harold and Maud, reversed. Fred's funeral is giving them a legitimate situation in which to express their continual and inexplicable grief over nothing. They will sit in the same seats later in the afternoon, for another funeral. Father Reilly has his fans, though his new angle on things has shaken them a bit.

Joe's blood pressure is aiming for an all-time high: yet another blunder to add to the history of Snelling fuck-ups he has witnessed. Leaving his wife behind! Robbie is to blame; he always is. Carson, however, is still smiling, her love for Snellingdom and the world in general vibrating through her and making her feel giddy and in the right place. Robbie has his defensive I-did-too-do-my-chores look, and Georgia-May is wishing she'd brought her youngest so she'd have an excuse to sit at the back and nurse. Her breasts are killing her; on the verge of gushing out all over the altar. Great lakes of milk that the priest could slip in. They hear Morag, but do not turn around. This particular branch of humanity are not truly interested in anyone else. Not today.

Father Reilly drones now; the creative part is over. Tells them to sit, stand, genuflect. The Latin version has been a special request phoned in by June, for whom understanding words is secondary to comprehension. No-one knows what the priest is saying. A sort of medieval stupor drops over most of them.

Morag blows her nose loudly, and feels tired but better because she's just had an important realisation. The last twenty-three years suddenly seem like a mere bleep on her life register: a hiccup, an aberration, an experiment. Her heart is not here, and that explains her cancer. Her own cells have rebelled against North America!

Forgetting her fear of the cold and her new appreciation of Golden Hills Mall she decides, yet again, that she'll just go back to Scotland and that'll fix everything. Reverse all the carcinogenic effects of Marin. Of course, she'll use the ticket she bought with Carson. She blows her nose again, loudly enough to distract Carson from her own realisation: I am in the right place after all, thinks Carson. I am a Snelling in my bones and this is my home. I will not go to Scotland. She gives Robbie a wink, which he misinterprets and hands her a disgusting piece of toilet paper.

At the end, when it finally comes, Joe almost claps his hands. He's gone so far into his angry-at-Robbie dream that he's forgotten he's at a funeral and not at yet another boring long amateur theatre production. The relief is so intense that it's almost worth the agony.

The casket, destined for cremation, is taken back to the hearse by the funeral home men, six strangers who disguise their opinion of a family whose members don't want to carry the casket themselves. Joe and Robbie and all the other males present assume that the six strangers *are* family. Joe catches himself wondering, not for the first time, if they slip the body out of the expensive coffin before the flames to sell again and again. Half of him hopes they do. He would. Such a waste, otherwise. The other half of him plans to report his suspicions to the sheriff. He catches Carson's and Georgia-May's hands arrested half-way to applauding too, and they all exchange a quick smile. Well, that's laid Fred to rest; thank God it's over, and let's eat.

Outside the church Robbie and Carson, the only descendants of the Fred line, assume a grief-stricken look to meet the consolations of all the other guests. To accept the hugs, hand-squeezing, arm-touching, kisses on cheeks; to breathe in all the different perfumes, deodorants, perspiration and bad breaths. It takes a lot of concentration to remember to respond appropriately to the comments, not to mention what a grand thing it will be not to have to smell soiled diapers or be woken by midnight wanderings.

'It was a blessing in the end; now he's at peace,' is an acceptable phrase. But not, for instance, 'Thought he'd never buzz off, the old fart.'

Joe stands half-hidden behind the two Snellings, watching. So engrossing is this public display of funeral etiquette that he forgets he is angry at Robbie. He even forgets June and her absence.

'Joe! Here I am, Joe! Yoo-hoo!'

And there is an old lady getting out of a taxi, turning around to pay the driver; so he thinks for a minute that it's some old auntie come late. When June turns he thinks that the aunt looks familiar; then all at once June's features spin into June, and he shakes himself and is very relieved he's not said anything to give away the fact he sometimes forgets not just little things, but very major things too. Joe Johnson, officially, has no weaknesses. Especially silly girly weaknesses like senility. Johnson brains are invincible; Georgia-May and her children are proof. June, of course, not being born a Johnson, is an exception; is allowed humility and is patronised in the nicest possible way.

'Joe, dear, I'm afraid I have some bad news.'

She stumbles up to him, her face a picture of anxiety.

'No, no; it's all right, June: Robbie's here. It was his fault; he forgot to pick you up.'

'Oh, it doesn't matter about that. Robbie's just fine. How did the funeral go anyway?'

'Great, just great, June. Now hurry up – what's the news? I made a reservation at The Towers for lunch. We have to get a move on.'

'The news?'

'Yeah honey, you said you had some bad news for me.'

'Oh! Oh dear.' She fidgeted with her rings. 'Joe, this is really terrible. But I'm afraid Moze is, well, no more.'

Joe feels his heart literally sink. It slips down his shirt, under his belt, out of his trouser legs and starts melting on the hot heartless sidewalk. He winces. Moze! Mozey-Wozey!

'Are you sure?'

'Pretty sure, honey. I'm so sorry.'

'What do you mean, pretty sure?'

'Well, she' s not breathing, and when I stood on her, she …'

'You *stood* on her,' Joe says so loudly that Robbie comes over to see what the fuss is.

'Well, she was in the way, and I tripped.'

'June.' Joe puts his hands on her shoulders and speaks an inch from her face. 'June, tell me the truth. Did you kill Moze?'

'Joe!' says Robbie, moving protectively towards June.

'No! Of course not, Joe! I was just telling you. She's dead,' she whispers.

'Who's dead?' asks Robbie.

'June thinks she killed the dog.'

'I did not, Joe; that is so unfair. The dog, *your dog*, is dead.'

'Moze is dead too? Talk about bad timing,' says Robbie.

'But you're not sure,' says Joe, who feels dizzy.

'I'm sure. I mean, dead is dead, Joe. You know that.'

'Not necessarily,' says Robbie. They both stare at him. 'Sometimes death can masquerade as life. Or, or alive can, uh, look dead.'

'Robbie is right. Did you try artificial respiration?'

◆◆◆◆

Over by the palms Carson has just spotted Morag and instantly THE IDEA returns to her mind, causing her heart to race with guilt. The chance to travel with such an interesting woman strikes her as enormously lucky. Morag would ease Carson's way into the universe-that-does-not-know-Carson. If Carson actually went to Scotland with her, that is. If Carson left her brother, which she will not. But how to tell Morag? Then she notices Morag's puffy eyes and for two seconds comes to the same conclusion as Father Reilly. Wonders if indeed Morag is one of Fred's old flames, despite the age difference. Maybe her nickname is Obolomio. Or just Bolo, and he'd been saying Oh bolo mio! My Bolo. Maybe that was the true reason she'd been loitering in Gentle Valleys garden, and disease was just a cover story. Hard-core groupie, there for the last flashes of Fred. His soul streaking out of the window and dissolving in the glare of a September sun. Had he been a great lover? How surprisingly lovely to think so. But no. No. Fred may have been a great lover, but not with Morag. Look at her! She is an honest daytime kind of woman, and obviously chaste.

The two women smile at each other, incline heads and move away from the funeral crowd. Carson takes Morag's arm and faint girlish laughter is heard from their direction.

Robbie slaps Father Reilly on the shoulder and says:

'Nice one, Father. Not too bad at all,' and slips a few joints into his vestment pocket.

'Nice of you to say so,' he replies. Then adds, 'Do I have your number?'

Morag Orders Tea

She slips inside the restaurant door, feeling naughtier than she's felt in years. A funeral party gate-crasher, an uninvited guest! What if someone speaks to her? But Carson has insisted she come. Said she had something else to tell her, about the trip. Lovely girl, Carson. Reminds her of someone. (Herself.) They will have such a lovely time together in Inverness. Carson's face had looked so worried, nervous even, when Morag mentioned the trip, but that was probably because of the occasion.

She decides to chat to Carson later; leave her with her own family just now, and sits next to a sedate woman who smells of cat. Morag orders a pot of tea and observes the room calmly. Now the funeral is over, some kind of reaction seems to be setting in. But the nosiest mourner is not one of the grandchildren or relatives, but the hospice owner. Joe Johnson. His wife is patting him on the back and offering him clean tissues while he swigs down bourbon and howls and (there's no other word for it) howls. Carson and her brother, sitting at the same table, are simultaneously smoking cigarettes, swigging gins and picking at their tacos. It seems like a weird meal to serve after a funeral, but then all these Californians are a bit weird, she decides. She is getting out in the nick of time. A whole state of loonies. Well, she'll give them not another week of her life.

Her tea arrives and she tries to engage the cat pee woman in a conversation about the weather, but it peters out after the woman contradicts her.

'Hot today, isn't it?'

'Call this hot!'

At the mourner's table Joe is saying, between sobs:

'I don't think I can bear it. She was my best friend. I loved that goddamned dog.'

An ancient aunt, who mistakes Joe for a relative, comes up and takes his hand.

'My deepest sympathy. He was a good man. If there's anything I can do.'

'What? I can't bear going home and knowing she won't be at the door, slobbering all over my suit. The garbage will never be dragged across the floor again.'

'Yes, he had some endearing habits, didn't he. We'll all miss him.'

'Her.'

The aunt looks worryingly at the others, who quickly cover.

'He's just beside himself. Takes it all way too personally each time.'

'Wrong line of work, perhaps,' says June, pleased with her cleverness. 'I think I'd better get him home,' she whispers to Robbie.

Dog Ponds

It is surprisingly easy to forget unpleasant chores. Like telling people that you are going to stand them up. Carson not only forgets to tell Morag that she's changed her mind about Scotland, she forgets that Morag is in the restaurant, and has walked out, right past her. Still, she has a job to do. A very important job.

Carson, Robbie and Georgia-May between them lug yet another corpse, the body of Moze. They go out of the back door and down the steps into the blinding heat.

'Can't we just phone a dog corpse disposal unit or something?' whines Georgia-May.

'Or just hire a few Mexicans to dig a hole?'

'Look, we're almost there. Joe said to use the fish pond.'

'But Robbie, the fish pond has, like, fish in it. And water. You know, it's a pond. What are we going to do, launch Moze and sail her?'

'It's basically a hole, you dope. It's deep enough, and besides the ground is too hard in this heat to dig. Completely dried out.'

'Cremation's a pretty efficient way to deal with things like this,' mumbles Georgia-May.

'Georgia-May, just shut up, will you.'

'It's all right for you guys; I've got two kids waiting at home, and …'

'Yeah, yeah, we know, and we have no idea what it's like to be an adult, not having any kids ourselves.'

Georgia-May drops her end of the dog, which leads to the whole dog falling with a soft thlump and the dust rises. Fuck you, say Georgia-May's eyes.

'Look, Georgia-May, why don't you just go on home? We'll manage fine,' says Carson.

'Yeah, but first go out to the garage and see if your dad has run out of beer or if he's being sick, or whatever. Next thing, we'll have to haul his ass into the house.'

'Jesus,' says Georgia-May, marching off.

Carson watches her old friend's quivering indignant back, her frugal Mervyns' tennis shoes scuffing through the yellow grass. Georgia-May, despite all the trappings of maturity, is so endearingly not mature.

'What's her problem? You'd think Fred was *her* grandfather,' she says to her brother. 'We don't have to do this at all. It's her dad; her dad's dead dog. Spoiled brat.'

'Right, well, whatever. Let's get this over with,' says Robbie, pragmatic.

They drag the dog to the pond, where the whole idea starts to look strange. A dragonfly hovers over the lily pads, while under the surface gold-freckled fish hunker down on the cool muddy bottom. The tranquillity defies them.

'Are you sure this is the right thing to do?' asks Carson.

'Joe said.'

'Yeah, but Joe is a bit, you know. Today, especially.'

'No, he said it even before today. He always said Moze would end up a part of the landscape in this garden. This pond is just a temporary pond – it was always intended as a dog grave.'

'Bizarre.'

'Not really. I understand it,' says Robbie with superiority. As if she has no right to judge someone she is willing to abandon for a foreign country. By purchasing her air ticket she has abdicated opinions, and is only tolerated if she minds her manners. Traitors forever forfeit the right to doubt!

Carson sighs. It is so hot. She hates it being so hot.

'Oh well. Do you think Joe wants to say a final goodbye?' she says.

'I don't think Joe can move at the moment. He can't cope. He loved Moze.'

'I know.'

'No, I mean he really *loved* this dog. His heart is fucking broken. Moze was his child. His mother. His … '

'Not his wife.'

'No, not his wife. Or maybe a little bit. Still, he said we were to take over, he said he couldn't even look at her. Probably throw himself into the pond with her, and then we'd have a real job on our hands.'

'Right, well; you take her back paws and we'll swing her in.'

One two three, splash! The dog sinks three feet to the bottom; old hairs float to surface, as do panic-stricken goldfish.

'Shit! I'm soaked. Now what?'

'Here,' giving her a spade. 'We remove this flower bed and compost and dump it in. It's all loose soil, it'll be easy.'

'What, just fill in the whole thing? It'll be mud city.'

'Look, I don't know. It's hot. Do you think I've done this before? Just do it.'

Three minutes of digging.

'Wow, I'm boiling. How about a beer?'

'Yeah. Beer and a little break in the shade.'

'Oh bolmio.'

'What?'

'You heard me.'

'Oh *bolomio.* You didn't say it right. There's got to be two *o*'s in it. See, you're forgetting all that important stuff already and you aren't even gone yet. Moron.'

Carson opens her mouth, then closes it.

◆◆◆◆

Meanwhile, in the garage:

'Joe, oh dear Joe, do you think you can stand up? Oh look, here comes Carson to help us.'

'Georgia-May, Mom.'

'What?'

'My name's Georgia-May.'

'That's what I just said, honey, now do you think if you get Daddy's other side, we can get him up all right? That's it; now I'll open the door if you just prop him up for a second. Oh dear! I bet that hurt.'

'Mom, he's not conscious. He's not feeling any of this.'

'No. Well, maybe we'll just leave him here then, if he doesn't know any better.'

'What, right here, in the oil patch by the drier?'

'Well, I suppose I could go get a pillow and put it under his head.'

'Oh, all right. Let him sleep it off. Wake up for the memorial sunset service.'

'The what?'

'Nothing. Look, Mom, I've got to go; the kids will be starving. I'm real sorry about Moze.'

'Are you, dear? Why?'

'Because … oh, never mind.'

◆◆◆◆

Georgia-May gets in her Ford Fiesta with that familiar feeling that she is leaving insanity. Home, immersed in too long, is always detrimental to her mental state. Lucky old Carson and Robbie, they never get this claustrophobic feeling. No wonder all her favourite childhood books – in fact, all her generation's favourite books – have been about orphans. Well, it was all right for some people.

She grumbles out loud all the way back to her house, where her children wait to pull her into their own unique sphere of insanity. She quickly attends to their most pressing needs, nurses the baby, wipes bottoms, sets food out, switches on the telly, heats the kettle, then turns to her husband, who is hiding in a beanbag on the floor, playing with a Gameboy.

'What are you doing?'

'Uh. Peeling carrots. So how was the funeral? Fun?' Oh yes, he does have a voice, but still no name. Georgia-May pauses. Sarcasm is not his usual tone. It's hers, not his.

'Oh yeah. Fun, fun, fun! You know, *death*. Guess you're jealous. Well, thanks.'

'You're welcome.'

'I mean really, thanks a lot, looks like you've been working your butt off here.'

'You noticed, huh?'

'Oh yeah, sure, you really know how to get a job done. You know, finishing things off properly.'

He does a quick mental check list of the previous three hours, and instantly realises she is talking about: 1. The new toilet roll on top of the toilet, while the empty roll still sits in its holder. 2. The garbage that has been emptied, but not replaced by a new bag. 3. The dishwasher filled, but not turned on. 4. The washing machine – run, but not emptied.

'Ungrateful, that's you,' he says defensively.

'Tell me please, because I just really wonder,' she says, as hatefully as she can manage which is not difficult because she does really loathe him in this minute: 'tell me, does it take a special skill to finish these little jobs, and are you deficient? Or is it just that they are boring stupid chores, and you feel above them? That your time is more precious than mine?' She glares; he looks un-contrite and sulky. Both toddler and baby freeze, tuning into the tone. Georgia-May, perfect mommy and housewife, does not often use this tone.

'Oh fuck off,' says her husband, pleasantly enough, so Chloe goes happily back to shoving small cars into the video slot and the infant goes back to gnawing her own fist. 'What's your problem? I cleaned the windows last week.'

Georgia-May has been married five years. In that time, she has contemplated leaving her husband for Adam (or someone like Adam) one hundred and ninety-nine times. This is her two hundredth time. But this time, it is different because she has an epiphany. One of those short-lived bursts of clarity that occasionally come to the domestically-challenged and sleep-deprived. She realises that with each time she hasn't left him but stayed while things got bearable again, it has made it less likely that she will leave him next time. Like giving up cigarettes. She has got through the first two hundred unsatisfied cravings without collapsing, so why quit now? And then, while her toddler waters the carpet with milk from her bottle and her baby starts crying and her husband scratches his groin right in front of her, she sees that the days of her life rolling out ahead of her are not just her days, but their days as well. They will all continue together, accumulating common memories, imperfect, grating, alternating times of friction with times of unexpected ease. And yes, even times of gratitude, though these may never be expressed. Is this all right? Is it enough?

'Do you love me?'

'Jesus, Georgia-May, what kind of question is that? No, as a matter of fact. I can't stand you. What do you think?'

'Oh good, that's a relief, because I have to say I hate you as much as ever. Maybe more. Probably more and more with every passing day. In fact, you are my heart's repulsion. The hate of my life.'

'Guess we're well-suited then,' says Steven, smiling warmly. (He has just come marginally into sharper focus for Georgia-May, hence his acquisition of a name.)

'Go change that damn toilet roll before I give your Gameboy a virus. Gameboy! How old are you, anyway? Pathetic.'

'God, you are such a snob.'

And he heaves himself off the beanbag, scoops up the baby and blows noises on her soft fat belly, filling the house with infant hysteria. The toddler runs up to him and cries to be included.

This is how it will go, Georgia-May tells herself. Or how it might go, if they survive each other's bad tempers. They will have a back-assed marriage. Here they are at the beginning, hardly liking, respecting, or in her case lately, desiring each other. The opposite of how marriages are supposed to begin. Therefore the romance and passion bit is yet to come. Georgia-May and her husband will come out on the other side of several decades of indifference and mutual contempt, and not be able to keep their hands off each other in public places. They will embarrass their children and shock their grandchildren.

Well, it might be true. It is certainly the case that couples who start out with all the passion are doomed to mundane disappointment. And surely, a good ending is far more important than a good beginning. After all, it's the feeling you're left with at the end of the book that makes you think you've just read a good book or not. Isn't it?

Then the toddler screams because her little sister has just bitten her and her daddy won't spank her little sister so she does, and the doorbell rings and it's the paper boy wanting to be paid for sixteen weeks, and there's a smell of burning in the kitchen because she has let the kettle boil dry again. Georgia-May's grand epiphany fades away into nothing. But just before it does, during the second before she fully responds to all this external chaos, she smiles. Smiles from way down deep. Wasn't it the real redeeming beauty of being human, to keep having epiphanies and keep forgetting, so that you can discover them again and again for the rest of your life? Blessed forgetfulness; blessed trivia that distracts people from important truths. Blissful amnesia.

Part Fifteen

Your best souvenir is your body. No need for photographs or old teddy bears, just look at your hands – they were there at your birth. Look at your eyes – they saw your mama's very first glimpse of you. Imagine! Your feet, the feet you must have hidden somewhere, those same feet once let you walk for the very first time. And your heart, the very same heart, has not once, in all that time, forgotten to beat. I bet you never even think about it. And when you feel kind of fluid and not your age: well it's because, really, you are not. The you that is you. You're a bit like a river. You're moving in one direction, but you are also all the river. You know how the banks feel, and the stones on the bottom, and the rain. Every curve and waterfall, it's all you. All the lives you have lived, live within you. Dip in, dip out. You're five, you're ninety-five, you're forty-five.

Excerpt from *The Consuela Chronicles*, transcribed by Debbie McDougal, Terra Linda, California, 1958.
Consuela's estimated age: twenty-one.
Location of apparition: the parlour in Sycamore House.

What Happens

One more dinner at the Johnson table – the stage is set. Fabric napkins neatly folded, candles lit, jazz playing. All civilised, artsy, contrived and cosy.

Georgia-May, Georgia-May's husband Steven, Chloe, and the baby in her high chair fill four table spaces, observes Joe smugly. A growing tribe of Johnson ambassadors. Excellent. Carson sits next to Robbie, and Joe and June take their usual places at the heads of the table.

'What's for dinner, sweetheart?' asks Joe.

'I told you, Joe. Pizza. It should be here any minute.'

'Pizza? Oh honey, I would've cooked something.'

'But they all wanted pizza, and I thought, why not?'

'But is there even any salad?' Joe frets. The idyllic dinner scene is starting to fragment already. Can't his spouse do her bit, and provide the culinary backdrop to his wit tonight? He fidgets with the pepper grinder.

'Oh, Joe. If you want salad, you know where it is.'

'Have you bought any peppercorns, June? It's empty again.'

'Was it on the list?'

Georgia-May observes the undercurrents, the old familiar routine, the old tensions that rise quicker for being so familiar, yet fade quicker too for the same reason. It's possible that Joe even empties the pepper grinder himself to ensure that the ritual continues.

'Hey, Carson. Is this really your goodbye dinner?' asks Georgia-May.

'Well, yeah.' Because while technically she has changed her mind, she finds herself unable to tell anyone. A kind of paralysis. She can hardly breathe.

'And you're going with that lady from Gentle Valleys? Margo?'

'Morag. Morag McTavish. Yeah, we're going together. Dawn flight. A mere eleven hours.'

'Good for you, Carson,' says June.

Carson blushes, not from embarrassment but from confusion. What is it – some kind of pride that prevents her from admitting it is all a mistake? But no, the big ball is rolling; not only has she been squashed flat by it, she is stuck to it. Like silly putty.

The doorbell rings.

'Joe – it's the pizza boy!' Who is, in fact, a middle-aged Latino man.

'All right, I'll get it,' says Joe. 'How much is it? How much?'

'Fifty-four dollars.'

'Damn, June. Where's my money?'

'You don't have any, dear.'

'Well, where's my chequebook?'

'You're out of cheques. Don't you remember, honey? You went to the bank this morning about it.'

'Well, how the hell am I supposed to pay for these pizzas? Dear?'

Joe frowns at his wife, who adores him, and she knows that it's not a real frown so she just smiles, and everyone pays attention to this tableau, this encapsulating Joe-and-June scene. It is better than TV.

'I'll pay,' says Robbie, reaching for his wallet.

Joe's mouth drops open, then his eyes glaze with gratitude, then defensiveness, when Robbie says he'll take it off the money he owes Joe anyway. From last year.

Robbie goes to the door to negotiate the payment while Joe, June, Georgia-May and Steven debate this old debt and its authenticity. Carson watches the four of them. She notices every nuance, every detail. Even the voices are heightened, and the spicy aroma of the pizza, and June's overpowering perfume. She watches and thinks: this is what is always like here. Nagging, arguing, sarcasm, air thick with historic hurts but also with patterns of forgiveness and lust and affection and tenderness. They act like this all the time, and they will continue to do so. They will re-shuffle these chairs so there is no gap. These people are not friends, thinks Carson. I never chose them, or I don't remember doing so. In fact, I don't even really like them all that much. They must be my family because I can't think of any other reason I'm connected to them.

Robbie returns with the pizza and Carson zips back into life, full of distractions. Her napkin falls to the floor; she reaches over to fetch it, notices that June has bare feet and that they're not too bad for her age, and wonders whether June uses moisturiser on her toes. The thought soothes her. It would be typical of June, to pamper even her old toes in readiness for Joe.

The pizzas are eaten, then an ice-cream cake as well.

'A toast to Carson,' announces Joe, raising his glass of Beaujolais.

'To Carson! We'll miss you. When are you coming back?'

Carson smiles and drinks and cannot speak.

And by eleven it is too late for the truth. Georgia-May has departed with her husband and daughters, after much hugging. The dishwasher hums; June putters around the kitchen happily folding napkins. Carson and Robbie drink a last cognac with Joe.

'Here's to old Fred,' says Robbie. 'He would have been excited for you, Carson.'

'Yeah, in the old days maybe, when he knew what was what.'

'Still,' says Joe, who has sensed an occasion to be eloquent and risen from his drunkenness to answer it. 'Here's to a grand old man who loved you both so very much, and to whom we all owe a great deal. A very great deal,' he says meaningfully for effect, not meaning anything at all.

'Hear, hear, Gramps,' says Robbie raising his glass to the heavens. 'Hope you're finding lots and lots of bolomios up there. Or whatever. Wherever.'

'And here's to the marvellous Moze,' says Carson, anxious to extend the toasts. She is in an out-of-control car careering towards some crucial crossroads, putting on useless brakes. Burning rubber, screeching tyres. Just keep talking. 'Life will never be the same without her unique … her unique …'

'Smell,' says Robbie. 'Oh, Christ, Joe; I'm sorry. I thought you were over that phase. Here, take my hankie. Sorry man, it *is* a little used, try the other side. Wow. Maybe you should get another dog, man.'

◆◆◆◆

Finally, years later, the evening ends. Carson and Robbie stumble over to the yellow house, dark and cool. Carson decides she will not sleep at all tonight, but just wait for dawn and watch herself to see what she'll do. Since she seems incapable of informing herself of her intentions at all. Then a numbness descends on her exactly like a heavy blanket. An awareness that sadness or something very like sadness lay too close to risk being alert. Savour, savour! part of her says. But she can't; the blanket is too heavy, knows the dangers of savouring.

'Think I'll catch a few hours of sleep, Carson. Wake me up when it's time,' he says.

'Yeah, okay. Night-night old buddy. Gonna miss me when I'm gone.'

'I know you, Ryder.' Quoting Grateful Dead lyrics is the code that they use when overly emotional. 'If only you weren't my sis, we could have made such a damn fine couple.'

'Isn't it pretty to think so.' They also quote Hemingway a lot. Well, they are a strange pair.

She sighs and sighs. Hell, and all this angst is self-induced. What is she, a total masochist? And so self-loathing is added to her load. The blanket is so heavy now that she doesn't bother brushing her teeth, but does consider finding a penny to toss.

Cowardice or courage?

Stay or go?

Go, obviously. *Obviously.*

The trouble with epiphanies is that, unlike Georgia-May, Carson does not believe in them. Single moments of truth, of clarity and decision making – she distrusts these. Life, according to Carson, is a long disconnected series of moments which entice an accidental tumble, or cause a lop-sided gait that ends up forcing a person down one path and not another. Simple as that. The known or the unknown, that is the only choice.

Danger or stability?

Go or stay?

Stay, obviously. *Obviously.*

Half an hour later, she tiptoes into her brother's bedroom, notices his smell afresh because she has almost lost it forever, and whispers:

'Hey. Robs.'

'What? What? Is it time already?'

'I'm not going, okay? I changed my mind.'

'Right. Whatever. Turn off the alarm, will you?'

She goes back to bed and slips into a stupor of sleep. She has a second's consciousness to luxuriate in the skin-tingling which precedes oblivion, when oblivion is approaching faster than the loss of consciousness. As if her whole ragged being is being repaired by the knowledge of safety.

Cynthia Rogerson

Finally

Morag feels young. The furry animal is asleep and the low lighting is flattering, so she looks young too. She moves quickly about her room, double-checking that she has everything. Passport, ticket, money, gold credit card. Toothbrush, Lancôme lipstick, two diamond necklaces, a box of sparkly rings, and lots of clothes with the price tags still attached. She takes out one T-shirt. Puts the T-shirt back in. Sighs and paces. She is wearing pale blue silk trousers and a white short-sleeved shirt which, in this very early morning air, leaves her arms in goose-bumps. She finally zips the bag shut and surveys all that she is leaving. About four thousand, nine hundred and seventy dollars' worth of clothes, CDs, jewellery, bottles of booze and skincare products. (Try as she might, she hasn't managed to reach the credit limit. She hasn't bought anything really big, like a car. Yet.)

A wistful moment – a miniature echo of leaving her house. Which, in its turn, was a miniature echo of all her goodbyes. Every abode she has ever left, right back to her parent's house with her floral papered bedroom and view of back gardens. Every move has been a diluted version of previous moves, and so this one is a mere half second's flit. She gives her hair a quick comb and creeps to the door, which opens the very same second so that Manuel falls into the room and knocks Morag off-balance.

'Morag – are you all right? What are you doing up? It's the middle of the night. Are you all right?'

'Of course I'm all right. What are you doing here, Manny?'

'Oh, just checking to see you are all right. Not in any pain, or too … you know. Down. I wasn't going to wake you.'

'How sweet, Manny. But I'm fine, you see. Not even near killing myself, see? No tears, none. I'm fine.' She backs up to her bed and sits on it.

'Why are you dressed? Have you packed your bags? Where are you going? Moragita,' reproachfully.

'Why, yes, I guess I am going. Might as well tell you, Manny. In fact, it saves me sending a letter later, because I wasn't going to not tell you. Just thought it might be better to wait till I was there.'

'There where?'

'Sit down, Manny,' patting the bed beside her.

'Tell me, Moragita. You look cold,' he says, pulling her to him. The time of night and low lighting allows him the courage for this simple act. She stiffens but does not pull away. Leaving California changes the rules, and touching, within bounds, is allowed. Takes a sharp breath, realises she has stopped breathing. He strokes her face with his other hand, trying to turn it to his. His fingers move along her chin, find bristles and freeze.

'I need a wee shave,' she whispers, humiliated.

'Hey, so do I.'

'Thank you, Manny. You always know just what to say.' Then curls into him 'Oh, this is good. Your shirt smells just like you. I'm going to miss you.'

'Where are you going?'

'Oh well, Manny, good old Manny Welly-Belly. Haven't we become good friends?'

'*Sí, sí,* very good *amigos*. Now talk to me,' he says, tightening his arm around her shoulders. She is so small, such a light fragile woman. She smells lemony and buttery and like something tantalising from the kitchen that he has always wanted to eat.

'It's hard to explain. You know some things just don't come to light till you get a fright?'

'Like your disease, you mean?'

'Well, of course. What's more frightening than cancer?'

'Because that's what I've got to talk to you about. I think there might have been some kind of …'

'No, no, Manny. There's no need to soften the blow for me any more. I've accepted it, I understand, and I am living my life accordingly.' She pats his hand, leans her cheek against his neck. Feels his delicious pulse. Has a momentary understanding of vampires.

'Oh my. This is hard, Manuel, but that's why I'm going home.'

'Home?' He thinks of Baja. Blue sky, white sand, the taste of chillies and shredded beef, enormous turtles for some reason, and the sound of his own language on everyone's lips. Home is a lump in his throat. Home is the absence of homesickness.

'Scotland. Inverness,' she says, and instantly his hot blue pictures are replaced by cool black and white foreign dreariness. Variations of grey.

'But, but … Morag. Scotland is so far, and it's been so long that you would not like it any more, I do not think …'

'Well, I've made up mind, anyway. I know it won't be the same place in many ways, but I'm going anyway. So is Carson Snelling. Do you know her? Such a nice girl. We're going together. But I've booked a taxi to take me to the airport; let her brother drive Carson, give them that wee bittie privacy they'll be needing. Hey, what's the matter? You're not in love with me, are you?'

'Tell you the truth, Morag, I don't really *want* to be in love with you. It is a problem.'

'Yeah, because I'm dying and that might depress you.'

A shudder goes through Manuel, then another. Morag absorbs his shudders, but does not know what else to say. What can she say? Then, although she is leaving and has about thirty-three minutes till the taxi comes, *because* she is leaving, and this will be the last time, first and last, she gets: THE LOOK.

Without moving a muscle, a mere dilation of her pupils, a slight swelling of her lips, she gets the *I would not vomit or scratch you if you kissed me* look. But do it right now. This is a minuscule window, and fleeing fast. Already her pupils are beginning to contract again. So he plunges his face towards hers, hurls his lips onto hers. Quickly, empty-minded, they both lie back on the bed as if the wind has been knocked out of them and the instant contact is made ... well, it's like all the fires that ever were, that she had ever imagined, pouring over her, and Manuel is not a body but a lake to pour herself into, to extinguish herself. The fire rips through them both, renders them both senseless; their eyes are shut, which is fortunate as they are not a pretty picture, either one of them. But then fire is not about beauty.

'Moragita!'

'Manny!'

Morag and Manny!

'Don't go, Moragita,' he pants. 'You must stay with me now.'

'Ah no, Manny, that's where you're wrong. I must leave you, and especially now.'

'Will I never see you again?'

'Never. Not even once. This, my dear *hombre*, is it. Goodbye.'

'Moragita!'

'Manny!'

'Say it again. That word.'

'Goodbye. Goodbye Manuel, forever.'

'Ahhh, no. Do not go.'

'I will go, dear Manny. Shh ... I am going home.'

They lie sideways to each other; he crushes her to him, to all of him, to his toes, his forehead, his belly, and do you know what he feels like? He feels like he is going home too.

Dawn Nurses

'Psst, Liz! Listen to this.'

'What?'

'Come here, listen.'

'Goodness me! Look at that wall! Are we having an earthquake?'

'Listen!'

'But that's Miss McTavish's room! Quick, she must be having a seizure. What are you laughing at?'

'Listen.'

Then, as all the fuses in the house blow, the two women stumble in the pitch dark, and say things like 'Oh dear!' and 'Oh my!' and hold each other's arms.

In the Air

She straps herself in. Puts on the headphones and waits for the taxiing run and the moment they leave the ground. It comes with Jerry Garcia pouring into her ears, and she thinks that the miracle of flight is nothing compared with the shock of hearing Jerry through British Airways headphones. The plane tips a tentative nose up into the air, falls back, then up and up again, and stays up; seems to find a sky on-ramp, and swerves on upwards till it comes to the main sky freeway, east-bound. North and east to colder places, the silver wings shiver. Six thousand miles to go.

She feels empty. Her brain is too tired for thoughts; too full of rushing air and the proximity of dangerous misgivings, but her bones and muscles and blood know. She stretches while they acknowledge certain facts:

That she will never again live in the bosom of her odd makeshift family, but will love them with a powerful nostalgic yearning from a great distance all the rest of her life.

That she will not believe this for many years, and she will never understand it or be rid of it.

Ever.

Everyone is different. There are people who settle down and marry; there are people who settle down unmarried; and there are people who get lost. Who disappear. Who move through one door to another, and so on, and by the time they look for their way back it is too late. They cannot find a way back. But not because of an absence of sentimentality. Their hearts do ache; they do feel love; but it is an unfocused love, and it is sufficient that they feel it. A diffuse promiscuous benevolence. For Carson, it will not matter who she loves, only that she manages to love. Loving is the feat. Above all, she will not waste love.

Something else. (Even her bones don't know this yet.) That she, like Morag, is quite good at moving. In fact, it will be what she excels at, so she will continue to do it because she can. The centrifugal force of her motion will shed all vestiges of triviality, all notions of nationality, and she will be no more and no less than herself. A shining Spartan pilgrim soul. A *good* Spartan pilgrim soul, because no-one is as good as a person who has been bad.

The man on her other side makes overtures of conversation, looks at the book she has on her lap, tries to make eye-contact – but she ignores him. It is interlude time, time for nothing, time of nobody.

'Well, well, Morag,' says Carson, under the noise of the engines. 'Here we go.'

On the Ground

Morag notices the silver jet pluming out in the blue sky and watches it, even though she knows it cannot be Carson's. Carson will be in Inverness by now, maybe even knocking on Aggie's door. She hopes that her sister won't be too angry that Carson is alone. And if she is, that she won't take it out on poor Carson, who is only trying to find a life and for sure will not need a crabbit old Highland wifey telling her off.

'What did that sign say?'

'What sign?'

'*Ay caramba*, Moragita! Will you please pay attention, or we will never get there.'

'Ach, shut up will you, Manny. What's the hurry? Slow down and I'll look at the map. What do you think the sign said?'

'Something with a lot of *s*'s and *f*'s in it.'

'Well, that's a fine help.'

An hour later, Morag is feeling annoyed with the way that the map will not fold back into a flat accordion, and her hair feels dirty and keeps getting in her eyes, and the scenery, even the sea, is flat and uninspiring. So she asks, almost as a reflex,

'Am I dying, Manny? Am I really really dying?'

'Oh yes,' he says. He puts his hand on hers for a second.

And with his words the map becomes irrelevant and falls to the floor, the sun flares into a vivid fireball, the sea regains its fluorescence, the air pings into elixir, and Manny's hand sends her swooning into heaven.

All this beauty with no purpose. She is dying, but the world is such a beautiful place to die. 'I'm dying,' she whispers.

'We're all dying,' he whispers back.

Consuela Gabriella Garcia

Connie sits in the window seat and gives one last exhalation, without falling. Leaning against the wall, head tilted. The girl outside in the Vietti garden, the stunning dark girl giving a plate of bread and eggs to a young man under an oak tree, notices the old woman, but does not notice that she is no longer watching her, or indeed, breathing. She simply carries on talking to the man, consigning the old woman to the realm of things that do not impinge, that do not matter. Orange blossom petals drift on the lawn, flies buzz and the dark girl swats them. She gets on with life. The old woman comes and goes. She's died before.

And Connie Gabriella Garcia's life – the life that she led from her marriage at Sycamore House till her arrival back on the door steps of Gentle Valleys? It happened, like all lives happen. And also, like most lives, it will remain unrecorded and forgotten.

Part Sixteen

Goodbye. Do not be sad. Live, while you live.

In the time you have taken to listen to me, to scribble down what I say, some minutes and hours of your life have gone and nothing is going to bring them back. Time may keep happening; it may eddy and swell and flood, but it moves one way only, and that is the way of decay. For this reason, if no other, I hope you've enjoyed our visit.

Excerpt from *The Consuela Chronicles*, transcribed by Cynthia Rogerson, formerly of San Rafael,1967.
Estimated age of Consuela: twenty-one.
Location of apparition: the upstairs window seat in Sycamore House.

True Answers

On the tip of Baja in Mexico, on a promontory jutting out into the sea, there stands a white adobe chapel, blinding white at mid-day. And inside stand a man and a woman, in front of a thin young priest with a dark moustache and yellow teeth.

'If there is anyone present who knows of a legal or moral impediment to this marriage, may they please come forward now or forever hold their peace,' says the priest in Spanish, to the almost empty church.

The silence howls for a moment but then remains silent. Manuel feels impediments whisper past him. They feel like moths – un-pretty, but light and soon gone. Morag's red lipstick mouth stays shut, her eyes sparkle, till the right question comes, the question she wants to answer truly.

Cynthia Rogerson

THE END

really does come.

Recent Titles from Two Ravens Press

Titles Published in April 2007

Love Letters from my Death-bed.
Cynthia Rogerson

The adventures of a Scottish bigamist dying – or is she? – in California. There's something very strange going on in Fairfax. Joe Johnson is on the hunt for dying people while his wife stares into space and flies land on her nose; the Snelling kids fester in a hippie backwater and pretend that they haven't just killed their grandfather; and Morag, multi-bigamist from the Scottish Highlands, makes some rash decisions when diagnosed with terminal cancer by Manuel – who may or may not be a doctor. Meanwhile, the ghost of Consuela threads her way through all the stories, oblivious to the ever-watching Connie – who sees everything from the attic of the Gentle Valleys Hospice.

£8.99; ISBN 978-1-906120-00-9

Highland Views. David Ross

Military jets exercise over Loch Eye as a seer struggles to remember the content of his vision; the honeymoon is over for workers down at the Nigg yard, and an English incomer leads the fight for independence both for Scotland and for herself … This debut collection of short stories from a gifted writer provides an original perspective on the Highlands, subtly addressing the unique combination of old and new influences that operate in the region today.

£7.99; ISBN 978-1-906120-05-4